TO
Betty &
From
george gauci
5/9/13
on gozo

THE CROSS

BY

GEORGE GAUCI

To the people of
Malta and Gozo

Chapter 1

The Gawchi Family

The island I speak of is Malta. It is the largest of three beautiful islands right in the middle of the Mediterranean, two hundred and ninety kilometers from North Africa and only one hundred kilometers from Sicily. Malta covers two hundred and forty-six square kilometers; another smaller island called Gozo, (Ghawdex in Maltese and sounds like 'Awdesh') covers sixty-seven square kilometers; and lastly Comino, which is the smallest, covers only two and a half square kilometers.

The story begins in Qormi, one of Malta's largest villages, sometimes referred to as the 'City of Pinto', after the Grand Master Pinto, who formed part of the religious and military Order of the Knights of St. John the Baptist. The Knights were given the Maltese Islands in the early fifteen hundred by Charles V, the Head of the Holy Roman Empire at the time. They arrived on the twenty-sixth of October, 1530, with full power to take over. The village of Qormi was divided into two parts; the larger part was protected by the patron saint, Saint George, and the lower and smaller area was protected by the patron saint, Saint Sebastian.

Giorgio, a fifty-six year old carpenter, was born in Qormi. Giorgio made furniture for a living in his large workshop next to the house, which was situated right on the main street, a few minutes' walk from St. Sebastian's Parish Church. The house itself consisted of a large hallway with a door to the left, which led into a spacious bedroom with a window which opened directly onto the main street. The next room, straight ahead, was the kitchen which housed a table, a cabinet and a large amphora that stored freshwater from which to drink and cook. The kitchen had two exits: one doorway led into a

5

smaller room, full of wooden shelves displaying pottery bowls and other kitchen items including a wood burning stove, (which the Maltese call a kenur) and the second led into the backyard. To the right, there was a well where the rainwater from the rooftops was trapped, which was essential for daily needs, especially during the many dry summer months. They shared this underground well, which passed under the wall separating the house from the next door neighbour's, and there were many times when a member of either family might open the wooden covers of both wells at the same time and see each other's reflections in the still water and call out a greeting.

Giorgio's first wife, Rita, had died some years earlier. They had shared twenty wonderful married years together before Rita became ill. Sadly, it was an illness that had taken her life in just a few short months. Rita had never borne Giorgio children but they had found comfort in the neighbours' children with whom they had come into contact. Rita was a very kind woman and when she passed away, Giorgio felt totally empty and lonely. Life seemed so meaningless. The nights were the worst. Lying on his bed, he would reach out to touch the only photograph he had of them together, which had been taken on their wedding day. Kissing Rita's face and caressing the photo, he thought his heart would break in two. It was not the first time that while holding it, he begged God to take him to be near his beloved wife in heaven. Giorgio felt that he did not have any future to look forward to, but six years later, during the first week of 1908 to be precise, his entire life changed. Walking along the seafront of Marsa, the next village, and enjoying the sound of the strong waves crashing against the rocks and the smell of the fresh sea air, his eyes caught sight of two people walking in his direction. One was a young woman dressed in traditional dress (a feldetta,) who was walking with an older man, who seemed weak and could hardly walk. Only her arm and a cane seemed to be keeping him in balance.

As they walked past Giorgio, the lady lifted her face just enough to catch Giorgio looking at her. Even at first glance, Giorgio felt his heart turn over. It was as though a magic spell had come over him and he could not take his eyes off her, even as they crossed the road.

'Surely they can't live very far away,' he thought; 'the man is too frail to walk a long distance.' His heart was telling him to follow them, so he crossed over to see where they were heading. At this point, he caught sight of them entering their home. Had he paused and waited any longer, he would surely have missed them. Giorgio was in luck. There, just a few steps away from the front door where they had entered, with his back resting on the wall, mending a few holes in his fishing net, was a fisherman. He walked over to the man.

"Good morning. My name is Giorgio," he said, introducing himself. "Could I ask you a question please?"

"It depends on what you want to know," replied the old fisherman, without even removing his pipe from his mouth.

"It's about the lady who has just walked into that house over there, Number Five. I have never seen such a beautiful woman, and…"

"I've never seen you around here before. You're definitely not from this village," the fisherman interrupted, before Giorgio could continue any further.

"I only want to find out if the lady is still unwed. It would save me the embarrassment in case she is already married or spoken for."

The fisherman lifted his cap (a beritta,) took a deep puff on his pipe and said, "So you're looking for a wife? In that case, I might be able to help you. The young lady's name is Angela, a perfect name for such a lovely woman. She is an only child. She lost her mother many years ago and has been taking care of her ill father ever since. So many men have admired her beauty, her innocence and the qualities she carries. If you go and knock on her door, I'm sure her

7

father will tell you that he is not interested, just like he has done with the other men who've asked before."

"Then, what do you suggest?"

The fisherman now stopped mending his net. Looking Giorgio over, this time from head to toe and observing him a little more, he said, "You seem to be a good man. I like you and I think I could help you. Perhaps I could be your matchmaker. Her father and I go back to childhood days. Please sit down and tell me all about yourself. Later, I will go and visit Pietru, her father, and I will inform him about you and your intentions. If he agrees, then we will see what the future holds for all of you. By the way, my name is Frencu," the fisherman said, and they shook hands.

Matchmakers were very common on the Maltese Islands. These men were paid money to bring a proposal to the father of the woman who was being asked for in marriage. The father would then meet the intended husband and the daughter would honour her father's wish. They would marry the man their father had chosen, even if they had no idea who he was or what he looked like.

When Giorgio answered all the questions the fisherman had to ask, he was told to return the following day at around the same time. Giorgio felt that he had taken the first step towards his union with Angela. His head was still spinning with her innocent looks and beauty. So caught up was he in his thoughts, that on this day he did not even stop to chat with anyone who greeted him. He was in his own little world, surrounded only by the magic of her eyes.

That evening he prayed to God to give him his wish. The clock that ticked away on his bedroom dresser seemed to go too slowly. At one in the morning he was still awake. Eventually, he did fall asleep but not for long. At four o'clock he woke up, and getting out of bed, put on his best clothes which included his only winter jacket, and headed up the street to hear the first Mass at five. It was a foggy morning and the only sounds around were those of a few crickets, a cat crying and some roosters crowing far away.

Once at the church's front doors, he found them closed. He had arrived there too early. The village Sacristan had yet to arrive. When Emmanuel, the village Sacristan, finally appeared, Giorgio's greeting caused the poor man to jump in fright. "Giorgio, what are you doing here so early? Is something wrong?" he asked.

"I have something very important on my mind," replied Giorgio, "and I need to pray."

No sooner had Emmanuel opened the door than Giorgio rushed past him. On this day Giorgio heard Mass services, one after the other. He prayed and prayed as he had never prayed before, until the time came for him to return to the village of Marsa to meet Frencu the fisherman. Walking at a fast pace he was relieved when he arrived to see Frencu sitting on the same stone where he had left him the previous day.

"Please tell me that he did meet you," Giorgio asked breathlessly.

"Calm down Giorgio, please calm down. Yes, I did meet Pietru. He listened very carefully to what I had to say. When I finished, he asked me for my personal thoughts about you and for my honest opinion. I told him that I judged you as a good man. After sitting quietly for a few minutes, he then asked me to bring you over to his house."

"God bless you. Thank you," Giorgio said, shaking the fisherman's hand. "So when will it be possible for me to meet him?"

"We could go now; they have just returned from church. Shall we?"

Making sure that he had no dust anywhere on his clothes and that his hat was in place, Giorgio straightened himself up, took a deep breath and looked to Frencu for approval. They then walked to the house. The moment Giorgio saw Angela at the front door, his

9

blood rushed to his head, his body became weak and he stood speechless. She was more beautiful than ever.

"Good morning Angela," Frencu greeted her, politely. "Your father is expecting us. Could you please tell him that Giorgio and I are here?"

"Yes certainly, please do come in," she said in a warm voice. As soon as she had closed the door behind them, she asked for their hats and then showed them into the sitting room.

"Please sit. I will go to get my father," she said quietly, stealing a shy glance beneath her lashes at Giorgio, who was by now totally mesmerised by her.

Very slowly, Angela walked her father into the sitting room and after she had helped him to sit down in his favourite chair facing Giorgio, he told her to leave so that the three men could talk in private. Pietru looked older than he actually was due to his illness, but his mind was as sharp as ever. He asked Giorgio a lot of personal questions, one after another. The more they talked, the more he liked what he was hearing, especially the way Giorgio spoke of his late wife Rita. Through his voice and his eyes, Pietru could feel and see the love and respect this man still had for her, even though many years had passed since her death. Losing his only love himself, Pietru and Giorgio had something in common. This deeply touched Pietru, as he too had wished to find love again but it was not destined to be. With this in mind, he came to the conclusion that if this man in front of him came to love and respect his daughter with even half of what he still carried for Rita, then his Angela was going to be in good hands. The fact that Giorgio was twenty two years older than Angela did not matter to him at all. On the contrary, this worked to Giorgio's advantage, as in Pietru's eyes age ripened a person in maturity, respect and personality.

When the questioning ended, they sat in silence. With every moment that passed, Giorgio awaited Pietru's decision with trepidation. Silence fell upon them. After a few minutes, Pietru picked up his pipe, lit it, relaxed back into his chair and said, "If you don't mind, I am feeling a bit tired and I need to rest now. We have to finish here for today, but can I suggest we meet here again, in seven days' time?"

Giorgio knew very well that Pietru was not going to give up his daughter to anyone until he had investigated that person thoroughly.

"Yes, I understand," Giorgio said. "One week, a week today; I will be here."

"Come round at the same time. Is this alright with you Frencu?"

"Yes, that's fine."

Pietru picked up the little bell he used regularly when he needed his daughter's attention and summoned her into the room. The moment she entered, Giorgio and Frencu stood up in respect and then her father asked her to show Giorgio out.

Giorgio felt such warmth within him just being around her. He wanted so much to tell her personally how he felt about her but this would not be proper. So, after putting on his hat he gave her a quick gentle look and with a smile, wished her a good day, said his goodbye and left.

Angela too had admired his looks and as she closed the door slowly behind her, she was really sorry to see him go. Taking a deep breath, she walked back to her father's side. Her father asked her to fetch another glass of wine for Frencu and a glass of water for himself. After this Angela left the room so that they could talk again in private.

"I like Giorgio," Pietru said when they were alone. "I have a good feeling about him, but I have to make sure who he is. Frencu, you are my loyal and trusted friend and again, I need your help. Will you go to the village of Qormi to enquire about him? I don't have to

11

tell you how or what to do; you already know very well what I mean. You have a week. If by next Sunday you tell me that Giorgio is a suitable match for my Angela then I will allow him to marry her."

"My dear friend, thank you for trusting me again. I will give you my honest findings," replied Frencu, as he tipped back the last of his wine and left.

That same afternoon, Frencu walked all the way to Qormi to start his research on Giorgio. Day after day, Frencu mingled with the villagers, sat near matchmakers, listened and watched. He even followed Giorgio's movements from afar. Frencu himself had never married. Growing up with Pietru and living only a few doors away, Angela was very special to him. Finding out that Giorgio was a kind gentleman and loved by all pleased him immensely. He had only good words and praise to report to his old friend Pietru.

During these seven days, it was not easy for Giorgio. Each day seemed longer than the one before, but finally Sunday arrived and it was time to return to Angela's house. That Sunday morning he was so nervous; he fussed over his clothes but nothing seemed to look good enough. However, he was not the only one. Unknown to him, in house Number Five on Triq Santa Katarina (St. Catherine's Street) in the village of Marsa, Angela was having the same problem. As soon as her father told her that Giorgio was to come by that day, the wonderful news made her excited. She wanted to look her best. She put on her favourite dress and then tried on all her head scarves, but on this day none of them seemed right. In the end, she decided that she would not wear one at all. She wanted Giorgio to see her long curly hair simply as it was.

When she answered the front door, Giorgio felt he was looking at the most beautiful face he could ever have imagined.

"Good morning Giorgio," she said, welcoming him. "Please do come in. My father and Frencu are waiting."

In the sitting room the men greeted each other. "Would you

like a glass of wine, Giorgio?" Pietru asked.

"Yes, thank you," Giorgio replied, hoping that some wine would help to calm his nerves. Angela fetched the wine and then left the room, closing the door behind her.

The meeting went well, with all three men enjoying each other's company. The conversation touched on many areas which even included politics and the current situation of the times. In the end, Pietru looked calmly at Giorgio for a moment and then announced his approval; that George would be welcome to marry his daughter.

Giorgio's eyes widened with pleasure but before he could celebrate his good fortune, Pietru continued; "but on two conditions."

At this moment Giorgio's heart almost stopped. What conditions could there be?

"Due to my illness, as you must have already noticed, I constantly need my daughter's assistance. I know that you run your own furniture business from your garage and I know that you have to live there. If you want my daughter's hand in marriage, then you have to take us both permanently into your home. The second condition is that as I haven't worked for many years, I cannot finance any wedding expenses. You will have to take care of all the expenses in this matter. If you don't find any objection to these, then God bless you both. You can marry my Angela on any day."

These were not conditions; Giorgio was already prepared to take on both of these responsibilities. Excitedly, he walked over to Pietru and said, "Sir, it is my pleasure to take both you and your daughter into my home and as for the wedding costs, I will gladly take care of these. Sir, I can honestly promise you that you will never ever regret the decision you have made here today. Thank you, thank you!"

Pietru now picked up the little bell and rang it. This time when Angela entered the room he asked her to sit down, because he had a very important announcement to make. Angela felt very nervous and she could not wait to hear her father's decision.

"Angela, Giorgio has asked me for your hand in marriage and I have agreed." Angela's heart quickened. She could feel her face burning with shyness and pleasure and she could barely lift her head to look at him. She liked Giorgio and throughout the exchange of questioning and answers between the men, she had sat in the next room working on her lace, hoping that her father would agree to this man's proposal. Taking care of her father for so many years meant that she had had doubts as to whether she would ever marry. Honouring her father's wish to marry this man was a lovely dream come true and she accepted happily with all her heart.

The custom of the island was that the wedding mass would take place in the village church of the bride's residence. A small celebration with family and maybe some neighbours and close friends would then take place in the church hall following the ceremony, if finances allowed. After the bond of marriage, a few newly-wed brides would then return to their respective homes for at least a day. In this case, however, with Pietru moving into Giorgio's house and Giorgio being an older widower living on his own, both parties agreed that the wedding would take place in Saint Sebastian's Church, in the village of Qormi. Then, from the church they would begin their new lives together on the same day.

Giorgio was so grateful for the help that Frencu, the fisherman, had given him that he paid him as soon as they walked out of Angela's house. Now he had a wedding to plan. With this in mind he headed straight to his village church, first to thank the Lord Jesus Christ in his own house, and then to share the wonderful news with the Kappilan; the parish priest. Dun Salv was more than happy to hear about Giorgio's new bride-to-be, and together they sat down to set the wedding date and time. This did not take long because Pietru gave Giorgio the choice. The wedding was arranged to take place in just two weeks' time, on a Sunday, at three in the afternoon. Giorgio was in such a happy state that afterwards he walked straight down the road to tell his neighbour, Martin. He had kept Angela a secret because he knew that if things had not worked out, Martin would have felt sad. Now, on hearing about Giorgio's future nuptials, Martin and the family were overjoyed. When he asked Martin to be his witness on the day, Martin could hardly contain himself.

"Giorgio, you can't imagine how happy you've made me! I am honoured. Yes, I will stand as your witness. I wouldn't miss it for the world." Everything was going so well. Giorgio was sure that this was one of the luckiest days in his entire life. He felt so young and so full of life. He walked all through the neighbourhood, telling everyone he met. The wonderful news spread quickly through the village. This occasion gave the villagers something new to talk and gossip about. There were a few who thought that Giorgio should not marry again at his age but the rest were more than happy to hear about it and a few even grouped together to see how they could help. It was not long before some of his male friends called by to congratulate him. His oldest friends recalled the many times he had helped them whenever they had been in need, and now they wanted to give him and his new bride a wedding day to remember.

During the next two weeks, Giorgio and Angela met daily for a short time and yet even at their age they were always chaperoned by her father. It was forbidden for a man and a woman to have any physical contact with each other before they were bonded in the sacrament of marriage. There were parents who were so afraid of premarital relations, that from early childhood, they would tell their daughters that by just touching a man's hand, a girl could become pregnant. Some went even further, terrifying their daughters by saying that if they became pregnant they would not only dishonour the family name for generations to come, but would also never enter heaven.

On Saturday, the afternoon before the big wedding was to take place, Martin and a few of Giorgio's friends walked with him to the village square to share a glass of wine.

With Giorgio's permission, while he was with his friends, Karmena and her daughters went to his house to wash all the floors, polish the furniture and to iron his wedding suit. Dun Salv, the Kappilan, wanted to do something special too. With the help of a few altar boys, he draped some of the church's interior walls in red damask, usually used only on the big feast day.

On Sunday, the wedding day, after the noon mass ended, a few women stayed behind to decorate the church with freshly cut flowers and with polished brass holders containing plants which some of the villagers had brought for the occasion, while a few altar boys helped the Kappilan to roll out a red carpet along the central aisle. Everything was in place and all were satisfied. They returned to their homes to get dressed. They did not want to miss the moment when Giorgio's bride would be arriving; they wanted to see Angela so much.

As the church bells struck three, Angela and her father arrived at the church steps in a one horse carriage which Giorgio had hired. Angela wore a lovely, simple white dress, a dress she had sewn herself and a white hat that she had borrowed from a neighbour for the occasion. Like so many other brides, Angela had always hoped to marry in front of a church full of people, but she had begun to think that this would never happen. Throughout the years of caring for her father around the clock, she had lost contact with most of the childhood friends with whom she had grown up. The only ones she did see were the few who attended the same Mass Services. Besides this, Angela hardly ever went anywhere and she did not see many people during the course of her daily life. The only other times she came out of the house were to buy food, and even this was from the street hawkers who stopped right outside her front door to sell fresh fish, vegetables and milk. Even the oil and the kerosene were delivered straight to her door. Arriving to a full church, Angela was overwhelmed. There were so many people present. When she entered, everyone turned their heads in her direction. She looked so lovely. Everyone had to agree that Giorgio was a very lucky man indeed. Standing within the entrance of the wide church doors, Angela was more nervous than ever before, but the moment her eyes caught sight of Giorgio waiting at the altar steps, she focused on his handsome face and felt better. Lifting her head high, she took a deep breath. Holding tightly to her father's arm, they slowly began their walk down the aisle.

When they got to the altar, Pietru kissed Angela on both cheeks and placed her hand in Giorgio's.

Dun Salv started the Mass service and before they knew it, the special moment to bond Giorgio and Angela in marriage had come. Blessing the rings, the Kappilan asked; "Giorgio, will you take Angela to be your lawful wedded wife, in sickness and in health, for better and for worse, for richer and poorer, until death do you part?"

"Yes I do," answered Giorgio, full of emotion as he slowly slid the wedding ring onto Angela's finger.

Then he turned to Angela and repeated the same question.

"Yes I do," Angela answered, as she put the wedding ring onto the finger of the most wonderful man she had ever met.

"In the Name of the Father and the Son and of the Holy Spirit, I now pronounce you husband and wife."

Everyone within the church had fallen in love with Angela. The Kappilan now proceeded with the Mass. When it finished, the parishioners waited outside to meet Angela. Small children threw rice over the newly-wed couple for good luck as congratulations filled the air.

During this time a few of the women decorated the carriage. To Giorgio's surprise, Martin and some other close friends had hired a four man band to walk behind it and to play a few local tunes. Once the newly-wed couple and Angela's father were seated in it, they proceeded down the main street towards the house, while children of all ages ran ahead, throwing freshly cut flowers in front of the carriage. What a special day it was.

When they arrived, Giorgio helped Angela down and then they both carefully helped the fragile Pietru. The three of them now thanked the small crowd who had followed them and then entered their home. Everyone kept clapping to welcome Angela and her father into the community. Today Angela's dream had more than come true.

With marriage, Angela's world changed completely, for although she had dreamt for many years of married life, nothing could really have prepared her for being a wife. She had lost her mother when she was only eleven years old. There were no female influences in her life to guide her in the intimate relations that occur between a man and a woman, though Giorgio was patient and very gentle with her in this respect.

Pietru handled the change very well. After a few days, he felt very comfortable and content in his new home in Qormi.

As their lives together progressed, with one day following another, daily routines set in. Angela loved to cook and Giorgio loved all of her meals. After she had prepared dishes such as pork chops, chicken, macaroni and pies, Angela would take them to the baker just around the corner to bake in the big oven, along with the fresh bread. Mario the baker had agreed that Giorgio did not have to pay for this and instead would repay him by repairing any wooden tools.

Slowly Angela grew to care for Giorgio deeply and their admiration and respect for one another became mutual. Rainy winter days passed into spring, bringing with it all kinds of different and beautiful wild flowers. Various birds from Central Africa were migrating to the North, to the countries of England, Germany and even all the way to Finland. Turtle Doves, Quail, Honey Buzzards, Lesser Kestrels, Purple and Grey Herons and Golden Orioles filled the air with song and colour. Angela made new friends who loved being around her. Karmena, her neighbour, had become Angela's best friend. Karmena and her husband Martin were in their forties and they had six children; all girls. Martin was the son of Giorgio's late school friend. Martin and his sister were born and grew up in the house next door, though his sister was now married and living in Birgu. Martin worked at a printing press in the village. Karmena herself was one of five children and she was born in the village of Qormi too, but in Saint George's area. They were married young and Martin's parents had passed away while they were both still middle aged. Every evening Karmena gathered her family together to recite the Holy Rosary. Her neighbours could hear her voice from their own back yards and prayed along with her. After the Rosary, other prayers followed; for the intentions of the Pope, the Church, for all the Saints, for the poor and needy, to thank the Lord Jesus Christ for the day, and to look over them through the night. Every second Thursday, Karmena cooked fresh coffee beans in a canister over the fire. Just like a craftsman, she knew exactly when to lift the canister to give it a shake before any of the beans could burn. The aroma of the coffee beans filled the air around the house, as if telling the neighbours who had placed an order with her to come and collect it the next morning. Angela was very lucky to have such a kind and loving person as Karmena next door, and they met at Angela's place on many afternoons to share a cup of coffee, a few biscuits and a quiet talk. Giorgio was acquiring new contracts in his furniture making business and everything seemed to be going his way.

In the month of April, after only a few married months, Angela gave the greatest news any wife could give her husband. She announced that she was pregnant. The baby was due to arrive around the end of October. Giorgio was so surprised at Angela's words, that he actually asked her to repeat what she had just said.

"I am pregnant!" Angela responded joyously.

There was no doubt; he had heard her right the first time. He felt that a miracle had taken place. He had been married to his first wife Rita for over twenty years and she had never conceived, yet now, after just a few months of marriage to Angela and he was on his way to becoming a father. He kissed and stroked her cheek and then he knelt down in front of her to kiss her swelling belly.

Together they told Pietru, now totally bedridden, the wonderful news. An emotional Pietru cried tears of happiness as together they prayed to the Holy Lady for an easy pregnancy.

On the twentieth of August, just four months later, Angela went in to wake up her father but he did not open his eyes and did not move. Pietru had died in his sleep. Yes, Angela cried for her father because she loved him so. She had so hoped and wished that he would live long enough to see his grandchild, yet she had to accept that this was not meant to be. Giorgio was very sad, for in a few short months of living together he had become fond of the old gentleman, but there was nothing he could do. The only consolation was that Pietru had passed away peacefully and without pain. Arrangements were made and the next day a very solemn funeral took place. Pietru was then buried with his late wife in the Marsa cemetery.

Two months later, in the early hours of the thirtieth of October, Angela's labour started. It began so quickly that there was no time to take her to the hospital. Giorgio rushed next door and Karmena sent one of her daughters to fetch the midwife. Exactly on the stroke of midday and in her bed, Angela gave birth to a very healthy baby boy. The bells were ringing in all the churches around Malta and Gozo to remind all the Islanders that it was midday, time to stop working and to say prayers in thanks to God and to have a bite to eat. Yet to Angela's and Giorgio's ears, the bells ringing all around the island were sounds of joy from the heavens above, welcoming their son into the world. The moment the midwife placed the crying child into Giorgio's arms, Giorgio lifted the little one up to the painting of the Holy Trinity which hung over the bed, presenting the child to all above. Then, he turned towards the statue of Saint Sebastian, on top of the dresser and prayed:

"Dear Saint Sebastian, I have asked you to protect my wife and baby from the moment she told me that she was pregnant. Here he is, my healthy boy. I thank you and I'm more than grateful. I will have him carry your name. I am calling him Sebastian. Please, I beg you, protect him throughout his life."

This was the greatest day of their lives because together and out of their love, they had brought a human being into the world. Having Sebastian, their daily life was now filled with pleasure. He was a big baby, very quiet for the first weeks and asleep for most of the day, but as the months passed by he became quite a handful. They loved him dearly and Giorgio spent most of his spare time holding the little one.

On November the seventeenth, 1910, Angela gave birth to her second child, this time a very beautiful, healthy baby girl. Now they were really blessed with everything, because God had given them both a son and a daughter. They could not be happier. They named her Mariella, after Angela's grandmother.

21

Then, only a few short months later, Angela discovered that she was expecting again. Three pregnancies in just a few married years! Who would have thought that Giorgio at his age would be blessed with such treasures?

Chapter 2

A Death and a Birth

On the day of the nineteenth of December, 1911, it rained all morning but eventually the clouds cleared and the sun that afternoon was more than pleasant. Giorgio kissed Angela and then went for his usual evening walk. Lately, he had been experiencing some chest pains and these seemed to be getting worse. It frightened him but he did not want to worry Angela. He could not tell his family doctor either. There was a small chance that the doctor would admit him to hospital. He was also being a bit selfish. He did not want to miss the birth of his third child.

Ten minutes into his walk, Giorgio felt a twinge followed by a very sharp pain. The next was even stronger. His left arm stiffened and he felt out of breath. He became very worried as he sat on a stone nearby. Even at such a moment, his thoughts were all about Angela. Thinking only of her, he attempted to pull himself up onto his feet.

Ganni, a villager, whose job was to light the street lamps, noticed a man crouched over and walked up to him to help. He was very surprised to find that the man was Giorgio, a man he knew very well. "What's wrong?" he asked. Seeing Giorgio in such difficulty, he offered to help. "Let me help you get onto your feet. Let me take you to my house, it's closer than yours. You need a doctor."

On hearing the word 'doctor', Giorgio, making a big effort to talk said, "No, please. I beg you, no doctor. Ganni, as you very well know, Angela is expecting. I don't want to worry her. Please, help me to get home. Once there, I promise I'll go straight to bed. Tomorrow, I'll be fine. Please, just walk me home." Ganni was sure that Giorgio needed a doctor urgently but at the same time he did not want to upset him. Gently, he helped his friend up and step by step they walked down to Giorgio's house, but once at the front door Giorgio's legs gave way. Ganni tried to hold him up but his body was a dead weight and they both fell onto the street. Ganni panicked. He needed help and quickly. Getting back onto his feet, he started to knock as hard as he could on Martin's front door.

"Open up, Martin! Quickly, open up, open up!" he yelled at the top of his voice. It did not take long for Martin to appear at the door, but Martin and his family were not the only ones who had heard Ganni's loud voice and knocks; these had also been heard by Angela.

Wondering what all the noise was about; Angela too came outside to find out what was happening. At the sight of her husband lying on the floor, she threw herself beside him, calling out his name, but Giorgio did not respond.

"Giorgio talk to me, please talk to me, talk to me!" she cried out repeatedly. Ganni and Martin tried to pick her up but she started screaming hysterically. "Leave me alone! Leave me alone!" she yelled over and over again.

Her screams brought other neighbours to the scene. It was not easy to persuade Angela to move away from her husband, but once they told her that he was still breathing and that they needed to move him off the damp floor, she let him go. Two women walked her inside, while a few men who had gathered there carefully carried Giorgio into the house and placed him onto his bed. Someone had already run for the doctor. Angela's screams and all the commotion outside had woken up Sebastian and Mariella. They were both taken into the kitchen to their mother but then moved to Martin's house. Oh how Angela prayed that the doctor would arrive soon.

When Doctor Muscat arrived, he realised that Giorgio's condition was very critical. It was obvious that Giorgio had suffered a massive heart attack. His heartbeats became weaker and weaker and then stopped; Giorgio could not hold on. Doctor Muscat tried to revive Giorgio but to no avail. Giorgio had passed away. Sadly no one could do anything. All those in the room made the sign of the cross in prayer as Doctor Muscat gently pulled the blanket over Giorgio's head. Complete silence followed, but not for long. Angela was about to enter the bedroom to check on her husband's condition. Little did she know that she was about to face one of her worst nightmares. Seeing her beloved husband's head covered, her heart could not cope. Like a volcanic eruption she screamed out in pain. Taking all her strength with it, she fell to the floor before anyone could even move to help her. Doctor Muscat quickly opened his bag to find his salts but his instincts now told him differently. Was Angela ready to face her husband's dead body again? Would she miscarry? No, he could not take the risk.

"Pawlu, Ganni, Pietru," Doctor Muscat called, putting the salts back in his bag, "help me to move Giorgio out of this bed and onto the one in the hallway before Angela comes round, hurry! Pinu, go and tell Dun Salv and the police about what has happened. We need them here as soon as possible."

Like clockwork, everyone did as the doctor ordered and just in time too. The moment they placed Angela onto the bed, she started to come round. As if the doctor did not have enough to cope with already, Angela's waters broke right there and then.

"Oh, my God, the baby, it's on its way! Angela stay strong; you will need all of your strength and concentration. Karmena, go for Anna. Tell her the baby is coming," instructed the doctor.

Anna was one of the parish's midwives who helped Doctor Muscat with other deliveries and she lived just around the corner.

At the parish church, Dun Salv was devastated to say the least upon hearing the news of Giorgio's sudden death. Quickly, he stopped what he was doing and rushed down to the house, arriving almost at the same time as Constable Pinu. Dun Salv headed straight to pray over Giorgio's body. Thanking the small group for helping, the policeman politely asked them to return to their homes. Then, another serious problem occurred; the baby was now in a breach position and was going to be born feet first. At the moment of the delivery, Doctor Muscat asked Angela to push, but she did not have the strength. She was too weak. The situation had now become alarmingly dangerous; the baby could easily die. Doctor Muscat was determined to do all he could to deliver the baby, hopefully alive and healthy, but in all his professional years he had never encountered such an experience. In the end, with God's will, Angela gave birth to a baby boy. His skin was bluish in colour and he was having spasms, shaking violently. It seemed that the shock of his father's death had somehow been transferred to him. Doctor Muscat checked him briefly and then he passed the tiny one over to Anna, to her care. Angela was now bleeding heavily. Doctor Muscat had to stop the bleeding before she bled to death. After heavily sedating Angela, he began to operate.

Anna cleaned the baby's air passages and succeeded in getting him to cry, but she was very concerned. The baby was still shaking. Believing that a newborn could never enter heaven unless it had been baptized, she took the little one, now wrapped in a white cloth, to Dun Salv, who was still praying beside's Giorgio's dead body. Dun Salv agreed that the newborn had to be baptized, and right away. Turning to Martin and his wife Karmena, he asked them to stand in as the child's godparents. "What names do you choose for the child?" Dun Salv asked, holding a small silver jar containing Holy Water over the baby's head.

"George. Yes, George," Martin replied. "God has taken our beloved neighbour Giorgio away from us, but He has given us this baby to carry on his legacy. George for his first name and Emmanuel for his second, being born so close to Christmas."

"You couldn't have chosen better. I name this child George Emmanuel, in the name of the Father and of the Son and of the Holy Spirit, Amen."

Sometime later the doctor came out of the bedroom to tell the little group that he had managed to stop Angela's bleeding. Asked if Angela was going to make it through, he said that he had done all he could and that now, only time would tell. As he took the little baby from her, Doctor Muscat asked Anna the midwife to stay with Angela.

"Dun Salv has just baptized him. Karmena and I are his godparents. His name is George," Martin said proudly. "Doctor Muscat; about the baby, he will live, won't he?"

"He is underweight, bluish and having spasm attacks from shock, but he does seem to be a fighter. We will have to monitor his progress. One thing I'm sure of though, the baby is hungry!"

"I'll take care of that," Karmena said, as she in turn took the little one into her arms.

With Angela sleeping for many hours to come, the men in the house had a lot to discuss. Giorgio's body had to be buried sometime in the next twenty four hours and Angela was certainly not in any condition to organise her husband's burial. As Giorgio and Angela had no next of kin, the men took matters into their own hands. Doctor Muscat wrote the death certificate, prepared Giorgio for the burial and took it upon himself to organise the coffin. Dun Salv took full responsibility for all the funeral arrangements, including finding the six poll bearers and preparing the parish church ready for the Noon Mass the next day. The policeman went to see Loreto, the cemetery caretaker, to ask him to prepare one of the available government plots in Qormi. Anna, the midwife, offered to stay overnight but Karmena volunteered to stay, just in case there was another delivery that same night and Anna was needed.

Sebastian and little Mariella were now sleeping next door under the care of Karmena's daughters.

By the early hours, the death of Giorgio and all that had taken place, spread around the village like wild fire. By seven in the morning Doctor Muscat was back at Angela's house with a nurse to attend to Angela. Karmena had not slept a single wink. She had spent the whole night praying and crying and seeing to the baby. The doctor sedated Angela again. He wanted to keep her sleeping; at least until the coffin carrying Giorgio's body was carried out of the house.

Sometime later, Luigi the carpenter, one of Giorgio's best friends, arrived with the coffin. Being a carpenter himself, Luigi and Giorgio had shared many a walk to discuss the new tools of the trade. Luigi was lost for words. They had planned to meet up that coming Sunday. Now all he could do was give Giorgio the best coffin he had in stock for free. Once Giorgio's body was placed inside the coffin, the front doors of the house were opened for those who wanted to pay their last respects. On this sad morning, farmers and shepherds left their fields and animals unattended. Craftsmen put down their tools and others kept their businesses closed. Women who were usually hired and paid to walk and weep behind the coffin (Il-Bikkejja) showed up too. On this day, they came freely to weep, to suffer, and to represent Angela, who was not able to be present. Black pieces of material could be seen hanging on many front doors along the main street. This part of Qormi was in mourning.

At eleven thirty the parish priests, altar boys and the six pallbearers appeared, walking down the main street. The large crowd moved to the sides to make way as the parish bells tolled. Dun Salv said some prayers and then he blessed Giorgio for the last time. The coffin lid was put in place and the procession proceeded up the street. The large crowd followed, leaving Doctor Muscat, Karmena and the nurse to take care of Angela. In the church, Giorgio's coffin was placed in the central aisle at the steps of the altar, in the exact

28

place where he had married both of his wives, Rita and Angela, and where he had baptized his own children, Sebastian and Mariella. On those special days Giorgio had shared many smiles and happiness with most of the people here today, but now everyone present was weeping for their loss. After the service, most of the crowd followed the coffin all the way to the village cemetery.

Back at the house, when Angela opened her eyes, she tried to focus or to move but she could not. She then realised that she wasn't pregnant anymore.

"What happened? Did I lose the baby?" she asked Karmena, worried.

"No. You've had a baby boy. He is fine."

"Where is he, where's my baby? Can I see him?"

"Of course. Katarina! Bring the baby! Angela is awake," Karmena called out to her daughter.

"Oh look at my baby, he is so beautiful! Thank you all, thank you. My God, the baby looks like his father. Where is Giorgio?" she asked, "oh my God! Now I remember. Giorgio! My Giorgio! I saw him! I saw him on this bed with his face covered. Oh my Lord! Oh my Lord! Nooooo!" Angela cried out.

"Angela, in the last hours you have experienced the greatest ordeal any woman could ever endure. If it wasn't for the love of God, you and the baby would have died too," the doctor told her. Poor Angela, her heart wanted to break but looking at her newborn in her arms encouraged her to stay strong. As hard as it was going to be, she had to face the fact that nothing would bring her husband back to life.

"Where are my other two children? Where are Sabastian and Mariella?" she asked, still sobbing.

"They are at my house," Karmena replied. "I'll go and bring them."

"Please," Angela said, trying to control her emotions.

"Mum! Mum!" Sebastian yelled as her ran to her side.

Having her three children with her, Angela managed to stay strong. She was the only one there for them now. She had so many questions but for today, all she could do was cry and pray. These would have to wait.

Katarina, Karmena's eldest daughter, asked for her mother's permission to take care of Angela until Angela could regain her strength. "Yes, that will be wonderful. The children know you well and they love being around you."

The next morning Katarina and Karmena told Angela about what had taken place in the last twenty four hours. Angela's grief stricken face and her crying said it all, but she was pleased to hear that at least Giorgio had been given a very respectful burial. With every day that followed, Dun Salv personally came to give Angela the Holy Host and to pray and encourage her. He said that God would always be with her. Many neighbours came to visit and to show their respect; showering Angela in her time of need with all of their love, generosity and kindness.

Chapter 3

Angela and the Family Cassar

Angela's biggest discomfort was the loneliness she felt without Giorgio's companionship, love and affection. A union such as theirs, solid and strong, left a huge emptiness which was impossible to replace. In marrying Angela, Giorgio had been very lucky. Not only had she filled his loneliness with the same love and respect his first wife Rita had, but she had also given him the children he had wanted for so long. Giorgio had looked his age, but to Angela, he had been the most handsome man on earth. He had had the most beautiful eyes and a smile that had melted her in seconds, and he had loved her dearly. He had cared for her and had made her feel a complete woman. She would not have changed him for anyone in the whole world. His sudden and unexpected death had been a complete shock. Sleep continuously evaded her and she was haunted by the memories of their few short years together. She always went back to that January day, when their eyes first met. She could still see herself stealing that quick look at him and the warmth she had felt when she had opened the front door to find him on her doorstep. Oh how she missed his warm touch, the way he had held her at night and the way he had run his fingers through her hair while they had lain holding each other. She missed everything about him. She was a very religious and devout woman who repeated the Rosary day in and day out. Yet, being only human, in some of her weaker moments she too demanded spiritual answers. There were moments when she did ask God; 'why, oh why of all the men, did You have to take away my husband?' But then, realising that she had no right to question God's will, she would then reach under her pillow for her rosary beads to pray for forgiveness. Due to the complicated delivery and the lengthy and reoccurring infections, Angela had to stay bedridden for months.

On the first day Angela was able to get out of bed, she waited until everyone in the house was sound asleep. Walking very slowly and holding onto her late husband's pillow, she passed by Katarina who was snoring away in her bed and walked out into the small backyard. Here, she sat on the same bench her Giorgio had made for them; the same bench they had spent many nights holding one another. Looking at the stars, she remembered how Giorgio had told her that the stars were souls of family members who had passed on. Looking at the large shining moon, she could now hear his voice telling her that the moon and the sun were signs from God that He was always there to look upon all mankind. She now put her face into the pillow to cry so that no one could hear her. The pillow carried Giorgio's smell, such a wonderful smell. Oh how she missed her husband, how she wished she could be near him. Only the thought of her children kept her sane, after all they did give her courage, so sweet and innocently unaware of her grief as they were. Baby George had all of his father's features. The same shaped face and his father's eyes. The bluish colour of his skin was now slowly fading and his spasms had now stopped. He was just adorable. Mariella's hair was black, as black as it could be and very curly, just like her mother's. She was such a sweet child. Sebastian was fair and had bright blue eyes and short blond hair. He took after Angela's father's side of the family, being tall for his age.

It was now June and over six months since Giorgio's passing. The warm weather on the islands had been around for weeks but today, the twenty first of the month, meant that summer had officially started. The strong winds that had hit the islands during the night had calmed down. On this early Sunday morning, the sky was blue and there was not even a cloud in sight. On this day, Angela told

Katarina that they were going to attend the nine o'clock Mass and that directly afterwards, she wanted to visit Giorgio's grave. Katarina was more than happy to hear that Angela was getting out of the house, but not so sure about the visit to the cemetery. Quickly however, she helped dress the children and they were on their way. When Mass ended, whilst most of the congregation waited outside to greet Angela, Katarina took a minute to find Dun Salv and to tell him about Angela's intended visit to Giorgio's grave. Dun Salv had seen many widows and widowers break down at gravesides. Picking some flowers out of a vase that was in front of the statue of the Holy Lady in the church, he came to find Angela and said, "Angela, I am going to the cemetery to put some flowers on my mother's grave. Katarina tells me you're heading there. Can I join you?"

"Yes, please do. I don't even know which grave my Giorgio is buried in, but Katarina is going to show me."

"Let me go back inside and get a candle and some more flowers to put on Giorgio's grave."

At the graveside, Angela handed the baby to Katarina and then slowly knelt on the stone slabs to lay down the flowers and the candle. Here she started to gently touch the surface as though she was caressing Giorgio's face. Suddenly she broke down, sobbing, crying and calling out for him.

"Giorgio, come back, why did you have to leave us?" she cried in pain, as though her heart was breaking in two. "Why, oh why did this happen? Look at your three children, look at them, oh my God, why did this happen to us?" Seeing their mother crying, Sebastian and Mariella started to cry too. "I love you my Giorgio, I always loved you and I always will. Please look over us and give me the courage to carry on. I beg of you, please help us." Dun Salv and Katarina were trying to stay strong. They felt choked with emotion and they could not stop the tears running down their cheeks. Angela now took out her rosary beads and still sobbing, started to say prayers with Katarina and Dun Salv for Giorgio's soul, but it wasn't long before she threw herself down onto the surface of the gravestone, kissing it. After giving her some time, Dun Salv decided that Angela had suffered enough and he gently helped her onto her feet. As they all slowly walked away, Angela kept crying and looking back. "The children and I will come and visit you my love," she promised.

When they got back to the church, Dun Salv invited them for coffee. Afterwards he made a suggestion. "Why don't you all stop at the public garden for a while? A bit of sun and a little more fresh air will do you and the children the world of good." Angela had to agree, and after all, the Armier Garden was only a short walk away. This garden was always full of beautiful flowers at this time of the year and it even had a large children's playground with swings and pathways for children to run freely in and enjoy. No sooner had they walked in, than Sebastian ran off to join the other boys who were playing Cat and Mouse. There were a few older boys playing football. A small group of girls were playing with beads, while another smaller group of children were involved in a game the locals called 'Passio'. There were women crocheting lace and others knitting woollen jumpers. Nuns and priests and the usual elderly gentlemen were looking at the local newspapers and debating the issues of the day. The Armier public garden was a place for everyone young and old alike.

Katarina took little Mariella straight to the swings while Angela sat on one of the benches shaded by a big tree, nursing baby George. The surprise of the day was the energy Sebastian had, running happily all over the place nonstop. Angela was overjoyed, but with it being such a hot day she did not want him to overdo it, so she began to call him over. But Sebastian would not stop. Surely he would exhaust himself soon, she thought to herself. Just then, a couple strolling by stopped to greet her. It was Paul Cassar and his wife Rosa.

When Paul was a child, he had sometimes spent time at Giorgio's home during the years when Giorgio was married to his first wife Rita. Unlike Giorgio and Rita, Paul's parents had raised seven children. Knowing how much Giorgio and Rita had wanted to have a child, they had allowed Paul, their youngest, to stay at the Gawchi's house for days at a time. Giorgio and Rita had loved Paul dearly. After Rita passed away, Paul would still make regular visits to see Giorgio.

Angela had met Paul and Rosa on only one occasion, on their wedding day. "Good morning Paul and Rosa. Thank you so much for your kindness over these last months. I don't know what I would have done without people like you."

"You are more than welcome," Paul said, "it's the least we could do. Angela, if you ever need anything, anything at all, please let us know; I have a better idea, we're on our way home now, why don't you come and join us for lunch?"

"What, today?" Angela replied.

"Yes. My mother is preparing meat pies. As you know, we are a big family, so she always cooks big meals. I am sure there is plenty for everyone. Please say yes. I'm sure my mother would love to see you and the children again."

Being her first day out and still recovering from the visit to her husband's graveside, Angela did feel a little tired and she was going to refuse Paul's generous offer, but when his wife insisted, Angela told them that she would consult with Katarina.

On hearing Angela calling, Katarina took Mariella off the swing and walked over to the group. "Oh, this must be Mariella. She looks like a little angel, she's so beautiful," Rosa said, as she knelt down to hug the little girl.

"Paul and Rosa have invited all of us for lunch at their farm. Would you like to go?"

"Yes, of course. I haven't seen Paul's mother for quite a while now. It would be wonderful to see her again. Did you know that I was once courted by his oldest brother, Toni?"

"So what happened, if you don't mind my asking?" replied Angela.

"Toni decided to go to work on a merchant ship and I never saw him again. That was many years ago of course. Paul, did Toni ever marry?" she asked.

"My brother Toni, marry? No, he's travelled to many exotic destinations all over the world but he never found the right woman I guess. Maybe that's why he's back home!" Paul added. Angela was sure that she saw a sparkle in Katarina's eyes.

"You mean; Toni is back in Malta? When did he return?" Katarina asked.

"About a month ago, didn't you know?"

"No, I didn't. Imagine that! Toni back, after all these years!"

"Listen, if you think that meeting Toni would make you feel uncomfortable, we don't have to go. I don't want to put you in an awkward position, if you know what I mean."

"I am a big girl now. I'm sure I can handle it."

"Fine, then let me call Sebastian over."

"Could I hold your baby for a minute?" Rosa asked Angela.

"Yes of course." Angela replied, handing her the baby. Angela called out Sebastian's name once more, but again, the child totally ignored her.

"Let me try. Let me call him," Paul suggested. "Sebastian! Sebastian! Please come here!" Paul called out.

When Sebastian heard someone new calling his name, he stopped running instantly and then ran as fast as he could to his mother. But once there, instead of clutching to his mother's dress, as

Angela had expected him to, Sebastian just stared at Paul.

"This is Paul and this is his wife Rosa," Angela told him, "they have a very big farm not very far from here and they want us to go there for lunch."

"Would you like that?" Paul said, smiling at the little red faced, breathless boy in front of him. Sebastian was gazing up at him, speechless. "Sebastian, do you like animals?"

"Yes, I do," he whispered.

"Then come and see the farm and I'll show you all of them."

All excited, Sebastian grabbed his mother's hand. During their walk, Paul played some of the games Giorgio had played with him during his own childhood years. He lifted Sebastian high up into the air and sat him on his shoulders. Sebastian loved all of the attention.

"Do it again! Do it again!" the little boy begged, giggling.

When they arrived at the farm, Paul called out to his mother. Lucia could hear the excitement in her son's voice and she quickly came into the hall.

"Katarina! What a lovely surprise. It has been so long. Welcome my dear," she said, hugging her. "Angela, how are you? It's so good to see you. Oh look at those children! They are just delightful. Paul, take them into the sitting room. I need to put the pies in the oven, and Paul, see what they want to drink."

"Mum, I've invited them for lunch. I hope you don't mind."

"Mind? No, not at all! Please get comfortable. I'll be back in a moment."

Rosa gave the now sleeping baby back to his mother. As promised, after serving drinks to the guests, Paul took Sebastian down to see the animals. "Sebastian is so comfortable around Paul," Angela said, seeing her son holding onto Paul's hand.

"All children love Paul. Whenever any of our families meet, the first thing the children do is run to his side. They know that he will give them all his attention. He has great patience too. Oh, I can't wait for our baby to arrive," replied Rosa.

"Are you pregnant?" Angela jumped in and asked.

"Yes, I'm due in November," Rosa answered.

"Why didn't you tell me? I wouldn't have let you carry my baby all the way here!" Angela replied, full of concern.

"Oh, I enjoyed every minute of it. You have three beautiful angels. I do hope that I will have lots of children too."

"You and Paul are wonderful together," remarked Angela, "I'm sure God will bless you with a fine family."

Here the topic of conversation continued on about pregnancies and babies. When Lucia returned to the room, the conversation then moved on to Katarina's earlier years. Talking about this time brought a discussion regarding the late Giorgio and his first wife, Rita. When Lucia realised that this could in some way upset Angela, she apologised.

"I am sorry. I shouldn't talk about the past like this. I haven't seen Katarina for such a long time and I got carried away. We can talk about something else."

"No, no, not at all," Angela said, "I am enjoying it. It is good to hear about the life Giorgio had before I came along. He was such a gentleman. I am more than happy to find out more about him. The day will come you know, when the children will grow and start asking questions about their father. The more I know about Giorgio and his life before he met me, the better."

Meanwhile, visiting the animals, the first thing Sebastian came face to face with was Paul's very own horse, named King. He was tall and noble looking, brown in colour with a beautiful shining black mane. Huge black eyes looked straight into Sebastian's little ones but Sebastian was not afraid. To Paul's surprise, Sebastian walked right up to King so that he could touch him. It was as if the horse and Sebastian could understand each other. "The horse likes you. Do you like him?" Paul asked.

"Yes very much, he's so big and strong," the boy replied. Sebastian had seen many horses of different breeds used by farmers in their fields or by the street hawkers, but this horse was very different.

"I have another horse. Actually, it's a little white pony. Would you like to see him?" All excited, Sebastian followed Paul down to another barn. When they entered, Sebastian was looking at the smallest pony he had ever seen, all white and munching away on some hay.

"He's so white and beautiful! Can I touch him?"

"Yes, but be very gentle," Paul warned.

Again Paul could feel the bond this little child seemed to have with animals. Just like his other horse, Snowy stopped eating his meal and lifted his head up as if to greet the new visitor. Sebastian patted its head and Snowy just stood there enjoying it. Paul asked Sebastian if he wanted to ride Snowy. Sebastian could not believe his ears and his eyes lit up in anticipation. "Yes! Please, could I?"

In a few minutes, Paul saddled up the pony. Holding Sebastian secure on Snowy, Paul carefully started to walk Snowy around the barn. This was Sebastian's first ever pony ride but it definitely was not going to be the last. There he was, sitting up high and confident and not at all frightened. After a while, Paul took Sebastian off the pony and together they went to feed some of the sheep.

Back at the house, Lucia took the freshly baked pies out of the oven and then started to call the family and guests to the table. When she knew they had heard her, she went to call Toni, who was busy milking the cows. Rosa took Angela into a bedroom next to the kitchen to lay the sleeping baby George down on the bed, while Katarina helped to set the table.

The moment Sebastian and Paul entered the kitchen, Sebastian quickly let go of Paul's hand. For a moment Angela thought that the magic between Paul and her son was broken, but to her surprise, all Sebastian wanted to do was to tell her about Snowy and his pony ride. Angela was speechless. Sebastian carried on telling her about the sheep, the chickens and the little kittens he had been playing with. "Look Ma, I picked up this egg myself!" he said, his little face so full of life. This moved Angela almost to tears. Once finished, Paul took Sebastian to wash his hands.

Entering the kitchen, Toni was totally surprised to see Katarina standing there before him. Their eyes locked onto one another and the women in the room could feel the energy between them. Could it be that the magic they had shared so many years ago was still this strong?

"Toni, I am sure that you remember Katarina. This is Angela, Giorgio Gawchi's wife and the little girl is her daughter, Mariella," his mother said. Toni could hear his mother's voice, but the vision of Katarina made him deaf to what she was saying.

"Katarina! What a wonderful surprise!" Toni said in a choked voice, "so, what brings you here? I mean.... are you staying for lunch?"

"Yes. I hope you don't mind."

"Mind, no! It is so good to see you again. You look well."

"Thank you," Katarina said hesitantly, "you look well too."

Lucia and Angela didn't want to interrupt them or to spoil this special moment but now Paul and Sebastian had charged back into the room. "Why is everybody still on their feet? Isn't anybody hungry?"

"Of course we are," answered his mother, smiling.

"Sebastian! You sit here near me," Paul said, seating the

40

little boy on the chair. Toni realised that he had been somewhat rude in not acknowledging Angela's presence. They had never actually met.

"Angela, I want to tell you how sorry I was to hear of Giorgio's passing. May I convey my deepest sympathy. Your children are lovely, what's the little girl's name again?"

"Her name is Mariella. I have another boy, a baby called George. He is sleeping in the other room," she answered.

"And this is Sebastian, her eldest son," Paul said, to introduce his new and youngest friend.

"Hello Sebastian, did Paul show you the animals?"

"Yes, he did," replied the boy, smiling, with eyes full of happiness.

Angela placed Mariella onto her lap and Rosa sat on the opposite chair while Katarina helped Lucia to serve the food. Lucia had always loved Katarina and she felt very sad on the day her son Toni had broken the engagement to leave her and the island behind. But today they were all under the same roof again and she was going to do her very best to reunite them, even if only a flicker of a chance remained. She placed Katarina right opposite Toni. When everybody was seated, Paul looked at Sebastian and asked him to honour them by giving thanks for the meal. Sebastian stood up, put his little hands together, closed his eyes, and in the sweetest voice said the short thanksgiving prayer his mother had taught him.

During dinner, Lucia loved the way Katarina and Toni kept looking at each other. Her son Toni was a good man but being the first born child, Lucia and her husband had pushed him into helping them on the big farm they owned from a very young age. Toni had worked very long hours with his father, so had never had the typical childhood fun the other children enjoyed. The only time that Lucia ever remembered him being carefree and youthful was when he had

41

courted Katarina, but then somehow he had become scared of the idea of marriage. Maybe he had needed the time to find himself because when the opportunity to go away came along, he had left the island and his family. Even on his return he carried on just as before, acting introverted and closed. The animals seemed to be all he cared about, preferring to be alone. But now on meeting Katarina again, his face looked vibrant and happy. It was remarkable. After the meal, the ladies talked a little more as they cleared up, while Paul took Sebastian down to the barn again. As for Toni, he did not want to leave the kitchen now that Katarina was there. He remained in his chair, just looking at her. Katarina could feel his eyes following her but she did not mind the attention. He was the only man she had ever cared for and having his presence in the same room felt incredible. It was now siesta time. Many families usually rested during the hot afternoon hours for a short while. Mariella had fallen asleep in Angela's arms and she was now resting next to her baby brother. It was no surprise to see Paul walking into the kitchen, holding little Sebastian asleep in his arms too. The child had fallen asleep on the hay. Now Lucia came up with a great idea, but this could only work if Angela stayed for a while. If Angela left the farm, then Katarina would have to leave too, so Lucia suggested that Angela should have a short rest with the others. Angela's first outing had proved to be eventful and she was indeed tired. She took up Lucia's kind offer and went to have a lie down next to her children. Rosa and Paul went into their bedroom too. Usually Lucia would do the same, but not on this occasion. Her instincts were telling her to keep Katarina and Toni together.

"Are you tired?" she asked Katarina after she had made sure Angela was comfortable.

"Not really," she replied.

"Toni, what about you; are you tired?"

"No I'm fine."

"Good. I was hoping that the three of us could go for a short walk." Katarina stole a look at Toni but remained speechless.

"I am waiting for an answer," Lucia said.

"I wouldn't mind," Toni answered, "that is, if Katarina wants to, of course."

"Yes, I'd like to," Katarina answered.

"Good, we'll go right away. I'm ready."

As they walked through the lane with many wild prickly pear trees blooming with beautiful yellow flowers, Lucia talked about the two families and the early days. She reminded both of them of some of the family gatherings and celebrations which they had shared. Some of the memories she conjured up had them laughing. It was so nice to have them together again. Toni had been so lonely and Lucia was sure that her son's only chance of happiness was with Katarina. Toni and Katarina were not youngsters and they had courted before. Lucia wanted to give them some space.

"You both go ahead. I'll catch up with you soon. I need to cut some wild herbs," she said, as she opened a wooden gate to enter one of the family fields. Toni shook his head and smiled to show her that he realised what she was up to. Katarina too, understood her intentions and she smiled shyly. A short distance away, Toni asked Katarina if she wanted to sit down under the big olive tree nearby, the same tree where they used to sit so many years before. "The tree, it's still here and we are back here too. Isn't it amazing? I feel as if I am dreaming. Yes, I would love to sit under it again."

After all these years, destiny had brought them together again, and now that they were finally alone Toni could not keep his feelings to himself. "Katarina, you are just as pretty as the day I left you," he said.

"You look good too Toni; you've hardly aged at all," Katarina replied, full of happiness. Then there was silence. Toni wanted to tell her so many things but where should he start? Then he broke the ice with a heartfelt apology.

"Katarina, I want to tell you how sorry I am for what I did to you all those years ago. I am very sorry. I had to go away. I felt so trapped by my family and I just couldn't take it anymore. I felt so restless. It was an opportunity to leave everything behind and I did. But I found myself missing everyone, especially you. I travelled to many exotic places and met lots of fascinating people but I was never truly happy. None of them ever made me feel the way you did. I just couldn't get you out of my mind."

Katarina answered him immediately and said, "You must believe me when I tell you that you are the only person I have ever truly cared about. My heart was and still is yours."

Upon hearing these words Katarina stole his heart all over again. They were sitting in the most idyllic of surroundings, in such a still silence, with an abundance of butterflies flying all round them. He so wanted to kiss her. His heart was beating so loudly. Familiar desires of long ago stirred within him, but it was not to be as yet. Not on this day anyway.

"Do not turn round," she said shyly, "your mother is coming."

"So, how's everything?" Lucia asked.

"Fine," Toni and Katarina answered, embarrassed.

"I think that we should be heading back home now. I do have guests at the house after all!"

Toni gently helped Katarina to her feet and they began to walk home. The stroll back was quiet, but Lucia knew that they were going to be fine. They had hardly entered the house when baby George started to cry. His loud cries woke up everyone. Angela knew that cry very well; her baby was hungry. Lucia and Katarina attended to Mariella and Sebastian, while Angela dressed the baby.

As soon as Paul and Rosa came into the kitchen, Sebastian ran to hold onto Paul's trousers.

"Sebastian, it's time to leave now," said his mother. "Say thank you and goodbye."

"No, I don't want to go, I want to stay here! I want to stay with Paul! I want to see the pony again. I want to play with the kittens!" he cried.

"I promise we will come back another day. George is hungry; we have to go home."

"I want to stay here! I want to ride on the pony again!" Sebastian repeated.

Paul did not want Sebastian's first visit here to finish on a sour note. Quickly, he said a few words in Angela's ear and Angela understood.

"If you stop crying and obey your mother, you can have one of the kittens to take home, how about that?"

"Can I? Can I really have one?" Sebastian asked tearfully.

"Yes, but only if you stop crying and you thank your mother."

"Thank you Ma," the little boy said, drying his tears on his sleeve.

"That's a good boy. Now, which of the kittens would you like?"

"The black one, I want the black one," Sebastian replied. When Paul returned, he gave Sebastian the little black kitten. "And what are you going to name it?" he asked.

"I want to name it Fluffy because of its fluffy hair," the little boy replied, with a big smile on his face.

"That's a very good choice. Here, take some food and don't forget to feed it. You take good care of it, ok?"

As they were at the front door ready to leave, Lucia handed Angela a kitchen towel with a few pieces of pie wrapped up neatly inside it. "Take this with you for later. I want to tell you again how nice it was to have you over." Lucia then caught Toni's sad face. Thinking quickly, she turned to Angela again and said, "Tomorrow I am cooking the lamb Toni slaughtered this morning. Why don't you all come over again? The lamb will definitely be too much for just us. We would love to share it with you all." Angela didn't know what to say at first but when she saw Lucia wink, she got the message. Angela didn't want to look so obvious so she asked, "Are you sure? Two days in a row is maybe too much for you."

"Would I suggest it if that were true? Paul would love to spend more time with Sebastian, wouldn't you Paul?"

"Yes, please come," and turning to Sebastian he added. "And I can take you for another pony ride."

"Yes! Ma, please say yes!" Sebastian said, nodding his head as if to persuade his mother.

"Katarina, you must come too, I insist," Lucia said.

"I will. Thank you," she replied, stealing another look at the now smiling Toni.

They parted company, but not from their thoughts or their hearts. Throughout the rest of that day and well into the night, both Katarina and Toni thought only about the few wonderful hours they had shared together.

Chapter 4

Toni and Katarina

When they met at the farm the next day, events continued where they had left off. All of them talked, joked, laughed and ate a lavish meal. It was as if they were indirectly celebrating Katarina and Toni's reunion. For the second day in a row, Lucia chaperoned Toni and Katarina on a short walk. Once again, she gave them time alone by telling them that she had been asked to pick some more herbs for a neighbour. This time Toni did not want to miss the opportunity, and as soon as Katarina sat down, Toni knelt in front of her and kissed her. Katarina did not object at all. It was so wonderful to feel the same way again; young and wanted. Katarina's smile and the happy shine in her eyes said it all. Toni asked if he could court her once again. Katarina could not believe it; the only man she had ever loved had come back into her life. Her twenty ninth-birthday was coming up in just a few weeks' time. Needless to say, she excitedly said yes.

"Great! Tomorrow afternoon I will come to your house to ask your father's permission." Katarina could not have felt happier. The minute Lucia came up to meet them they gave her the news.

"I'm so happy I could cry!" Lucia said, throwing the bunch of herbs she had just collected into the air and clapping. "You have my blessing."

"You don't think your father would refuse, do you?" Toni asked Katarina.

"My father is a very good man. He won't let us down."

"Everything will turn out fine," Lucia interrupted, "but don't tell the others at the house just yet. Let's take things one step at a time. Oh, I am so excited. I think I am the one who will have the hardest time keeping this secret," she said. "Now, let's return to the house."

It was such a wonderful walk back, all smiles and good feelings. Toni hated letting go of Katarina's hand once they approached the farm. Katarina wanted so much to share the great news with her best friend Angela, but for once she had to keep a secret from her. On the walk down to the main street, Angela noticed the change in Katarina's behaviour. Katarina, the usual chatty person, was lost for words. She just smiled and nothing more. Back home, Katarina asked her parents to sit with her in private. Katarina was all nerves but she came right to the point. "Toni, Lucia's son, has recently returned to Malta, have you heard?"

"No. I guess we have been very busy looking after Angela and her family these last few months" replied Martin.

"Well, he has, and he's still single. Father, as I mentioned, Angela and I went to his mother's farm yesterday and he was there. We went for lunch there again today and it's still the same. We feel we belong together. Toni has asked me to court him again."

"That's wonderful! I mean, that's good news, but I need to have a talk with him first," said Martin.

"Of course father. Toni is coming down here tomorrow morning, at around ten o'clock. I hope that's fine with you."

"Yes, we'll be here."

Katarina did not have to worry about her mother's approval. She could see that she had tears in her eyes. The truth was that both her parents were happy to have Toni back in their lives, but they were somewhat apprehensive to see him. After all, Toni had hurt their daughter. This time around, they wanted to be sure that he was serious about his courtship with Katarina. Once Martin left the room, Karmena sat with her daughter to have a woman to woman talk. Katarina listened very carefully to all her mother's advice and when her mother had finished, asked for permission to go next door to tell Angela all about it.

"Yes, go. Angela is the person who got you back together again; she deserves to know. Make sure you give her my love."

"I knew it! I knew it!" Angela cried, and jumped up, hugging Katarina. "Oh my Lord, I am so happy for you I want to cry. Let me put the kettle on so we can share a coffee," she said, taking down a tin in which she stored buskuttini, the aniseed flavoured biscuits to eat with the coffee, as if to have a small party.

That night, Katarina could not sleep at all. She wanted to see Toni so much. She wanted so much to look her best for him that she got out of bed and tried on all her dresses. In the end, she decided to go with the yellow dress that had lace around the collar. Everyone always said how much it suited her.

That morning Toni was a nervous wreck himself. "What's wrong with you?" Paul asked, noticing his strange behaviour.

"I'm not supposed to tell you but I can't keep it a secret any longer. This morning I'm going to Martin's house. I'm going to ask Martin if I can court Katarina again. I asked her yesterday and she happily accepted."

"That is great news. Does mother know?"

"Yes, of course, but please don't tell her I told you."

"So why are you so nervous?"

"Martin might still be mad at me, for the way I broke off my engagement with Katarina."

"But that was such a long time ago! I am sure that Martin will think about Katarina's happiness first. Even I can see that you both still adore each other. I'm sure that things will work out for both of you. Martin is still the same kind man. Just don't worry; it'll work out I'm sure."

"Thank you Paul, I really mean it," Toni said.

Toni now went to look for his mother to have her blessing.

"Katarina is the woman for you. You two belong together. Martin would be a fool not to see it. Go. All my thoughts and my prayers are with you. I will be waiting." During the walk, Toni tried very hard to think positive, but negative thoughts kept creeping into his head. What if Martin scorned him for the way he had deserted Katarina so many years before, once they came face to face? His head was full of negative thoughts and he was scared, but before he knew it, he was standing in front of Martin's home.

"Come in Toni," Martin said as he answered the door.

Toni remembered the house very well and nothing seemed to have changed. Everything was in the same place as he remembered. It was as if he had moved back in time. It felt good to be here again for he knew only love in this house. Yes, Martin had gained some weight and had lost some of his hair, but it was so nice to see him again. Taking off his hat, Toni started to apologise even before he had sat down. He continuously told Martin that he had never stopped loving Katarina. He assured him that it was a time when he was very young. Only the arrival of the pot of coffee stopped him from going on forever.

Karmena served the coffees with a greeting and a smile and then she left the room.

"Toni, I do believe you. I do believe that you feel sorry for what happened, but you have no idea what your break up did to Katarina. It was extremely heart breaking for all of us to see her so hurt. She was unwell for many weeks; for months in fact. She loved you and I believe she still does. She's never looked at any other man. I did have a few offers for her hand in marriage, but you were always the love of her life. I didn't want to force her into an unhappy marriage. Now that destiny has bought you back together, I will not stop you. We are all older now, with no time for games or disappointments anymore. I only want happiness for all my children and you are Katarina's happiness; my heart knows this. So yes, you can court my daughter and may God bless you both."

"Thank you Martin. I promise you, I will take very good care of her. I know that Katarina is the only woman who can fill the emptiness in my heart." Toni's sincerity had shone through. They shook hands and then they walked into the kitchen to tell the rest of the family. Congratulations were in order. Karmena and the rest of the family hugged the couple. Martin opened a bottle of his special homemade wine. They talked, laughed and shared some stories. Before Toni left, Martin told him that they would stop at his mother's house the next morning. "Please give your mother and the rest of the family our love and regards, and Toni, welcome back!"

"You've made me a very happy man. See you tomorrow."

Katarina stood at the door, watching Toni walk away. She adored his walk. She loved everything about him. When he was out of sight, she ran next door to tell Angela that all had gone well.

Back at the farm, Lucia's nerves were shattered in anticipation as she continuously prayed for good news. "Mother I'm back!" Toni shouted, as he entered the front door. Lucia could hear the energy in his voice; this was very good. One look at his happy shining face and she knew it had all gone well. "Katarina and I are courting again. Martin has given us his blessing. Isn't it wonderful?" Lucia opened her arms wide to hug him, as only a mother can.

Rosa just happened to come into the kitchen and Toni took her hands and turned her round in circles. "I'm going to marry Katarina! I can't believe it, I'm so happy. I'm going to marry Katarina!"

"Congratulations," Rosa said, "I like her. She will be very good for you."

"Before I forget," Toni said, turning to his mother; "Martin and Karmena are coming to see you tomorrow morning. They were

51

so wonderful. They treated me with so much respect. Mother, I want us to prepare something special for lunch. I want them to eat here."

"Don't you worry about a thing; leave it to me. Oh Toni. I am so happy for you." When Martin and Karmena came to the farm the next day, they all talked for hours and hours. With Toni and Katarina courting every day, Angela started to adjust to her new way of life without having Katarina's continuous help. Each day was a new challenge, trying to raise her young family on her own.

After courting for three months, Toni asked Martin for Katarina's hand in marriage and Martin agreed. The families went to see the parish priest and the wedding was arranged to take place on the first Sunday of October. Angela had always wanted to find a way to repay these families for all they had done for her during these many months, and with the impending wedding, she had her chance to do so. She immediately offered to sew the bridal gown. Katarina accepted Angela's kindness with open arms. Lucia was overjoyed. She was going to prepare a wedding party that no one would ever forget. She would invite everyone she knew. Nothing was more important to her than her son's happiness. On the wedding day, all the villagers waited on the church terraces to see Katarina. She looked beautiful in her exquisite dress. They had never seen such detailed lacework before and the other brides-to-be envied her. They waited eagerly to hear about the identity of the seamstress. By the time Angela walked into the elaborately large hall which Lucia had rented for the reception celebrations, Angela's name was being whispered on the lips of all the upcoming brides. A five man band played a variety of local folk music. Simple romantic melodies followed one after the other and everyone had a great time. They ate, drank and danced. Nobody seemed to want to leave. Lucia had succeeded and she was very pleased with herself. This was a wedding that no one would forget for a very long time indeed. From the wedding hall, Katarina and Toni went straight to their new home, a house that Toni had bought from some relatives a short distance from his mother's farm.

Chapter 5

Angela

Yes the wedding was over but none of the women present on that evening would forget Katarina's wedding dress, and as early as the next morning two mothers, whose daughters were engaged, arrived at Angela's home to speak with her. Angela was delighted with this new business venture which had literally sprung up overnight, and she gladly took the orders. As time went on even more orders came her way. The income was more than welcome but Angela was a very humble person and she did not let the idea of riches go to her head. Her prices were very reasonable and her children always came first.

In 1914, the Great War broke out. The Maltese nation voluntarily offered to contribute help and many thousands joined the Empire. Malta was not attacked but war casualties arrived daily to the island. On some days, hundreds arrived at a time. At one point the hospitals became so full that the Government asked the Islanders to help out by taking in some of the injured soldiers. The people responded willingly. Lucia and her son Toni were among the first to help by filling all the rooms on their property. To protect her children from any diseases, Angela stopped visiting. Malta became known as 'the Nurse of the Mediterranean,' with the Victory of the Allies in 1918.

With the war over, Angela started to sew a new set of designs. These caught on so well with the locals, that through word of mouth, her name was on the lips of all the upper class who approached her with many elaborate requests, and these proved to be popular. Joan, an English teacher who lived just across the road, loved her clothes. She too had become one of Angela's regular customers, but for her, this was becoming rather an expense. So she approached Angela with a proposition. She was ready to teach English to her three children in exchange for free sewing. Angela readily accepted Joan's proposition.

Mariella and George loved their learning, but not Sebastian. All he wanted to do and all he thought about was riding Snowy, the pony on Paul's farm. No matter how hard Joan tried, she could not make him pay any attention. He would cry and distract his siblings. In the end he got his way and stopped going.

The years passed and the children grew. Mariella was now ten years old, going on eleven. She was a very bright girl, memorising everything her mother and Joan taught her. She took to the needle and thread quite naturally too. She went with her mother everywhere, but by far her favourite places were the fabric and textile shops in Valletta, the capital city of Malta. George was nine and he had become a very independent boy, full of energy. No one could keep him in one place for more than a minute. That October, 1921, Sebastian was turning thirteen. For the special day, Paul planned to throw a big birthday party for the young boy he had grown so attached to.

On the day, the birthday meal was enjoyed by all. Asking for everyone's attention, Paul then asked Sebastian to cover his eyes. When Sebastian was told to open them, Paul was right in front of him holding Snowy by his reins. "Take him; he's yours," Paul said to the young boy whose eyes opened wide in disbelief; "Happy birthday Sebastian." Angela was so overcome that she could not contain her feelings, crying tears of joy. What more could this family do for her and her children? Sebastian was so proud to own his own pony that he rode Snowy all the way home. He then tied him up inside the garage his father had used to make his furniture, right next to the house.

The next morning, Leli the blacksmith, (nicknamed 'Il-Ggant') 'Giant', because he was tall and heavily built, came to see Snowy. Leli knew horses and he was very impressed. "You've got a fine animal here but he does need new shoes. I will make him them for free."

"You will?" Sebastian answered, delighted. "I'll tell Mother. Please wait here."

"Are you sure?" Angela said on meeting Leli, "you have so much work."

"A small belated birthday present for Sebastian. I'll have them ready by the end of the week."

Guzeppi, another friend of Giorgio's, now a retired carpenter, had heard about the pony too. Seeing that the animal needed a stall, he offered to build one in the garage, next to the house. Sebastian felt that he was the luckiest boy in the village.

Chapter 6

Meningitis

For the past few years, life had been fulfilling for Angela's family but unfortunately, sad times were just around the corner. Seven weeks to the day that Sebastian had celebrated his thirteenth birthday, the boy woke up complaining of a very bad headache. It progressively worsened. Within just a short time his whole body was burning hot. Angela immediately sent Mariella to fetch Karmena. Karmena quickly took Sebastian out of the bed. Placing him into the large stainless steel clothes wash tub, she soaked him with cold towels to break the fever, while George ran for the doctor. But the doctor arrived too late. Sebastian had died. The doctor's diagnosis was Viral Meningitis. Just like on that night, the night her husband had died, Angela's heart was ripped apart. She screamed and called out Sebastian's name but her adorable boy had passed away. The doctor covered the boy's body and told everyone to leave the room.

Filippa, another of Karmena's daughters, ran to tell Paul and he came as fast as he could, only to arrive and see Angela, crying uncontrollably sitting on one of the chairs in the kitchen, totally bereft. Tests on Sebastian's body confirmed that he had died of Meningitis. Immediately, a curfew was ordered in the small area of St. Sebastian. Children were to be kept inside their prospective houses and the parish school closed until further notice. The government did not want this to become an epidemic.

Paul asked Angela's permission to take care of the funeral arrangements. Angela was too distraught to think clearly and she accepted gracefully. Paul purchased a small white coffin and hired the white hearse.

The next day the funeral left the house at around noon, taking Sebastian's body straight to the cemetery. For the second time in her life Angela was not able to accompany a member of her family to the graveside. When young Sebastian was lowered into the ground, Paul said a few words to the boy he loved so. "Rest in peace my young boy. I thank you for the wonderful times we've shared together. You will always be in my heart."

A few days later Angela asked Paul to take Snowy back to his farm. She did not have the time or the strength to care for the animal. With no other cases of Meningitis reported, the curfew was shortly lifted and life returned to normal for the villagers, but not for Angela. She closed herself at home working on the orders she had fallen behind with. This was the only thing that kept her mind occupied. She now stopped visiting Paul's farm altogether for the place brought back too many memories of Sebastian; it was simply too much to bear. Mariella and George asked many times for their brother's whereabouts. Angela tried to explain that he had gone to be with God in heaven; a very wonderful place where everyone would meet again, but they did not understand why their elder brother was not there.

Chapter 7

George and David

The Narcissus, the Sulla, the wheat, the hay and other crops had been cut and already harvested. Now it was time for the village feast to begin. On the Maltese Islands, the feast days were eagerly anticipated by everyone, with each village celebrating their own day in a very big way. On the feast day, the whole of the village would unite. Only the clothes distinguished the upper and lower classes. The rich men wore suits and vests. Expensive gold pocket watches could be seen on many, young and old. The women wore intricately detailed gowns specially sewn for the occasion with new handbags and shoes to complete the ensembles. The less affluent men wore a cap, a shirt and an open jacket, showing off their suspenders. The women wore many different kinds of traditional headdresses and blouses. The poor wore anything passed down from an older sibling or relative, and some did not even own a decent pair of shoes. But today, it was the feast day and all classes came together. The community were there to honour their village saint and in this part of the village it was Saint Sebastian. The patron's statue was carried out of the church on the shoulders of eight proud men. The Pinto Village Band played the specially written music to honour the saint, while villagers sang along to the traditional lyrics. The procession then proceeded through the streets as petard after petard shot into the air, filling the night sky with vivid colours. Before the statue was placed back into the church there was still the big ending, the last box of fireworks to set off, and no one dared move until it had all ended. For this year's feast, young George asked his mother's permission to help out with the village preparations. Although still in mourning, Angela gave him her blessing. It was during this time that George met David, another boy from the same area. Being the same age, thirteen almost fourteen, the two got along right away and they soon became firm friends. By far, their favourite place was a valley the locals called 'Wied Ic- Cawsli,'or 'the Valley of the Berries'. In season, the trees were abundantly laden with juicy blackberries. Like monkeys, George and David would climb up the tree trunks to cut and eat the ripe fruit straight from the tree. Like rabbits, they played and jumped from one stone to the next, challenging each other in a race, then undress down to their underwear and dive into the large water reservoir to cool off.

In winter, this valley filled up with mud and rain water which ran down from the high fields, though this did not stop them from having fun. They now played different games in another valley nearby called 'Wied l' Kbir' or 'The Big Valley'; a very rocky valley with high cliffs on both sides. It was a pleasure to challenge the cliffs and to race to the top. In doing this, they came across several birds' nests. These fascinated David and in time he became an avid bird watcher. Bird watching was definitely not George's idea of having fun however, as George could never stay in one place for long enough. While David watched the nests, George would walk along the paths and explore the caves in the area. What caught George's attention were the ponds full of tadpoles. He found the frog's life cycle quite amazing. Tadpoles were not the only things he found either; caterpillars and other insects found their way into his pockets. There was many a time when he took home a chrysalis to watch transform into a butterfly. George was a thoughtful boy and he always picked a bunch of pretty wild flowers to take home to his mother. They were such simple hobbies and yet each delighted the boys. This was such an innocent time in their lives. They did not know what fear or danger was, it was simply a time to enjoy their youth to the fullest. Their interest and excitement in all that lay around them was to the same degree, yet their characters developed in different ways.

In time David became totally obsessed with bird watching and was outside continuously, yet George on the other hand preferred to stay at home more and more. Woodworking was in George's blood and so with the help of a local carpenter he started to learn the trade. Even though George's father had died many years ago, there were those still loyal to the late Giorgio. On hearing that the young George was interested in following in his father's footsteps, they started to come to him with a few small orders.

Chapter 8

Angela's Last Moments

With Mariella's help, Angela's little enterprise thrived. Sometimes their work continued well into the night. However, lately Angela would wake feeling thoroughly exhausted and unable to get out of bed like she used to. Eventually she had to talk about it and Mariella sent her brother George for the doctor. The doctor could not see or feel anything but after consulting with another two doctors they had Angela admitted into hospital for tests. The news that came back devastated Mariella and George. The test results showed that Angela had a tumour and there was nothing anyone could do. They decided to take her home to care for her themselves. Mariella and George had agreed beforehand that they would not tell their mother, but in just a few short weeks, Angela's health became considerably worse. She felt herself deteriorating and she knew that something was very wrong. Even so, through her pain she kept quiet so as to not make life any more difficult for them. In turn, Mariella and George never gave up hope and prayed daily to the Holy Lady for a miracle, but their mother continued getting weaker.

During the early hours of July the twentieth of that year, 1927, Angela felt a presence in her room. At first she thought it was Mariella who was sleeping in the same bedroom, checking on her as she often did during the night. But before she could turn around, a bright light appeared. After staring at it for a few seconds, the light turned into an image, the image of a very beautiful woman with a halo around her head. Angela could not explain it but she was sure that this could only be the Holy Lady, the Madonna. Angela wanted to wake up Mariella but she could not move a muscle. It was as if the presence of the Holy Lady wanted it this way. In seconds, two more bright shining images appeared, of her husband Giorgio and her son Sebastian. Oh how happy they looked and she wanted so much to jump out of bed to embrace them, but her body would not move. Without moving his lips, she could clearly hear her late husband telling her that on this same morning she was going to be reunited with them in heaven. Angela was overcome to hear such news as she had missed them so, but she then remembered that she also had two beautiful children who she would be leaving behind. At this moment it was as if Giorgio had read her mind. He assured her that they were going to be fine. Angela now looked straight at the Holy Lady and just as the Madonna had accepted the death of her son Jesus on the cross, she too accepted that her time had come. Giorgio slowly lifted his right hand and pointed to the corner of the room, as if to tell her something. She turned her eyes to see where he was pointing; it was the dresser in the corner. When she again turned her eyes to look back at him, all three images had vanished. The room fell back into darkness and they were gone. Where had they gone? She did not want them to go. 'Was it just a dream or had it really taken place?' she asked herself.

Mixed in her thoughts, she then remembered Giorgio pointing to the dresser and she understood the message. Underneath the dresser there was something hidden, a small treasure only she knew about and which she had promised her husband she would pass onto the children before she died. Yes, now she was sure that the vision had taken place. She noticed that her body could now move freely. The continuous pain she had been experiencing these last few days had suddenly passed. She turned around to reach for her rosary beads and quietly started praying.

The first thing Mariella did each morning was to open the only window for sunlight and fresh air. After, she would sit at her mother's side for a little while to ask her what she needed. But on this morning, it was different. To her surprise, her mother's face showed no pain. Angela was smiling. Mariella immediately thought that the miracle they had been praying for had taken place and she started to call out to George.

"George, George, quickly come here!" she said in a loud voice, "hurry George, hurry!"

"What, what is it?" George asked as he entered the bedroom.

"Look at Mother! Look how good she looks!" she cried happily. It was true. Angela had a happy peaceful face. She looked so well. As they sat on the bed, one on each side, they hugged and kissed her.

"Good morning my children, I do feel well today, it's true," she said, even though she knew in her heart that this would be the last time they sat together.

"Mother, let me call Karmena over. George you stay with her. I'll return in no time and then George, you can go to fetch Doctor Muscat."

"No," Angela said, "don't go, not yet anyway. I have something very important to tell you. Please sit and listen."

"What is it Mother?" Mariella asked.

"George, go to the dresser and run your hand underneath. You will feel a small box. Pull it towards you; it should slide out easily. Please get it and bring it here. Your father once hid something there and the time has come to tell you about it." Mariella and George looked at each other in confusion. 'What was their mother talking about'? 'What box was under the dresser and why hadn't she ever told them about it before'? However, George did as his mother asked. Kneeling on the floor, he ran his hand along the bottom ledge.

"I found it!" he said in a loud voice.

"Good, now bring it over," Angela answered. George sat on the bed near his mother.

64

"Open it," Angela asked.

Inside the box, George saw something wrapped in a red cloth. Mariella watched George unfold the fabric. When the object was revealed, they could see that it was an eight pointed cross. It appeared to be made of pure gold with a large precious stone in the centre on a long thick chain. One did not have to be an expert to know that it was priceless. Why was it hidden, how did it get there and who did it belong too?

"Listen very carefully," their mother began, just like in their childhood days when Angela would tell them fairy tales and stories from long ago. "One of the reasons I used to read you so many historic passages when you were small was because of this cross," she said. "As you well know, during the end of that horrifying time here on Malta, the Turks attacked non-stop. The people under the orders of the Knights fought bravely but they suffered many casualties. It was during these uncertain times that one of your ancestors happened to see a small group of knights fighting the Turkish soldiers. His name was Salvu and he wanted to help the knights. So, taking out his stiletto, he rode his horse as fast as he could to the scene. When he reached it he noticed that the fighting had been going on for some time and there were many dead. It had been reduced to only two knights against five Turks. Salvu was tall and thickly built, strong as a bull so they say. Quickly killing one of the astonished Turks with one swing, he now entered the fighting. At the end of it he was the only one still standing. He looked for the other two knights and found them on the ground."

Here Angela stopped and asked them for some water. "Mother, I think you should stop now, we don't want you to get tired," Mariella said, as she helped her with the water.

"No, I have to tell you this and I am fine, really I am. Now where was I?"

"You were telling us that the knights were killed and lying on the ground."

"Yes, well, that's what Salvu had thought but when he checked them, one of them was still breathing. Salvu could see that this soldier was bleeding heavily and in pain, but he managed to open his eyes and in a very weak low voice told Salvu to take out a scroll he had tied to his leg. The knight then told him to take it and give it personally to the Grand Master Jean de La Valette and nobody else. No sooner had he finished these words than he died in Salvu's arms. For some reason, Salvu felt that he could not just leave this knight behind, so, lifting the body from the ground, he placed him on one of the stronger horses and rode quickly towards the Grand Master's palace. What Salvu did not know was that this knight was not just any ordinary soldier but a Spanish Grand Master who happened to be carrying a scroll, detailing strategic battle plans. When the Grand Master was told about Salvu's arrival, he asked them to bring him into his private chamber right away. Meeting the Grand Master Jean de La Valette, Salvu felt honoured and handed him the scroll. Without a second to spare, the Grand Master unfolded it, but to Salvu's disbelief there was nothing on it. The Grand Master however, walked over to one of the burning candlesticks and when he put the scroll over the flames, words started to appear. Salvu had never seen anything like it before. Then the Grand Master started to speak and told Salvu that he had done his country and all of them a great deed. He said that for his courage and service he wanted to give him something. Then the Grand Master walked to his armoire, took out this cross and he gave it to Salvu. This same cross has been passed down through the generations ever since, always to the eldest son. Had your brother Sebastian, God bless his soul, been here with us today, this would have been passed onto him. George, it is yours now. No matter how poor you become, you have to promise me that this cross will always stay in the family."

The story was fascinating. George felt so proud to possess such an important heirloom. "I promise," George said, "I will always take care of it and cherish it."

Angela now reached for Mariella's hand and said; "I wish I had something for you, but this is the only thing your father left behind. I hope that you understand why I had to give it to your brother."

"Ma, I understand, really. I am very proud of Salvu and happy for George, but I am happier just to see you looking so well. Let me go for Karmena. She will be so happy to see you like this, in no pain."

"Pain? I haven't had any pain for hours, which reminds me. Did I tell you about the three visitors I had during the night?"

"Who?" Mariella asked.

"The Holy Lady, the Madonna Herself. She came first and then your father and your brother Sebastian came too. They were all here, just a few hours ago."

Mariella and George looked at one another. Their mother had in detail recalled a story from the past and now, just a minute later, she was speaking of ghosts. She must have been hallucinating. Angela saw the looks on their faces.

"They were here, really! You don't believe me, do you?" she said, "The Holy Lady, She is so beautiful, just like I always imagined Her to be."

"Ma, stop talking like this, you're scaring me. You must have had a nice dream that's all," Mariella said, looking at George, but Angela insisted that it had happened that way and it was not just a dream.

"I love you both so much. I'm very proud to be your mother. Come, come closer, both of you and give me a hug." She embraced them, one on each side of her and just like the Maltese proverb says, she died right there in their arms, like a little bird.

Later Mariella and George could swear that they had felt their mother's soul leave her body. It was a moment that they could never explain or forget. Mariella very gently lowered her mother's head onto the pillow. The room suddenly went cold. Mariella started crying, but as the full impact of what just had happened deepened, she went into shock. She started screaming hysterically, hitting and knocking everything her hands could reach. She was completely out of control. George had to stop her before she seriously harmed herself. He grabbed her by the shoulders to steady her, just as she fainted at his feet.

George ran to Martin for help. Together they put Mariella onto her bed and then Martin went to fetch the doctor. Once again Doctor Muscat was called to the Gawchi residence under tragic circumstances.

Later that day, George went to the village cemetery to check if his mother could be buried with his father and his brother at the Qormi cemetery, only to be informed that the particular government plot they were in was full. Angela had to be buried in another grave nearby. That day many villagers dropped by at the house to offer their condolences, bringing with them food to ease the difficulties of the following days. Angela had moved so many people. Her death at the young age of only fifty-three was a loss to everyone who knew her. George and Mariella were very touched to see so many different people there for the funeral service and the large crowd that followed the coffin all the way to the cemetery. Malta had lost a wonderful human being. In solidarity they prayed for her soul.

Later on that week Mariella and George, even at their tender young age, felt that their mother should be laid to rest with her father and brother. So they went out and bought a plot within which to lay their departed family. It was the least they could do for a mother who had given them so much.

Chapter 9

Mariella

With her mother's passing, Mariella fought her depression by dedicating all of her time to her sewing. In the New Year of 1928, she started with a new line of designs. Her fashion sense was exciting and fresh. Many young affluent women appeared at her doorstep. As Malta's port was being used as a military base by the English, by the summer, Mariella had a steady stream of clientele among the servicemen's wives and expatriates. Paula's English lessons helped her tremendously and everything was going well.

In the summer of 1931, Mariella had two new visitors. Everything about them was different; their hairstyles, the cut of their clothes, and even the way they spoke English. They had an accent Mariella had never heard before. Unbeknown to her, they were from the United States of America and they had been on the island for a week, mixing business with pleasure. Being very well known designers working with famous stage shows back in America, they were on the lookout for new ideas and talent.

During their few days on Malta, they had already attended various social functions. Intermingling with the prominent business sector and top level politicians, Helen Armstrong could not help but notice a few particularly special dresses. These gowns had been made by Mariella. So impressed was she, that she sought out Mariella's address from one of her new acquaintances. She had been informed that Mariella spoke very good English. Together with her husband Bob, they located the house and to their delight, found her at home. They introduced themselves as potential clients and found her to be ever so charming and humble.

"We've seen your work and heard many nice things about you and we are very interested to see more. Can you spare us a few minutes of your time?" Helen asked.

"By all means, please do come in. Please, make yourselves comfortable," Mariella said, as she seated them at the kitchen table.

"Well, we would love to see some of your designs," Helen asked.

"Of course," she answered, "but first of all, shall we have some tea or coffee?"

"Why yes," Bob said, "that would be excellent. Tea for both of us would be just fine."

"You look so young to be married," Helen asked, catching sight of a man in the back yard painting the wall.

"No, no, I'm not married. I live with my brother," she giggled. "Both of our parents have passed away."

Mariella prepared and served the tea. Her total candour surprised the American couple and the more they talked the more they liked her. After tea, Mariella cleared the table, went to wash her hands and then she brought in several of her latest creations. Both Helen and Bob were enthralled with her expertise. This was exactly the kind of work they were looking for. Once she had finished showing them all of her designs, they informed her of their true mission in Malta and introduced to her their idea of buying these outright for the American market. Mariella was speechless and she did not know how to respond.

"We are very sorry if we caught you off guard, but your work is extremely unique, though surely you are aware of this," Helen said.

"My work has always given me much pleasure and it is truly not work at all, although it does help pay the bills, along with my brother who is a carpenter. Our life is simple but fulfilling."

"Well, we really have come upon you like a thunderbolt, haven't we?" Bob said. "How about we let you think about this and talk it over with your brother. We're prepared to offer you a very substantial amount of money. Let's say we return in a couple of days to discuss it further".

"All right," stammered Mariella, "it would be really amazing to think of my clothes being worn all the way over in America." She then showed the Armstrongs out and went immediately to tell her brother.

George was equally surprised but very much intrigued by these American visitors and the whole situation. However, George advised his sister to think carefully about it and told her that he wanted to be present the next time they met.

Over the next couple of days, Mariella pondered everything Helen and Bob had told her. In between these thoughts, she had several orders to complete which kept her mind occupied. She eagerly looked forward to seeing the Armstrongs again.

When as promised, Helen and Bob came back, Mariella introduced them to George. They all sat at the table and, over tea, talked for a long time. The subject was finally broached as to why they were all there. Bob told Mariella the amount they were ready to offer for just six of her designs. Mariella and George looked at each other in astonishment. This figure indeed sounded astronomical and now, if anything, she was more confused than before.

"I assure you that this is a very fair amount," Bob interjected.

"No, no. You misunderstand. It just seems that things are going too quickly for me. I've never had much of a business sense. It's just all so overwhelming," Mariella explained.

"Take your time and think it over. By the way, on Monday the Embassy has arranged a private car to take us around Valletta.

Why don't you take a couple hours off and join us? Please?" Helen asked. Mariella had to admit that she liked their company and Valletta was after all, her favourite place. Her instincts were telling her to accept, so she did. "Fine," Helen said, "we'll pick you up at nine, shall we say? I am sure that we're going to have a great time."

"Thank you Mariella for your hospitality, and it was good meeting you George," said Bob, as he and his wife stood up to leave and head back to their residence.

That Monday morning, when the chauffeur driven car arrived at the door, Mariella was ready and waiting. Soon they were on their way to the capital city of Malta. What she did not know was that the driver was Anthony Sultana, a historian from the University of Malta, who was going to explain Valletta and its history in detail. When they arrived at the entrance gate of the city, Mr Sultana parked the car right in front of the famous Royal Opera House. He explained to them that this enormous building was one of the richest opera houses in all of Europe and was built in 1860, designed by the English architect Edward Middleton Barry. Bob then told Mariella that they were going to attend an opera there that Saturday evening.

"We'll walk from here," said Anthony.

As they passed the sweet carts on both sides of the main street, they had to stop to purchase some of the wonderful pastries. At this particular time of the year there were several different fleets in the harbour. American and English sailors could be seen everywhere walking around in their brightly coloured uniforms which distinguished them from their ranks and from each other. The establishments along Kings Way Street were buzzing with business. Happy shoppers lined the streets in the brilliant sunshine.

A few minutes later, Anthony stopped them to show them the city's foundation stone. This, he informed them, had been laid on the twenty eighth of March, in the year 1566. The city was named

Valetta by the Grand Master of the time, Jean de La Valette. His knights were that of the Order of St. John, who with the help and courage of all the Maltese people, had triumphed over the powerful Turkish Armada, the Ottoman. For everyone, young and old, the Grand Master had wanted to build a city as a reminder of their great feat. This area, then called Mount Sceberras, had been chosen. La Valette had approached the Holy Pope Pius V with his idea and the Pope not only encouraged him but he even sent his own engineer Fracesco Lapparelli to help him draw up the plans for the new city. On the morning of the twenty-eighth of March, 1566, the Grandmaster Jean de La Valette, in the presence of Bishop Cubelles, Knights of the Order, clergy men and all the people who had flocked from all over the Maltese Islands to be a part of this historical day, laid the foundation stone. The stone read:

'Fra Jean De La Valette, Grand Master Of The Order Of The Hospital Of Jerusalem, Mindful Of The Danger To Which, A Year Before His Knights And The Maltese People Were Exposed During The Siege By The Turks, Having Consulted The Head Of The Order About The Construction Of A New City And The Fortifications Of The Same, By Walls, Ramparts And Towers, Sufficient To Resist Any Attack And To Repel Or At Least, To Keep Away The Turkish Enemy. On Thursday 28th March 1566, After The Invocation Of Almighty God, Of The Virgin Mother Of God, Of The Patron Saint JohnThe Baptist And of The Other Saints, To Grant That The Work Commenced Should Lead To The Prosperity And The Happiness Of The Whole Christian Community And To The Advantage Of The Order, Laid The Foundation Stone Of The City On The Hill Called Sceberras By The Inhabitants And Having Granted For The Arms Of The City A Golden Lion On A Red Shied, He Wished It Will Be Called By His Name Valletta'

When Lapparelli returned to Italy, the work of the city was steadily carried out under the orders of the Maltese engineer Gilormo Cassar. Separate Auberges were built to house the knights of different birth origins and to hold their meetings. They were from Provence, Auvergne, France, Italy, Aragon, England, Germany, Castille, Leon and Portugal.

Jean de La Valette was Grand Master from 1557- 68. He died on the twenty-first of August 1568 from old age and a three week fever that never broke. He was seventy four years old. On this day a true soldier and a great leader died, but he was never to be forgotten.

Hearing Mr Sultana talking about the Great Grand Master, Mariella felt so proud that Salvu, the ancestor her mother had told them about on her death bed, had met such a man. The next stop on the tour was just minutes away.

"This is the Co-Cathedral of St. John the Baptist. Its construction was authorised in 1573 by the Grand Master Jean de la Cassiere and it was completed in the year 1578 by the famous Maltese architect Gilormo Cassar. Let's go inside, shall we? You are about to witness one of Europe's great treasures," Anthony said.

Once through its huge doors, Bob and Helen stood still with their eyes wide open in disbelief. The magnificent cathedral walls were covered in gilded limestone, marble works and mosaics, all crafted to the highest specifications. The ceilings were covered with paintings by Mattia Preti recalling episodes of the life of St. John the Baptist, the patron saint of the Order. Marble inlaid tombstones covered the whole floor, each with written scriptures of information about the person buried underneath, most of which were top dignitaries of the Order. Its altar was made of Lapis Lazuli and other rare marbles. There was also a great marble sculpture made by Mazzuli recalling the Baptism of Christ on its presbytery. The corridors on both sides led the visitor through consecutive small chapels, all adjoining one after another; chapels allotted to each of the Languages of the Order. The left aisle finished at the crypt, where a few of the Grand Masters including Jean de La Valette and La Cassiere, the builder of this cathedral, were laid to rest. In the oratory of the church, there was the famous masterpiece, a three by five meter painting of the Beheading of St. John the Baptist, by Caravaggio. Other rooms with endless walls lined with detailed tapestries, depicted various religious scenes. This cathedral made people of any religion or belief enriched. The small group could have stayed there all day but Valletta had many other magnificent places to explore. The day went well and they had a marvellous time.

"Thanks so much for a wonderful day," Mariella said to them as the limousine stopped at the door of her house. "I had a lovely time. Thank you again."

"It was our pleasure," Helen replied.

"Listen Mariella," Bob now said, "we don't want to distract you from your work but this Saturday, we are going to attend the opera 'Aida' by Verdi at the Royal Opera House in Valletta. We would be more than honoured to have you come along as our guest. All you have to say is yes and we will take care of the rest."

Mariella had always wanted to attend an opera, especially at the Royal Opera House and now that the opportunity presented itself, she jumped at the chance. "Are you sure?" she asked politely.

"Yes, of course we are. We'll pick you up at around seven."

"I'll make sure I'm ready and thank you," Mariella answered.

After they had left, she was so excited. She had to share it with somebody, but whom? As soon as Joan saw Mariella at her front door, she could see that she had something special to tell her.

"Can I come in for a minute?" Mariella asked.

"Yes, please do," Joan replied.

"So how can I help you?"

"I am just so happy about something," Mariella said.

Joan now put the kettle on the kerosene burner and then sat at the table. When Joan heard Mariella mention the names of Helen and Bob Armstrong, she was mesmerised. Could it be that Mariella was talking about the same couple everyone was talking about? As if this was not enough, she also told her that she had met them on several occasions and they had liked her work so much that they had offered to buy some of her patterns. Joan's eyes opened wide. "It's true!" Mariella cried. "They want to buy my designs!"

"Young lady, do you realise what anyone would give to be in your shoes? These people are big, I mean really big. They design for stage shows all over the United States! I always knew that you had it in you and this just confirms it. So, are you going to do it?" Joan asked, filled with excitement for her young friend.

"No, I mean…I don't know. Everything is happening so fast. I don't know what to do. They want to give me a lot of money for just six of my designs." When Mariella told her the amount Joan replied "My God! That's a lot of money. You have a great talent my dear. These people wouldn't dream of paying such an amount unless they were certain. They are very rich. If I were you, I would take it. Oh, how proud your mother would have been! I'm sure she is watching over you."

"They are very nice people and they have never pressurized me at all; as a matter of fact we haven't talked about it for some days now."

"Is your brother aware of the Armstrong's offer?"

"Yes, he is," Mariella answered.

"And what does he say?" Joan asked.

"He thinks as you do, that I should take it. But it's up to me in the end. Oh, I'm so confused!"

"Well if you are not sure, then don't rush into it. From what I have heard, they're staying in Malta for a few more weeks. I am sure that you will work something out by then. When do they plan to see you again? I would love to see what they look like," Joan asked.

"This Saturday I'm to be their guest. They are taking me to the Royal Opera House in Valletta."

"Are you joking?" Joan said in disbelief.

"No! You know me better than that."

"My God, you are serious. Mariella, you don't know how lucky you are! So, what are you going to wear for the big night?" she asked excitedly.

"I don't know. What do you think?" the humble Mariella asked.

"You have to wear the blue dress. The blue one you wore on the feast day; that dress is so you. Everybody was talking about it for days. If you wear it, I might even come to the opera myself. But not to see the opera, just to see the faces of everyone when you walk through the door. Oh, I am so excited for you!"

"Oh stop it now, you're embarrassing me. I'm sure that there will be plenty of other dresses better than mine."

"I wouldn't bet on it. The elite of Malta's opera world will be there and you will be in the spotlight with celebrities such as the Armstrongs. If you like, I'll come over on Saturday afternoon to help you get ready."

"Do you really mean it? That would be lovely. I'm sure I could use your support."

"Mariella, I wouldn't miss it for the world. Don't worry, I'll be there," Joan promised. They had another cup of tea and talked some more.

As promised, Joan went over to help Mariella on Saturday, taking her makeup box along with her. Mariella had never applied makeup to her face before and although she did not need much, the finishing touch was perfect. After helping her on with the dress, Mariella was ready. Joan stood back, convinced that she was looking at the most beautiful twenty one year old on the Maltese Islands. She was just about to say so, when George entered the room and stole the words right out of her mouth.

"You are the most beautiful girl I have ever seen, even if you are my sister," he said. "You're so beautiful, if only Mother were here to see you."

"Stop it! You're making me embarrassed."

"What? A brother can't be proud of his sister?"

When Bob and Helen saw Mariella walk out of her house, they too were stunned with her beauty and fell in love with her all over again.

"My God, look at you!" Helen said. "You look beautiful, doesn't she Bob?" Bob was at a loss for words. He too was mesmerised.

"Wonderful. Just wonderful," he repeated. Wishing her a great evening, Joan and George saw her to the limousine door and said goodbye.

When they arrived at the opera house, Mariella felt like she was in a dream. Cars and horse carriages were lined up one behind the other, dropping off the special guests for the performance, all of whom were resplendent in either elegant gowns or tuxedos and top hats. What a scene. As she walked along the red carpet in the entrance hall everyone was looking at her. Mariella stole the show. Whispers were to be heard everywhere as men and women alike were curious to find out who she was. They soon found out however, as Baronessa Inguanes and Mrs Margaret Beresford, a very well known English author were both dressed in Mariella's creations.

During the opera, there were still those who were watching her and during the first intermission several people took advantage of mingling with Helen and Bob just to be introduced to her. When the opera was over, there was still a party to attend. On learning that she was invited too, Mariella felt uneasy. She excused herself to Bob and Helen, telling them that she needed to return home. Bob and Helen understood immediately, so they called for the limousine to take her back.

"I hope that you don't mind me leaving like this," Mariella said to Helen. "I had a lovely time. The music was heavenly but I really must rest now. Thank you so much."

"Thank you," Helen replied; "you are wonderful. It's our pleasure being with you. Good night and we will come again to your house on Wednesday, if that's convenient for you."

"I'll be waiting. Thank you both and good night," Mariella said.

Mariella had enjoyed a wonderful time. She was filled with excitement. She kept tossing and turning in her bed and she just could not fall asleep. The Royal Opera House, the music, the clothes and everyone's compliments kept her awake and thinking. Did it really take place or did she dream it all? Then she would catch a glimpse of her blue dress draped over the chair next to her bed and smile. Oh, she was so happy. This had to be the best night of her whole life. She could not wait to see Helen and Bob again and that Wednesday she was ready to give them whatever designs they wanted. However, she was in for a very big surprise, much bigger than she could ever have imagined. For when they greeted each other at the front door, feeling as though they were old friends, Bob looked at Mariella and said, "Mariella, as you must realise by now we have become very fond of you. Both Helen and I like and admire you very much. Quite frankly, we have never met anyone like you. We talk about you all the time and we want to ask you a very important question."

"Why, you can surely ask me anything, anything at all."

"We would like you to come and work for us in the United States," Bob said, "what do you think of that?"

"What? Is it true?" Mariella answered, with wide open eyes.

"We wouldn't joke about something as serious as this. We want you to return with us when we leave Malta. We are ready to pay all of your expenses and have you settled in Chicago. You won't have to work all these hours that you are doing now. We promise that you'll have other women working with you. We know talent when we see it. We want your designs and are willing to take you on as a valued employee. But more than that, we regard you as a trusted friend. We could have some great adventures together in America."

"I am speechless. I wish I could say yes but how can I?" Mariella replied, "I have never been further than Valletta. I've never even left Malta! Come to think of it, I've haven't been to Comino or to Gozo either. Also there is my brother George. I could never imagine leaving him behind. He's only twenty years old and he needs me. No. Thank you very much but I'm sorry, I cannot accept."

"We knew this wouldn't be easy for you. I'm sure you know best, but we had to express our feelings. Just think about it and discuss it with your brother, by all means. Please know that if you should have a change of heart, the offer remains open. We promise we won't bring up the subject again."

"Yes, well I do appreciate what a great opportunity this would be and I too will miss you when you leave, but I just cannot do it. It's not possible."

At this point the conversation turned to the patterns they originally wanted to buy. Bob as previously agreed with Helen, handed Mariella the cash. "No, I cannot accept it. That is too much money," Mariella answered. Bob and Helen looked at each other, baffled. What were they to do now? "At least take something. You have to," Bob now said. Mariella did not want to embarrass them so she took half the amount. She felt that their recent generosity to her could not go unacknowledged.

When they parted, Mariella almost wished that they had never appeared on her doorstep that first day. Before then, they had been just fine. They had everything they needed. Since then however she had spent days feeling mixed up with thoughts of a new life outside her own little world. Oh, why had they come into her life? she repeated to herself. Then that little voice, deep down, would quietly tell her to stop thinking negatively. Helen and Bob had handed her the pot of gold at the end of a rainbow and she would be crazy or even stupid, not to grab the best thing that had ever come her way. If only she knew what to do. In her confusion, she needed help, spiritual help, so she turned to God. She told George that she was going to go up the road to the church and left. Holding her rosary beads, the same rosary beads her mother had used for many years to face her own problems, Mariella knelt down, closed her eyes tightly and in very deep thought, begged God and the Holy Lady to guide her. She was lost in her prayers for some time. After a while she could feel someone kneeling behind the chair next to hers. Mariella opened her eyes slightly to take a peek at the person. To her surprise it was Joan. Joan nodded her head and then gave her such a smile. It was as if she was assuring her that God had heard her and that things were going to be just fine. Joan now started to recite the Rosary in a low voice and Mariella began saying it with her. They prayed together and from there they went to Joan's house. Mariella opened her heart to Joan and Joan listened. Mariella asked for Joan's opinion and help. Joan told her not to worry about the situation too much. Life always had a way of working itself out on its own.

Bob and Helen kept in touch with Mariella and they went for walks and shared a few evening dinners together. Their friendships grew and the more they met over the following days, the more they learned about one another. As promised, the subject of moving to America never came up, but this did not mean that the Armstrongs had stopped hoping that something would change.

Mariella had not told George about the prospect of her moving away, but with just two weeks to go, the secret got the better of her. George had seen a change in her and had grown concerned about her health. He had started to worry that his sister was becoming ill with the same illness that their mother had died from. He just could not bear the thought of losing her too, but when he broached the subject, she jumped at him. "There's no need to be concerned, I'm fine! It's nothing!"

"You don't have to get upset; I'm your brother, the only family you have. I just want to know how I can help you. Please, can't you tell me what's bothering you?"

"I am not myself these days, that's all. I'm sorry. I don't want to upset you. Please don't be angry," she said, looking at his face, always so calm and sensible. Her brother had such a gentle face. He had always been there for her and she loved him dearly. He deserved to know the truth. So, one afternoon she told him to sit down at the table because she had something very important that she needed to share with him. Finally she told him about the idea of moving to America as the Armstrong's protégé.

George listened carefully and weighed every word in his mind. "Thank God I was wrong," George burst out in relief. "I had started to suspect that you were unwell. You are young and you are very talented. I have watched you grow. I saw you stitch your very first stitch and you have come a very long way. We have always been close and I have known you at your best and worst times. When you are around Helen and Bob, I can see how happy you are. You are very lucky to have made friends with such fine people. What we have, we shall never lose, no matter what life throws at us. We're bonded together forever. So there's no need to be confused. Listen to your heart. You have my blessing no matter what you choose to do."

With these encouraging words, the pressure on Mariella lifted instantly and she finally felt clear sighted. George was the greatest. She walked over to hug him. "Since I can remember, everyone has always told me how much you look like Father. I am sure that had he been here today, he would probably have given me the same advice. Thank you George, I will never forget this day."

"You're very welcome and always remember how much I love you."

When the Armstrongs returned to Mariella's home the next morning, she gave them the news they had been longing to hear. "Fantastic! I can't believe it!" Helen said excitedly.

"This is just great," Bob added. "You couldn't have made us any happier. Oh my Lord, we have to get things organised, and quickly. After all, we only have just over a week before we set sail."

"No. Please listen for a minute. I am going to come to the United States and I will work for you that I swear, but not next week. I have some dresses to finish and others promised. I can't let down the people who have put their trust in me; I have to honour my contracts. Besides, I have personal commitments that need to be dealt with here before I come. I need some time for all of this. I hope you understand."

"But of course we understand," they chorused. "We will help in whatever way we can."

The next morning, the three of them headed to Valletta, to find out when the next ship after theirs would be sailing to the United States. This turned out to be in two months' time, which was just perfect. Bob booked the passage for Mariella and paid for the ticket himself as promised. From here they went to the passport office to issue Mariella with her very first passport.

Bob and Helen's few remaining days were very busy with appointments. Before they knew it, they were standing at the docks to set sail from Malta. There were several important dignitaries and even some celebrities seeing them off.

"Goodbye," cried a tearful Mariella.

"It's not goodbye my dear. Just farewell for now; we will be meeting again soon. Now you take care," Helen said.

"I will," Mariella answered, as tears ran down her cheeks.

"Mariella, we will send you a telegram the moment we arrive home. See you in a few months!" Bob called out as they started to board.

"Goodbye!" Mariella shouted as she waved. "See you soon." The ship started on its voyage, leaving her feeling very sad. When she returned home she went straight to her sewing, working well into the night, barely able to keep her eyes open.

As the days passed by, she missed her American friends dearly and anticipated a joyful reunion, feverishly completing order after order. George stood by her to support her and her new venture.

The day Mariella was due to depart from Malta, some neighbours including Martin, his wife Karmena, and all their children and Joan the teacher were there to see her off. They came to wish her luck. They were all going to miss her but none more than her brother. George stood beside his sister and stayed there for as long as he could. When the porter called "last board", there was only time for one final hug. George put his hand into his pocket, took something out and placed it into Mariella's hand.

"Mother's rosary beads; I want you to have them," he said. "I know that I have the gold cross but I wanted to give you something more sentimental. Take them and pray for me every day as I will for you. Before you go, please promise that one day you will return."

"I promise," she answered, giving him a last kiss, thinking that another hug might make her change her mind and stay. She ran up the gangway. From the deck she waved her goodbyes and deep in her heart told her brother how much she loved him. George himself was already missing her and once home, the house seemed so silent and empty.

Chapter 10

George

In the following weeks George tried to work on his furniture, but he hated the loneliness he felt. Luckily for him, one day his teenage friend David came knocking. George was more than happy to see him. David told George that he was studying law. Of course he still had some years to go, but he was very confident that he would become a good lawyer. George told him about his sister Mariella and her new venture.

"What a shame she's gone," David said. "I always did secretly fancy her you know. She was always one of the most beautiful girls I'd ever met. It's been some time since I've seen her. If only I had come around earlier, I might have courted her. Well, she's gone now. I wonder if we will ever meet again?"

"Yes, I'm sure you will. Mariella won't stay away from Malta forever." David sighed and turned to matters now at hand. "How about you close up your shop and we head over to the Pinto Band Club for a while?"

"All right, I'll close for now. I don't want to be on my own anymore today. And it's been a long time since I had an evening out," George said.

George drank only cola, though David on the other hand could throw back a pint of beer in no time. They talked and talked about the good old days. Before they parted, David promised that he would come by more often. Then a few days later, George got the telegram he had been praying for: '*ARRIVED SAFELY IN AMERICA. I AM FINE. LOVE YOU. MARIELLA.*' He immediately ran over to tell his godparents next door. They were relieved to hear the news as they loved her and also missed her.

In the following months, letters were exchanged and Mariella's were always full of good news. Helen and Bob had kept their promise and she was now designing clothes for famous stage shows. In a few short months she had already become very popular in the entertainment world. More letters informed George that she also had four assistants and she was attending some important parties with very famous entertainers.

Mariella never stopped writing to George. He was more than happy to learn that his sister had also fallen in love. The young man was a very prominent artist, a young Italian emigrant by the name of Agustino Di Philippe. She told her brother that since his arrival in America, Agustino had changed his name to Austin as this was a lot easier for his business contacts to remember him by. He worked with the same stage company as Helen and Bob. George was so proud of her and yet he was not doing that badly either; he had secured several modest contracts, which were enough to keep him busy, at least for a while. Some of these were out of the village, so he had bought a horse and a cart to travel there and back. Working with a variety of heavy wood, he developed a very muscular physique and with his wavy black hair, long eyelashes and smiling face, George had many women's heads turning.

David and George met regularly in their spare time and had become regulars at the Village Band Club where they socialised and got to know many of the other regular clientele. David always tried to get George to have a glass of beer but no, George just drank his usual cola or coffee, though at least David could persuade George to play billiards with him.

In July of 1933, Mariella and Austin got married. A letter told George all about the day in every detail. George felt as if he had been present himself. Although he felt tremendously happy for his sister and her husband, a wishful thought did pass through his mind.

He wished that he too could be as lucky and find his own companion one day.

George was now twenty four, going on twenty five. He was happy enough but his life was missing the excitement young men go through at his age. He had his work and time with David to look forward to but it lacked what he really needed most. Yet all of this was about to change, for in the October of that year, 1936, someone came into George's life. A villager dropped over to his garage one day to let him know that a very wealthy gentleman, who owned several mercantile establishments along the main street of Valletta, needed a reliable carpenter to do some work around his estate.

"The estate is in Luqa," Alfred told George. Luqa was the next village. "If you are interested, we could meet with him tomorrow so that you could take a look and see what it involves." George had never refused a contract before and this sounded like a lucrative offer, so he immediately jumped at the chance. Arriving at the entrance, they rode through high trees on both sides. Once the house became visible, George could see a huge mansion and expansive grounds. The owners had to be incredibly rich. A butler answered the door. George had never been received in such a manner before. He was very impressed and a little bit intimidated if truth be known.

"This is George the carpenter from Qormi," Alfred said. This was not the first time that Alfred had come to the house and he knew Joseph the butler well. "I believe Lord Shembrie is expecting us."

"Welcome to Casa Ambrosia. Lord Shembrie did inform me of your appointment. Please follow this way." The butler showed the pair into the drawing room. "Lord Shembrie will be with you shortly," he added. The butler asked for their hats and if they cared for any refreshments.

"No, thank you," George replied.

"How about you?" he asked Alfred.

"I wouldn't mind a glass of wine; the usual please."

George began gazing about him and he was amazed at the antiques. He recognised priceless pieces, dating back hundreds of years. Then he looked up at the magnificent crystal chandelier. The sunlight coming through the wide bay window was hitting the hanging crystals, reflecting rainbow colours in all directions. It was like he had fallen onto another planet. "Why didn't you tell me that the house belonged to a Lord?" George asked Alfred.

"I was afraid that you wouldn't come if you knew, and it looks like I was right in my assumption. His Lordship asked me if I knew of a talented carpenter and naturally you were first to come to mind. Now don't disappoint me. He's friendly enough, so just relax and be yourself. I am sure you will do fine. He is a very rich man who has more money than he knows what to do with. He will pay you well for your services. Don't be shy; ask for what you're worth, and I wouldn't mind if you added something extra for me, of course."

Chapter 11

Grace

While the two men waited patiently for his Lordship to appear, Grace, his only daughter, happened to walk by. Through the drawing room's open doorway, she caught sight of George and Alfred. She stopped for a moment. From the clothes George was wearing, Grace could see he was of lower class and she was planning to totally ignore his presence and walk on. However, when George turned suddenly and walked over to look at a mirror, she caught sight of his face in the reflection. He was the most handsome man she had ever seen and she could not help staring at him. George caught her looking. Taken by surprise, she blushed and walked away, feeling embarrassed. Who was he? she asked herself. What was his purpose here?

Being an only child and the only heir to the family Shembrie, she was given everything by her parents and she had naturally grown into a very spoilt young woman. She had her father and mother wrapped around her little finger. She was a beautiful tall brunette with a stunning figure. She was twenty four years old, which was the same age as George, and very quick and clever. So, by the time her father appeared for the meeting, she had already thought of how she could meet this stranger again.

"Good morning father. I need to go to Elisabeth's. Could you drive me there?"

"Yes of course my sweetheart, but first I have some business to attend to. As you know, our carpenter retired last month and we need someone to replace him. I've asked Alfred to find us a replacement and he is waiting for me."

"Do I know him Father?"

"No. He is from the village of Qormi; a very good carpenter according to Alfred."

"I am very good when it comes to judging people, could I meet him too Father?"

"Of course my angel, come along."

As usual, Grace could charm her way into any situation. The butler appeared and introduced Lord Shembrie and his daughter to George. Although George was of a lower class, he knew that it was proper to kiss the outstretched gloved hand and he did. When their eyes met again, she felt a wave of heat going through her entire body, which she had never felt before. She had been courted by many elite young men, but none had made her feel so strongly. 'Why?' she thought. 'He is only a carpenter after all'. George for his part immediately liked her smile and her elegance. "It's an honour to meet you," George said in a reverent voice, making her blush again.

She had prided herself in being in command in any situation, but at that moment, she could feel her knees getting weak and she felt as if she was going to lose her balance. His eyes had flecks of green and gold and the longest eyelashes she had ever seen. She just could not take her eyes off him. His black wavy hair, his beautifully shaped mouth and muscular body made her dream. She had finally found what she had been looking for and she decided then and there that she was going to break all the rules to have him.

George was perceptive enough to sense her attraction towards him, yet he was here on business and he was smart enough to know that business and pleasure never mix. He could sense also that Grace and he would have nothing in common; the classes could never cross the lines.

Alfred now excused himself so he could leave them alone and the butler showed him out. They talked and talked and Lord Shembrie and George came to an arrangement. George was to start work on some doors the very next morning.

Grace was still at university and studying to become an actress. She certainly had it all; the looks, the smile, the passionate nature, not to mention the power and the riches of her family to back her up.

The next day being Saturday, she was at home when George arrived. She watched him from afar and while her father was discussing things with him, Grace went upstairs so that she could watch him from her bedroom window. George had hardly set his tools down when he caught her looking. This made him feel rather uncomfortable but he pretended that he had not noticed her. She pulled up a chair to the window and sat there, lost in her own little dream world, fantasising about the day when he would hold her in his arms. She was so caught up in her thoughts, that she had not even heard her mother calling out her name. Out of concern, her mother, Lady Jane, opened Grace's bedroom door. "Grace, are you alright?" she asked, startling Grace. "I've been calling your name. Why didn't you answer?" Grace was caught off guard but still managed to find the right words.

"I must be coming down with the Flu or something. I was just about to close the window and draw the curtains so that I could rest for a while."

"I am sorry to hear that my dear. Here, let me. Come away from the window and the draft."

"Mother, I'm going to stay in my room for today and then tomorrow I will see how I am feeling," Grace said, moving quickly to close the window and to draw the curtains herself so that her mother would not see George. Once in bed, Lady Jane fussed over Grace.

"Do you want anything to drink?" her mother asked again, as she touched Grace's forehead to see if her daughter was running a temperature.

"No," answered Grace, "not at the moment anyway. Thank you, I just need to rest." The second her mother closed the door behind her, Grace jumped quickly out of bed to peek out between the closed curtains at George, who was steadily working away.

Being such a hot day, George had taken off his shirt, and whilst working his muscles rippled with every movement. When he left that day she threw herself onto her bed, and clutching her pillow, started to scheme about how she could bring about a future with George. During the night she did not sleep much either. She kept seeing his face. The more she thought of him the more she wanted him, and somehow she was determined to find a way. She prayed that he had some feelings for her too. She wanted to wake early the next morning in order to be at the window the moment he returned. But when the morning came and she looked out, he was not there. Her mother knocked on her door moments later and Grace quickly jumped back into her bed.

"May I come in?" her mother asked.

"Yes of course," Grace replied.

"How are you feeling this morning? I hope that you are joining us for the Sunday Mass?" Lady Jane asked her daughter.

Sunday, did her mother say Sunday? she thought; no wonder George had not come to work, how stupid of her. How could she forget that it was Sunday? How could a man she had just met and knew nothing about, affect her in such a way? She tried very hard to get George out of her mind for the rest of the day, but her heart was aching to see him again.

The next morning she awoke early so she could have breakfast and return to her room to wait for George, but George was delayed on the way there, and she had to go to university without even a glimpse of him. In class, she could not concentrate. All she thought about was him. She wanted to go home, so she complained of a headache and left.

Her mother insisted on calling for the doctor and he was called. After a thorough examination, the doctor could not find anything wrong. Doctor Ellul had known Grace since infancy, and knew that look on her face. The girl was up to something. Today for what must have been the hundredth time, he had no choice but to play along with her game. "She might be coming down with Influenza. I think that she should stay home for a few days."

Her plan had worked, as expected. Now she could have some time to be with George and to get to know him better. Once left alone, she walked over to the window to watch George working away. The next morning, she waited for her parents to leave the house. Then the bedridden Grace put on one of her best low cut dresses, powdered her face carefully and summoned the maid to her room. "Lina!" Grace called out as the maid arrived, "gather the staff together in the drawing room. I will be there shortly."

From the chef to the butler, the waiters, the gardeners and the maids; they were all there. None were surprised to see her out of bed. This was not the first time that Grace had summoned the staff in this way and they were almost sure about what she was doing. The young Grace had orchestrated many such 'meetings,' using the servants to help her. This was to be another one of those days, but never could any of them have guessed that it concerned George the carpenter. "I'm going to be round the back of the house talking to the carpenter," she instructed. "When my parents return, come to inform me immediately. Is that clear?" she said, in a very bossy tone.

They all knew that should something go wrong, her threats of dismissal would be carried out. Grace was on a mission and she walked over to where George was busily working away.

"Good morning George."

"Good morning," George answered, grabbing at his shirt hanging over a piece of wood.

"I'm sorry that you caught me like this. It's already such a hot day that I had to take off my shirt."

"You don't have to apologise."

She could not stop staring at his muscular arms and his bronzed back glistened with sweat. Oh how she wished she could touch him, but she was careful and she did not want to scare him away.

George tried to concentrate and work but she kept distracting him by asking him all kinds of questions. George answered every question in all honesty and she quickly found out that not only was he handsome but intelligent as well. The more they talked, the more she liked him, but just when it seemed that she had made some progress, Lina came rushing over to tell her that her mother had returned. Grace quickly said goodbye and ran back to her bed. George now could sense that something was not right and he was glad to see her go. After all, he was here to do a job and she was becoming a nuisance.

The next day, Grace repeated the same behaviour but this time wanted all of George's attention.

"Are you hungry? Would you like something to eat?" she asked George.

"Well, it is almost midday and I will stop for a bite to eat soon."

"So, you are hungry, good. I will call Lina over to get us some lunch."

"Please, you don't have to go out of your way. I have my bread," George replied.

"Nonsense, you have been working nonstop all morning. You deserve a lot more than just a piece of bread." "Lina!" she shouted, "Lina!" The maid was there in a minute.

"Yes?"

"I want you to go and tell Joseph to prepare the gazebo. Tell the chef to make lunch for two; George and I will be eating there."

"Are you sure of this?" George asked.

"What do you mean? Don't you want to share lunch with me?" Grace asked.

"It's not that. What if your father comes home? What if he sees me sitting with you? I don't think he would approve."

"That's the least of your worries. Relax. I have already taken care of that. My parents will never catch us, trust me."

George did not like the sound of this at all and was beginning to regret taking on this job. 'How can I discourage her attentions?' he thought to himself. Grace asked one of the maids to show George where he could wash. Afterwards she took him to the other side of the garden to the gazebo. It was a wonderfully secluded area. Grace loved relaxing here and did so at every opportunity. The flowering borders were always kept neat and tidy. The trellises over the gazebo overflowed with brightly coloured bougainvillea and there were winding paths of limestone paving with tall shrubs and greenery in pots of all colours, sizes and glazes, spilling over with many different kinds of plants. The climbing roses and jasmine surrounded the archway where George waited awkwardly to greet Grace. Very quickly the table was set. The finest china was laid along with exquisite silverware and all were perfectly placed. Even the paper serviettes had fancy borders. He could not believe that this was all for such a simple lunch. The food was brought out; dishes of meat, chicken and vegetables. George could not wait to begin eating. Tony, one of the younger waiters, served them.

"Help yourself George. Go on; try it." Grace said.

George was not used to eating chicken with a knife and fork and he quickly grabbed the food with his hands and ate hungrily. On any other day, Grace would have been disgusted to see a man eat like this, but not with George. She started to giggle, realising that she actually enjoyed watching his teeth biting into the chicken, with the sauce dribbling down his chin.

"What is it?" George asked. "Why are you laughing?"

"I am just enjoying the wonderful view in front of me, that's all."

"What view?" George asked.

"You, you silly man; I could watch you all day." George now took another bite.

"It looks like you're enjoying that chicken."

"It's delicious. I have never eaten chicken prepared like this. The sauce is so different."

"Peter, our chef, is one of the best in Malta. He was the personal chef of the ex- British ambassador and the moment the ambassador returned to England, my father hired him before any other family had a chance to do so. You will be sampling more of his dishes I am sure."

"You haven't touched your plate. Are you not going to eat?"

"No. I am not hungry. I just wanted to be alone with you." Here George stopped eating. He did not like what he was hearing, but he did not know what to do or say next. His appetite seemed to have disappeared. "Why did you stop eating? Did I say something wrong?" she asked.

"No, not at all, it's just that I never eat like this, especially at this time of day. One piece of bread would have been enough. I am full, that's all. I hope you understand."

"George, could I ask a personal question?" she asked.

"Yes. What do you want to know?"

"Do you have a girlfriend, someone special?"

George was just about to answer when Lina came running to tell them that her father had returned. 'Damn' she thought, 'Just as I was getting there, Father had to come back and ruin it.' She quickly told George to return back to work. She then told Lina to clear the table, and running as fast as her legs could carry her, she returned to her bedroom.

"Good afternoon, George!" Lord Shembrie called, as he strolled towards the area where George was working to check on the work in progress.

"Good afternoon Sir," George answered. "So, how are things coming along?"

"Everything is going well. I'll have these doors ready by tomorrow afternoon, as promised."

"You're doing an excellent job. I do hope that you will like working for us George. I'd like to think that this may be the beginning of a long working partnership." George did like Lord Shembrie, but he was not at all sure that he should keep working here after what had just taken place. Grace was definitely a manipulative girl and he could sense trouble just around the corner.

"I do want to work for you, but as you know I have other contracts to finish too. Once I finish my work here, I'll have to honour those."

"What, you can't be leaving us so soon? I was hoping to show you some more things that need to be restored."

"I will look at them of course, but as I said I do have other unfinished projects to complete."

"I understand. Well how about something to eat? Why don't you stop for a short break and I'll send Tony over with something?"

This was the last thing George wanted to hear. "No, thank you. I have already eaten my bread. Thank you very much but I'm full."

"Fine, then I will let you carry on."

As Lord Shembrie walked away, George felt such a relief. He had to finish these doors and get away from this family as fast as he could. He felt uneasy. The next day, Lady Jane stayed at home the entire day and this interrupted Grace's plans. Grace could only sit by the window and watch George from afar. George had already decided that he would never return here. Tony the waiter found a few minutes to tell him certain details about Grace and she truly did seem to be a devious little minx. That afternoon George finished the job, was paid his dues and went on his way without even saying goodbye to Grace.

The next morning, Grace was very surprised not to see George anywhere. As the day passed she asked the staff if he was working in the grounds somewhere, but no one had seen him, so she went to confront her father.

"Why didn't George come today, Father?"

"Oh, didn't I tell you? He's finished the doors already and won't be returning for a while."

"What? What do you mean by finished? Didn't you say that he was replacing our old carpenter?"

"Yes I did, but he seems to have other orders to attend to first," Lord Shembrie answered.

"Since when?" she asked.

"Since when what?" her father answered.

"If you had wanted to keep him, you could have. If you had offered him a larger sum of money, then I am sure that he would have stayed. How could you lose such a good carpenter?"

"I didn't lose him. He'll be coming back at some point; I just don't know when."

Grace, distraught, returned to her room. What was she going to do now? When was she to see him again? She had to work out something, but for the first time her brain could not think straight. With each day that passed, Grace missed him more and more. She hardly spoke to her father and she was driving everybody around her absolutely mad. Nothing was good enough for her anymore and in the end her parents called for the doctor. Doctor Ellul could see that this time, there was something really wrong with Grace. He could see symptoms of depression setting in. He tried to make her open up about the problem, but she refused. He wanted to help her, and guessing that it had to be something to do with her studies, he decided to keep her home for a few more days to rest. This did not help Grace at all. Having so much time to herself, she progressively worsened. However, eventually a plan did begin to take shape in her mind and she began to feel sure that she would be able to see George again.

One morning, she told her parents that she was tired of sitting around at home and that she wanted to go out and do some shopping. Her parents were more than happy to hear this and they readily agreed. As both of them were too busy with their various committee meetings and social functions, they assigned Lina the maid to escort her. Grace could not have been happier. The moment they were off the estate and onto the main road, she managed to hail a one horse cab the locals call a 'karozzin,' and with Lina, they headed off to Qormi. Grace knew very well that it would be easy to find George's home, as she knew it was on the main street. When George saw the horse stopping at his front door, he assumed that a client had come to check on the armoire he had just finished restoring, but to his surprise, he saw Grace and Lina. 'What were they doing here? Could it be that her father had sent for him?'

"Good morning George," Grace greeted him joyously. "We were in your village purchasing some material from a shop at the square and I just couldn't resist seeing where you live and work. It wasn't difficult, was it Lina? Everyone knows you. So, we decided to stop by to say hello. How are you?"

"I'm fine thank you."

"I've been thinking about you and I was hoping that you could drop by the estate. My father needs some more things looking at."

"Did he send you for me?" George asked.

"No. It's just that he is still waiting for you to come and you did say that you would be back, didn't you?"

"Yes, but I have this job to finish and others yet to complete."

"You don't have to finish anything!" Grace said in exasperation. "My father will pay you a lot of money to become our permanent carpenter. Come and work for us, I promise that you will be very well looked after. Come and work for us and leave these little jobs."

Her attitude and her words were already making him angry. Who was she to come and tell him what to do and who to work for? He wished she would leave and the sooner the better. "Look, after I finish the next job, I will come by, but for the moment I have to keep working, so if you don't mind I need to continue."

"You promise you will come?" said Grace.

"Yes I promise," George said, just to see her leave.

"Good, and please, don't tell Father of my visit. He is a very proud man. He would be embarrassed if he happened to find out that I came looking for you instead of him."

"You don't have to worry, he will never know," George answered, making the sign of the cross over his lips with his finger as if to swear over it. When he saw them climb back into the karozzin which was waiting across the road, he felt relieved, and the moment they said their goodbyes, he stopped working and closed up the garage.

After this visit Grace frequently came by to see George, always accompanied by Lina. She was so persistent. She repeatedly asked how long it would be before he could return to Casa Ambrosia. Even though George was running out of patience, he was never rude. The locals liked a bit of gossip and her visits were raising a few eyebrows. It was not long before they found out the identity of the two visitors. Once the facts were known, the single women who had their eyes on George spread the news about the rich lady from the next village who had a crush on him. Through this gossip, it did not take long for Lord and Lady Shembrie to hear about their daughter's secret visits. At first her parents did not want to believe the rumour, but when they heard it from a very reliable source, they knew they had to confront Grace. Once summoned, Grace knew that she had been caught out, but not surprisingly, she already had a solid excuse ready.

"Your father and I have recently been hearing some very disturbing information about your afternoon outings," Lady Jane began. "Have you been going to see George, the carpenter?"

"Yes mother. Lina and I did visit George at his garage a few times," Grace admitted quickly, to her mother's surprise. "Let me explain. During the time that George worked at our villa, Lina fell completely in love with him. On the day she found out that George had finished his work here, the poor girl had no one to turn to. As you know, we have become friends in the last few weeks and I offered to help her."

Lady Jane was not totally convinced that her daughter was telling the truth and so Lina was summoned. Lina was shocked to hear about Grace's statement, but being a humble, poor and uneducated young girl who needed the small extra income to help out her widowed mother, she went along with Grace's statement. "Yes, my Lady. It is true," Lina replied, in a soft voice looking down at the floor.

"How dare you use my daughter to your advantage?" Lady Jane yelled coldly in a high voice, making everyone fearful, including her husband who had been sitting quietly all this time. "Your services are no longer required in this house. Gather your belongings and leave immediately."

Lina fully expected Grace to help her out, but Grace just smiled. Covering her mouth and feeling quite ill, Lina ran out of the room in tears. Grace had once again escaped yet another skirmish, but her luck would soon run out. Yes Lina was dismissed, but from that moment on Grace could not leave the grounds unless she was chaperoned by one of her parents. They did not want Grace and George to ever meet again. Lord Shembrie even went a step further. He dropped by to see George one day.

"George, you are a very good carpenter and you did a magnificent job on those garage doors, but I must have a full time carpenter. I came to tell you that for this reason I won't be calling on your services from now on; I'm sure you understand."

George felt so relieved. Grace was now definitely out of his life. The New Year 1937 had already begun but there was not a day when Grace did not think of George. Even with all the lavish parties and the invitations she had attended during the Christmas and New Year celebrations, her feelings for George stayed the same. George had become an obsession. She had to see him. She had to tell him how she felt about him before some other woman could steal him away. Again a plan came to mind and she called her new maid to her room.

"Victoria, I need you to do something for me."

"Yes my Lady," Victoria replied.

"I want you to go to the market. Buy a simple skirt and blouse, something cheap will do; pretend that you are buying these for yourself, but in my size of course. Buy a scarf and a pair of shoes, size thirty eight, as well. I want you to then sneak these into my room but mind you don't get caught. If anyone finds out, I will have you fired faster than you can blink an eye, just like Lina before you. Do you understand?"

"Yes my Lady. I will buy everything you've asked for," the very worried Victoria answered.

"Here is the money. Now go," commanded Grace.

On the day she was due to carry out her plan, Grace told everyone at home that she was going to rest all afternoon and that she was not to be disturbed. After changing into her peasant clothes, she crept out of the back door and out of the grounds. Hiding her face well in her headscarf, she hailed the first karozzin that came along and headed down to Qormi and George's house. At first, George didn't recognize her, but when she removed her scarf he just stared in disbelief. How far would this woman go?

"What are you doing here and dressed like this?"

"I had to see you. I had to come and this was the only way I could get out of the house. I have something very important to tell you."

"What is it?" George asked.

"I love you," Grace answered.
George was shocked. "Please, I beg you, leave me alone," he told her, but she grabbed him by his shirt.

"You have no idea what you do to me, do you? I love you so much. I need you," Grace cried. Some people walking by stopped to watch and listen and George lost his usual composure.

"Take your hands off me. People are looking. Please take your hand off my shirt!" he said angrily, but she still held onto him. George became so upset that he pushed her away from him. She lost her balance and fell onto the street. Feeling very embarrassed, she quickly got to her feet. Seeing a small crowd staring at her, she knew she had to get out of there before anyone could recognise her. A cab happened to be coming by and she tried to climb into it, only to find that it was already occupied. She then ran to the next one. Luckily this one was vacant. Once in, she quickly slid the curtains closed so no one could stare further. George had never lost his temper before. Seeing the crowd still staring, he closed the workshop and went indoors. 'Why was I so rude and unkind?' he asked himself as he sat at his kitchen table. 'Grace has always been so nice to me, so why did I treat her like that?' He was about to go to Villa Ambrosia to apologise but on second thoughts he felt that it would be better to leave matters alone, at least for the time being.

Grace asked to be dropped off some distance away from her home and then she walked the rest of the way, sneaking back into her bedroom unnoticed. She had cried all the way from Qormi and could not stop; no one had ever, ever, rejected her before. How could George do this to her? Closed in her bedroom, she caught sight of her reflection in the large mirror over her dresser. Her tearful eyes were all red and her hair was a mess. Her dress looked stained and ugly. She hated the sight of herself; she felt so low and dirty. She could not take this anymore and started to scream and rip at the dress. Her loud screams were heard from every corner of the house and everyone ran to her room.

Her mother was the first to get there. When she opened the door the first thing she saw was a woman dressed in a peasant dress, lying flat out on the floor, trying to catch her breath. Who was this woman, and how did she get into her daughter's room? Then she took a good look at the lady and realised that the woman on the floor was in fact Grace. "Louis, Louis, hurry, hurry!" she called out hysterically.

Lord Shembrie could not believe what he was looking at. What had taken place here? Why was his daughter lying on the floor and dressed in a peasant outfit? Grace needed a doctor and Doctor Ellul was sent for urgently. There was a moment when Grace seemed to lose consciousness.

"We need an ambulance," Doctor Ellul said as soon as he knelt near Grace, "we have to admit her into hospital as soon as possible."

"My God, how bad is she?" Lord Shembrie asked.

"Too early to say but it looks like she may have suffered a stroke brought on by stress or shock. I cannot say anymore until we run some tests."

"My God, hurry, call the ambulance!" Lord Shembrie yelled.

"We could admit her to St. Paul's, a private hospital. I know of a very good professor there who specialises in this kind of condition," Doctor Ellul suggested.

"Yes, only the best for my daughter, please, I beg you, help us," Lord Shembrie answered.

Grace was admitted to a private room and Professor Dalli took over. "How is she?" Lord and Lady Shembrie both asked, as soon as Professor Dalli came out into the hall.

"Well, we have given her medication and we will have to monitor her situation continuously. Have you any idea what may have caused this? Any sudden shock for example, or do you know if she's been under a lot of stress lately?"

"Well, she hasn't been feeling that well lately. If I find out that someone has caused this, my God, then someone is going to pay dearly, that I promise," Lord Shembrie answered.

"Revenge is not what she needs," replied Professor Dalli. "Right now what she needs is regular monitoring and a lot of prayers. Why don't you both go into the hospital chapel for a while?"

"Could we at least see her?" Lady Jane asked, devastated.

"Yes you can, but briefly. She will be asleep for some time."

"I understand," Lady Jane replied. Standing in front of their helpless daughter, their hearts wanted to break. "How could this be? My God, how could this have happened to us?" Lady Jane repeated, gently touching her daughter's forehead. In a very soft voice she told her daughter to hold on and that everything was going to be just fine. They had so many questions to ask. This was by far the worst day of their lives.

Everyone loved gossip, but none other than Guzeppa. Unknown to George and unluckily for him, she happened to be one of the people there when he had pushed Grace to the ground. Recognising Grace from the previous visits to the workshop, she was not going to keep the incident a secret and she started telling everyone she met. By the next morning, this had reached the village of Luqa and the Shembrie's villa. Lord Shembrie wanted answers. Getting into his car he drove down to Qormi to confront George face to face. George of course, had no idea what Grace and her family had been going through. Seeing Lord Shembrie at his work place, he honestly thought that he was there just to say hello.

"Good morning Lord Shembrie," George greeted him, with a smile.

"She was here? My daughter, she was here yesterday, wasn't she?" Lord Shembrie cried out in anger. George was not sure how to answer. He could have said no to keep his promise to Grace, but seeing him all upset, he opted to say the truth.

"Yes she was, but…..."

"What did you do to her to upset her so?" Lord Shembrie asked loudly. Then he lifted his cane and struck the surprised George over the head. Everything happened so quickly and unexpectedly. George felt dizzy and blood started running down his face. He tried to hold onto the bench he was working on, but he staggered to the floor. "You bastard, if she dies, if my daughter dies, I will come to finish the job!" he cried out, before getting into his car and speeding away. George's head was spinning. He was in great pain but he clearly heard what Lord Shembrie had said. Confused, he tried to figure out what this meant. What had happened to Grace and why was he being blamed? Struggling, he made it to Martin's door and knocked.

"My God, what's happened?" Martin said at the door.

"A big piece of wood fell on my head, that's all," George answered. "Please get the doctor. I think I need stitches."

"Come in. I'll call Karmena to clean up your face and to take care of you while I go and fetch the doctor." The cut was long but not as deep as they first thought. The doctor needed five stitches to close it. The doctor too asked George how it had happened and George stood by his story. Later, lying on his bed, George felt utterly confused about what had taken place and why. Then, his friend David came to mind. David was due to come round that afternoon, so he knew he should just wait. Seeing George at the door with his head bandaged up, David was very surprised and concerned. When George told him all that had happened, David wanted to file a police report and charge Lord Shembrie with assault, but George refused.

"From what you have told me, you haven't done anything wrong and even if you had, no one has the right to attack another person. Had he hit you any lower, he could have killed you. Let me issue a warrant for his arrest. You shouldn't let him get away with this."

"I have to know what happened to Grace. I have to know why he thinks I had something to do with whatever happened to her. You are the only man I can trust; please help me."

"Fine, I will. But if I find out that he has misjudged you in any way, I will press charges. Is that understood?"

"Yes," George answered.

Learning through law school how the higher class operated when it came to their private lives, David knew that it was not going to be that easy. However, the villagers always found things out somehow, so he went to the village of Luqa. Once there, he sat at the busiest village bar in the main square and ordered a beer. Luckily

Grace's story was on everybody's lips. "Lady Grace is a bitch," the unshaved old man said, "but she doesn't deserve this."

"Why do you feel so much compassion?" replied another from a table across the room. "Have you forgotten that she was the one who got your niece Lina fired? Let them have some bad luck. I say that Lady Grace deserves it."

"I don't want to hear talk like this," the bar owner jumped in, seeing David, a man he had never seen before, standing there. "My bar is open to everyone and I don't like this kind of talk." The whole bar turned to look at the stranger and the room went suddenly quiet.

David wanted to hear more about what people were saying though, so he moved to sit at the bar. He waited until he was all alone with the barman and over another glass of beer, cunningly managed to get the whole story. With his findings, he returned to George. George was stunned. No wonder her father was so angry. He wanted to help somehow, but David advised him to stay out of it.

"Don't go near the Shembrie's villa or to the hospital. Stay low, you hear. These people have a lot of power and they can buy anyone if they decide to destroy you. I pray to God that Grace does get better and when she does, I hope that she will tell the truth. With the same token, if her family comes after you, please inform me immediately. You are my friend and I will do my very best to help you if the situation gets ugly," David offered sincerely.

"Thank you David. You are a true friend," said George, as he sat there holding his head in his hands.

Grace was being looked after by the best professor available. The stroke had affected her tongue, her lip and her left eye. She needed a lot of rest, medicine and physiotherapy to recover. Her parents asked for permission to care for her at the estate and the doctor found no objection. Lord Shembrie even hired three nurses to be there for his daughter's needs around the clock. In the next few weeks Grace lost a lot of weight and her pretty face lost its charm. Amazingly and unknown to all, she blamed only herself for what had taken place. She was sure she had pushed George too far, too quickly. Even more amazing was that her heart still ached for George and she needed to see him. She had yet to utter one single word, but one morning while her father was next to her, she spoke. "Father I need to talk to you," she said, in a hoarse whisper.

"I'll get your mother," her father said, excited to hear her talk.

"No, please let me speak to you in private," she asked. Quickly, Lord Shembrie told the nurse to leave the room. No sooner had the nurse closed the door behind her than he moved to Grace's side.

"What is it my child? What do you want to tell me, my princess?" he asked, as he held her hand.

"I want to see George," she muttered in a very weak voice. Lord Shembrie could not believe his ears.

"Repeat that please Grace?" he asked her, now moving even closer.

"I want you to bring George the carpenter to me. I want to see him," she replied. Lord Shembrie pulled back in disbelief. This just could not be happening. "If you don't, I will not take anything, not even my medicine."

He asked her to be reasonable. He told her that her wish was impossible but Grace had said all she wanted. She closed her eyes and she kept them shut. Lord Shembrie suddenly felt ill and claustrophobic. The room suddenly appeared so much smaller and darker. He tried to stay calm but the walls seemed to be moving in on him. In the hall, he leaned his back to the wall to catch his breath.

"Is something wrong? Is …?" the nurse asked on seeing him.

"What are you doing out here?" he told her curtly, taking his frustration out on her. "Get in there and do your job!" he shouted. He had to find a way to tell his wife. Lady Jane was sitting in the large library, reading a novel to keep her mind occupied. One look at her husband's face and she could see that something was wrong, very wrong.

"Louis darling, what is it?" she asked. When there was no immediate answer, she thought the worst. She started to tremble and the book fell from her hands as she covered her face, ready for the news. "Don't tell me we lost her? Please don't say we lost our Grace."

"No. No. Grace is resting," he answered, walking over to hold her.

"Then tell me what's wrong!" she asked beseechingly.

He wanted to but he felt numb. How could he repeat what his daughter had just asked?

"I did have something to tell you, but now I forgot what it was. I'm sorry. I didn't mean to scare you."

"But you did," she answered.

"I'm so sorry. I really am," he said, apologising again and giving her a kiss on her forehead.

He had to think. He needed to be alone so he went to his bedroom, a room full of luxury. It had a large bay window, red damask curtains and embroidered white lace sheers. The large antique iron bed was gilded in gold, as were the matching side tables and other priceless pieces. Large paintings of past ancestors and others of religious saints hung all around. The floor was covered with a Persian carpet. Yet, laying on satin sheets and surrounded with all his riches, he felt so poor and helpless. What was he to do now? Who could he turn too? He wasn't a man of prayers but when his eyes caught the painting of the Madonna holding the baby Jesus in her arms, he knelt down and then threw himself prostrate on the floor. Humble and alone, he begged the Holy Lady for mercy. When, later that afternoon, Grace repeatedly made the same demand, he was at a loss once more about what to do. "But don't you know that this cannot be?"

"I repeat, I will not drink or eat anything until he is here next to me," Grace said again.

Definitely, no one knew Grace better than her father. She was the most stubborn person anyone could ever meet. 'But no, there are limits to everything', he thought, and what she was asking for was just too much. Giving her a sharp look, he stood up and left the room. Again he found himself alone, lying on his bed. There in silence, he recalled the many times when his daughter, through her stubbornness, had got everything she had ever asked for. Her threats were always her strongest weapon. 'Surely she isn't that stupid to want to kill herself?' he thought. In the next few hours, no matter how many times the nurse tried to feed her, give her water and the much needed medicine, Grace just would not open her mouth. This worried the nurse immensely and so she decided to talk to Lady Jane and tell her about the alarming situation. "Are you telling me that my daughter is refusing her medicine?"

"Yes my Lady."

"Let me try," she quickly suggested, rushing to her daughter's side. Lady Jane tried to get her daughter to co-operate but no matter how much she tried and how much she begged, Grace refused any nourishment or medicine. Lady Jane now sent for her husband. One look at his daughter and Lord Shembrie could see that Grace was still as stubborn as ever, but he was not going to give in to her just yet. "I'm sure she will take something soon," he said.

Lady Jane was more than surprised to hear him taking the situation so lightly. He had always fussed so much when it came to Grace's well being. He was the one to call the family doctor, even if she simply sneezed or mentioned that anything was wrong. Suddenly the butler came in to announce that supper was ready to be served.

"James, tell the kitchen that supper is cancelled," Lady Jane said, now using her finger to wet Grace's lips. "Louis, I'm very worried, please get the doctor," she begged.

"Jane, I need to speak to you in private." Taking her into the dining room, he explained; "This morning, Grace demanded me to bring George the carpenter to her bedside. She said that if I didn't, she would starve herself to death."

"But she must have been hallucinating! George the carpenter, never!" she said, in a loud voice.

"Believe me, she did and twice. That's what I came to tell you in the library. I've been trying to find a solution to the situation on my own ever since and I now realise that the only thing to do is to go and get George."

"I don't want to hear George's name again, do you hear? Now listen to me," she said. "There is no way in this world that I am going to let that man step foot on our land again, let alone into our house. I won't have it. God forbid, if our daughter dies, I want you to use all our power, all your contacts and all the money it takes, to ruin his life. Do you hear me? Now call the doctor."

In response to this, Lord Shembrie opened one of the showcases, filled a glass with brandy and downed it in one. All his life he had always given in to everybody's needs and wishes, but today, his only daughter's life was on the line. His patience had run out and his head felt like it was going to explode, he was so enraged. He lifted his arm high and threw the brandy glass against the wall with all his force, causing Lady Jane to jump in fright.

"You, our friends, power and money, for once you have to listen to me!" he shouted in anger, surprising her. "Our daughter, our only child is dying and George is our only hope. I don't know what his presence could do, but if it's George she wants, then I'm going to get him."

"Don't you know that I would give my life for hers?" Lady

Jane said, as she slumped backwards onto the sofa, "and even if you go for George, what makes you think that he would even consider helping us, or did you forget that the last time you saw him you hit him with your cane?"

"For God's sake, directly or indirectly, George is the cause of this. He will have to help us."

Lord Shembrie put on his jacket and ran for his car, leaving his wife tearful and slumped on the sofa. When he arrived at George's house it was in total darkness and it seemed as though George had already retired to bed. At first Lord Shembrie knocked very gently but this did not work, so he knocked a bit harder.

"Who's there?" George asked, from behind the front door.

"It's me, Lord Shembrie. Please George, open the door, I have to speak to you. It is of utmost importance. Please I beg you, open the door." George wasn't sure if he should open it.

"It's very late. Please go home. Come back tomorrow morning."

"No, George. Tomorrow might be too late. I need to speak to you right now. I beg of you, please open the door. Grace needs you." On hearing Grace's name mentioned, George had a change of heart, but remembering what had happened the last time, he held the big metal iron (a stanga) that kept the door barred in his hand for protection.

"George please, put that down. I come in peace. I am very sorry for the way I acted that day. I was wrong, very wrong. I know that this is not the right time to call either but I beg you to hear me out." Just like his father, George was a good man who would help anyone in need, regardless of the situation, be it day or night. "George, we don't have much time. Grace is fighting for her life as we speak. You must know by now that Grace has been very ill since she left your place that day. Well, this morning she spoke for the first time and she asked for you. She said that she would starve herself to

114

death if I didn't bring you to her side. George, she hasn't even touched a drop of water since. She won't take her medicine either. She is getting weaker and we are losing her. I beg of you to come with me. You seem to be our only hope."

Quickly, George washed his face, dressed and together they left. During the drive, George took the opportunity to explain his side of the story and the events that had taken place between him and Grace. Lord Shembrie believed George completely. The differences between the two seemed to have been resolved, at least for the moment. As they drove onto the estate, the moonlight was bright enough for Lord Shembrie to recognise the car parked right outside the front door. It belonged to the family doctor. Had he lost his only child? Were they too late? Pressing down on the accelerator, he drove the car as fast as it could go. No sooner had he stopped the car in front of the house than they jumped out and ran inside. "Is she still alive? Is Grace still alive?" Lord Shembrie quickly asked his loyal butler, who was at the bottom of the staircase.

"The doctor is with her Sir."

Inside Grace's bedroom, Lord Shembrie and George were met with grim faces. Everyone was focused on Grace. In total silence, the doctor was holding Grace's wrist to feel her pulse which, he said, was irregular. He was worried, very worried. Grace was in danger of having another stroke that could take her life. The situation was very critical. George instantly froze when he approached the bed. The last time that he had seen Grace, she was one of the healthiest and loveliest young women he had ever seen, full of life and vitality. Yet the woman on the bed was so fragile looking. Full of guilt, he was about to run out of there, but Lord Shembrie grabbed him by his shoulders and held him. "Grace, Grace," Lord Shembrie called out to his daughter. "I have George with me. He is here to see you. Please open your eyes."

"Grace. It's me, George. Can you hear me?" he asked.

That voice. That voice could only belong to George. She could recognise it in any crowd. Like the dead coming back to life, Grace opened her eyes to take a good look at the man she dreamed of, and even in the dim light in the room and at her weakest moment, she could still see his handsome face. She smiled. Very gently, George touched her face. His touch gave her such calmness and hope. Instantly her pulse became stronger, which took Doctor Ellul by surprise. "George, give her some water please," Lord Shembrie asked, handing George a small glass.

"Grace, you need to drink," George said to her, as he carefully lifted her head. Seeing her being co-operative, the doctor passed the medicine over to George. With her eyes gazing at the only man she had ever truly loved, Grace slowly drank the medicine.

"George, could you please stay with her, at least until she falls asleep?" Lord Shembire asked.

"Yes sir, by all means."

"Her pulse is a little better," Doctor Ellul said, as he put his instruments back into his bag, "I can assure you a small miracle has taken place here tonight, thanks to George."

When Grace fell back asleep, as instructed, the butler showed George into the sitting room, to see his Lordship. "George I don't know where to start. My wife and I cannot thank you enough. My God, the moment Grace heard your voice she started to feel better. Of course we do know that she still has a long way to go to fully recover, but the most important thing is that she is stable again. I have to say that we do need your help. George, we know that you have your orders to work on, but I beg you, please visit Grace regularly. I promise I'll make it up to you."

"I'll do whatever I can to help her to recover," George replied. At that very moment Lady Jane entered the room.

"George, thank you! Thank you so much. Tonight we are sure that you've saved our daughter's life. It's not easy for me to admit it but I have been very wrong and unfair. My husband told me about the obsession my daughter still seems to have on you, and now I have witnessed it. I do understand and I am truly sorry I misjudged you. Please forgive me."

"That's all behind us now." At that very moment the clock struck midnight. "It's late," George said; "I have promised to deliver a bench before six this morning and I still have to make some final touches. Would you be so kind as to drive me home?"

"Of course," Lord Shembrie answered.

"Good night Lady Jane."

"Before you go, you will come to see Grace again today, won't you?" Lady Jane asked.

"I will, right after the delivery. This, I promise."

"Thank you George and good night."

During the drive to Qormi, Lord Shembrie repeatedly thanked George over and over again. Once in his bed George just could not fall asleep. The image of Grace's face kept haunting him. How could that simple argument have had such an effect? He was not in love with Grace, but he was a compassionate human being, and he was going to do all he could to help her. When he returned again to Villa Ambrosia that morning, Lord Shembrie was waiting. "Good morning George," he greeted him, with a warm smile and open arms.

"Good morning. How is Grace?"

"Doctor Ellul said that she is better than yesterday. I was not surprised when the first person she asked for this morning was you. When I told her that you would be coming over, her face just shone. I'm sure she's anxiously waiting for you."

117

Once at her side, Grace's face lit up. The moment George held her hand; she placed it onto her lips and kissed it. "Thank you," she said in a very weak voice. Grace did not need to say more. She looked so content. George stayed with her all afternoon and made sure that she ate, drank and that she took her medicine. His daily visits took up all his spare time. Days turned into weeks, ending the outings with his friend David. Her parents became fond of George, and like their daughter, they never seemed to tire of his company. Grace was slowly recovering but her lip muscle was still weak, leaving her with a twisted lip whenever she talked or smiled. If it had not been for George's companionship, support and care, she may not have felt able to carry on. George had become her everything. On the twenty fifth of June, Grace turned twenty five. It should have been a day full of activities and presents, followed by a lavish party, but on this day she simply had a quiet dinner with George and her parents at the villa.

Outside the Schembrie's world, Malta's political situation was worsening and seemed to be heading into recession. As George's business was small, it was one of the first to suffer. The moderate orders stopped coming in and due to lost jobs, those who owed him money could not afford to pay their debts. It was far from easy for George and harder times ahead were predicted. Of course this did not have any impact on the Shembrie family. They had enough money to last them three more lifetimes. However, seeing Grace becoming totally dependent on George, and George still a single man, they dreaded the day when he would inevitably meet up with someone special and be taken away from their daughter's side. 'What will happen then?' they wondered, 'and to what extent will it affect Grace mentally and physically?' This terrified them. Knowing that George's business was struggling, they decided to take advantage of the situation and try to employ him full time. This would not only make Grace happy but it would keep George away from the eyes and reach of other ladies. Sitting to discuss this issue together, Lord and Lady Shembrie planned a way to broach the subject without being too obvious. Then, one day, while Grace was getting dressed, Lord Shembrie steered the conversation towards their plans.

"I remember the day you first stepped foot here, my, how time goes by. I remember telling you about all the jobs I needed doing. Then there was the time when I wrongly told you that I didn't need you. Nothing has been done since the doors you fixed, due to everything that's happened and I have totally neglected the estate. Now, what I need more than ever is a full time carpenter. George, it is never a shame for any man to admit when things are not going well financially. You have to admit that your business is suffering, what with the economic situation of the times. I have spoken to my wife at great length. Would you please consider coming to work for us full time? This would mean closing up your shop in Qormi. The pay will be more than you have ever earned, even in a good year. You can get paid weekly and you will never have to worry about being out of a job or money. Please accept. It would make us very happy." George seemed to hesitate. "George this is not a present. We are not offering you this out of pity. If you decline, we will have to offer it to someone else. We do need a full time carpenter and there are hundreds out there that would give an arm and a leg for what I am proposing. Shall I give you a few days to think it over?" George had to admit that over the last few months he had seen no new orders and his savings were dwindling. This and the uncertain future ahead of him had been worrying. He could not really afford to miss out on such an opportunity.

"I'll take you up on your kind offer," George said finally.

"Excellent! You are the best candidate for the post. We trust in you completely, thank you, thank you George," said a relieved Lord Shembrie.

Once served and alone again, they talked in detail. After supper, his Lordship made the announcement to the family.

"I'm pleased to announce that George is to be our personal carpenter. He will be starting right after the Christmas holidays, on January the second."

"Oh Father! That is the best news I could ever imagine. It's what I have been dreaming of for many months. Thank you," Grace said, with a sudden bright smile.

In January, Lord Shembrie gave George a list of jobs that needed to be done, but also left it to George's discretion to decide in which order to complete them. As they had anticipated, having him around helped Grace tremendously. With the best professional care Grace was recovering well, although she was not confident enough to leave the estate grounds just yet.

On May the twenty-seventh of that year, in 1938, Joseph the butler answered the door to Count Bartolo. The Lord and the Count had been very close, inseparable, that was until Count Bartolo decided to move his family to England. In the past, the two families had shared many special occasions together and Grace had found her siblings in their two children. The butler immediately showed him into the drawing room.

"Please have a seat. I will go and inform his Lordship of your presence."

When Lord Shembrie heard there was a visitor, he rushed down to meet him. "Peter my dear friend! What a lovely surprise, welcome! How wonderful to see you. How's the family and what brings you back to Malta?"

"Everyone is fine. They send their regards," the Count replied, as Lady Jane entered the room. "Jane. You're as beautiful as ever. You haven't aged a day; how do you do it?" he said, standing up to kiss her hand.

"Thank you for your kind words. You look very well yourself. Are the rest of the family here too?"

"No, I'm here just by myself on a short visit. Family inheritance you know. But, I do promise that on my next visit, we shall all meet together."

"Would you like a drink?" Lord Shembrie asked.

"Scotch, if you please."

"And what about you my darling?" he asked his wife.

"A glass of port will do fine." Lord Shembrie called the butler and drinks were ordered.

"Oh, I miss Paula's company so very much. How is she?" Lady Jane asked.

"You know Paula. She would settle anywhere as long as she has a good sized house with a big garden. With England's weather being so cold and the winter so very long, she had to have her own greenhouse. So now we have beautiful flowers all year round. In the summer our garden looks like heaven. You should come and visit. She would be more than thrilled to have you. You always loved the same things. You are two of a kind."

"Thank you. The idea is very tempting indeed."

"Our children have all grown up. Phillip is a lawyer now and Miriam has a serious boyfriend. Speaking of children; how's your Grace? Has she graduated? She must have landed at least one leading role by now. After all, not only is she talented but she is one of the loveliest young ladies Malta has to offer. Is she at home? I have a present for her."

For some strange reason, he could see that his last statement had brought a cloud over Louis and Jane. "She is here," Lord

121

Shembrie answered, after sipping the last of the whisky, "but she hasn't been well. About a year and a half ago, Grace suffered a stroke. She has almost recovered but she still feels uncomfortable around people. Please don't feel offended."

"I'm so very sorry to hear this!" the Count replied, "how very traumatic. Please, leave her be, but can I help in any way? I mean, I know some fine doctors in England. We would gladly accommodate her at our home. They might be of help."

"That's very good of you Peter, but she is doing fine. She is under a very good specialist and he has done wonders. There is also another person here who has helped her a lot and that's George. He is everything to her."

"George? Who's George? Do I know him?" asked Peter.

"George is our carpenter," replied Lord Shembrie.

"Sorry, but now I am confused," Peter said.

"You see, she fell totally in love with this man, this carpenter." Now the Count was more confused than ever.

Lady Jane could see where this conversation was going. Standing, she excused herself. "I shall leave you two alone." The Count was going to say something but she interrupted him and said; "it's fine, really. It's just that it hasn't been easy. I will let Louis tell you all about it. He needs to open up to someone and I'm sure that you're the right person." Over a few more shots of whiskey, Lord Shembrie told his long- time friend all about the trauma his family had been through over the last year and a half. Peter felt deeply sorry. "We want to help her to begin meeting people. We want her to become herself again, but we don't know where to start." Having known Grace since the day she was born and having watched her grow up, Peter knew her almost as well as his own children. He recalled the love that Grace had once shown for the other Maltese Island, that of Gozo.

"Why don't you take Grace over to Gozo? If I am not mistaken, her twenty-sixth birthday is only days away. Why not offer her a birthday trip to Gozo?" suggested Peter.

"You know that might be a good idea, thank you. Of course she has to agree and I'm sure she won't spend her birthday without George."

"Take George with you then!"

"That could work. She'd even get the chance to experience the new vessel, The Royal Lady. You know how much she loves being on the sea."

"The Royal Lady; I don't know this ship," Peter said.

"It's a steel twin screw motor vessel which the Gozo Mail Company bought last September from Scarborough, and seats around 500 passengers. It has a spacious saloon, tea rooms, and even ladies and gentlemen retiring rooms. Grace will love it. Thank you my dear friend, your wonderful idea has made my day."

"I'm glad I could help. I do wish her well," the Count replied.

This seemed to take the weight off Louis Shembrie's shoulders and instantly the topic turned to other subjects. Presently the butler came in to ask him what time they wanted dinner served. "My God, look at the time!" he exclaimed. "Peter you must dine with us. I insist."

"I wish I could, but not today. I have an appointment and I must be punctual. Thank you for the offer and your hospitality, but sadly I must leave." The butler went to tell Lady Jane that the Count was ready to depart. She too showed her disappointment to see him go so soon but Peter promised he would return again.

"Our house is always open to you. Drop in any time," Lady Jane said. During supper his Lordship discussed the Count's idea with Jane. "What a brilliant idea!" she said, "I love it. You must inform George. I'm sure he will come."

Lord Shembrie wanted to set things in motion as soon as possible. That Sunday, George's day off, he made a surprise visit to Qormi. George happened to have just finished re-reading a letter from his sister Mariella that he had received the day before. She had written to say she was fine. There was so much good news in the letter that he had to read it again twice over. She wrote to say that her husband and herself; had both parted from Helen and Bob's company. Of course they had parted on good terms and had only done so because they had decided to set up on their own. Mariella wrote that she had now added hats to her design skills, and that Austin had become a big name in the art world. With this success, they had moved into their own home; a large residence in a very chic neighbourhood. She went on to describe the new house in detail, room by room. George had to laugh. His place was so tiny and yet it was his castle. He was so happy for her though; she sounded so well and so excited about her new success. She ended the letter by saying that because they were so busy, they were not able to visit Malta, not yet anyway, but that if he wished to visit them instead, she was more than willing to pay for his fare. George missed his sister dearly but he knew that it was impossible to leave at the present time; his life was so busy and full. He had his home, a very secure job and he had grown surprisingly comfortable around Grace. Hearing someone at the door, he put Mariella's letter away in the tin with the others and went to answer it. Finding Lord Shembrie on his doorstep, he immediately became concerned. What had happened that could not have waited until later that evening when he was due to go for dinner?

"What's wrong? Is Grace alright?" George asked

"Grace is fine. Everything is fine. I just stopped by to have a word in private, that's all."

"Come in. I hope you don't mind the mess. The good news is that I do have something to offer you to drink. Yes, I just happen to have a very good bottle of red wine. It's a 'Ta Bertu,' I reckon one of best red wines on Malta. Have you heard of it?" George asked, excited that he had such a bottle.

"Yes I have, but to be honest I've never tried it."

"They say that once you taste it, you can't stop drinking until the bottle is totally empty. Yesterday I dropped by his place to see if I could collect the money Bertu owed me, and not only did he pay me in full, but he gave me this bottle for being so patient. As you know I don't drink, but I took it anyway. Do you want to try some now?" George asked. Lord Shembrie could never refuse a drink. He could drink at any time of the day and he was not going to say no.

"Hmmm, I have to admit, this is good, very good," he said, taking his first sip. "It competes, dare I say, with the many foreign wines I've tried. Now, let me tell you why I'm here. As you know, Grace's twenty sixth- birthday is coming up."

"Thank you for reminding me. I want to buy her a special gift this year," George said.

"This is not why I'm telling you this. Every year since her birth, we have always celebrated the day in a big way, except for last year, of course. That was very hard on us, but here we are now a year later, and thank God, Grace is almost as strong as ever. This year I want to do something different. I want to take her out for a special lunch, just the four of us, to Xlendi Bay."

"Xlendi Bay! But where is Xlendi Bay?" George asked, as he had no idea where this could be.

"Xlendi Bay is on Gozo. Don't tell me you've never heard of Xlendi Bay?"

"No, I haven't. I've never even been to Gozo. Come to think of it, there are many places here on Malta that I haven't been to either." "George, you are so humble. This is what I like most about you. You are so cut off from so many things around you and yet, you can be so happy. Sometimes I wish I could be more like you. Now, what was I saying? Oh yes. We have been visiting Gozo since Grace was this high," he said, placing his hand level to his knee. "Believe me, it's a magical place, a wonderful little island, very beautiful indeed. Please come with us. I am sure that your company would make her day even more special."

"Does Grace know about your plans?" George asked.

"No, she doesn't yet. I wanted to ask you first."

"Count me in. If Grace agrees to go, then I will be more then honoured."

"Wonderful. George you seem to never disappoint me. I can't wait until I get back home and tell her."

Grace wanted to fly with happiness when her father told her of the outing. Just the thought of spending the whole day with George on Gozo was magical. "I love you Father. I love you too Mother. Oh thank you both. Thank you so very much. You have been so wonderfully supportive," she said as she hugged them. Throughout that evening and for the next few days that followed, all Grace talked about was Gozo, and now, it was only a day away.

"It is going to be another very hot day tomorrow, so we are planning to have an early start," Lord Shembrie told George, preparing him for the trip as he was leaving the villa.

"We'll pick you up at around six."

"I'll be ready," George answered. "Good night then. See you tomorrow."

Chapter 12

Gozo

There was not a chance in the world that Lord Shembrie was going to take his car onto the vessel to Gozo. He still remembered the state of the roads there. He loved his Ford dearly and he always drove it carefully, but George swore his horse could go faster. They had told George that it would be a long journey to get to Marfa, the docking port at the northern point of Malta, but by now George was starting to think that this place was at the end of the world. They had already passed two fishing villages, that of St. Paul's Bay and Xemxija Bay, and now they were at Mellieha.

"I never realized Malta was this big. I've never been further than Luqa and Valletta. Where is this 'Marfa'? Does it exist?" George asked. They had to smile.

"Just up the hill George, we're almost there," Lord Shembrie said, laughing. He was right because as soon as they got up the hill, he pointed it out. No sooner had they arrived than The Royal Lady began unloading its passengers. Lord Shembrie stopped the car as close as he could to drop them off and then he went and parked. Very soon they were seated in the spacious saloon of the first relatively luxurious vessel on this sea route. Grace sat between George and her father. George was so used to caring for Grace by now, that she had become like his sister. He did not even realise that he was touching her arm. Just his touch gave her such pleasure. Oh how she already wished this trip would never end. The passengers on board included a few nuns, who had already started saying the Rosary, two friars, and many Gozitan countrymen. A few were speaking to a Gozitan family, who were obviously returning back to the island after a long spell in Australia. It was wonderful to listen and overhear their tales from the big country down under. Soon, the vessel was passing close to the smallest of the three islands, named after the cultivation of its cumin seed, that of Comino. "Look, there's…," Grace started to say, but as she turned to show George, her eyes caught his face and she stopped. The sunrays were shining directly onto his bronzed face and the light was filling his eyes with many different colours. He was so breathtakingly handsome that her heart fluttered madly.

"What?" George asked.

"There's Comino," she said shyly.

"Maybe one of these summer days we will spend a day there, right Father?"

"Yes, of course darling. Anything you wish."

"The island looks so small, how many people do you think live there?" George asked.

"Around eighty I believe, mostly of Maltese and Gozitan origin, but there are a few Sicilians too."

"It is a lovely island but too small for me. I could never live there," Lord Shembrie answered.

"Eighty people! What do they do all day?" George asked, curiously.

"Fishing, farming and hunting."

"Look George. That's the Blue Lagoon!" Grace said eagerly, "Oh George, I can't wait to swim there again. Do you know how to swim?"

"Swim?" George smiled, "No. I used to have a dip in the shallow end of a farmer's reservoir when I was a young boy, but that's about it," he answered coyly.

"Then the Blue Lagoon is the perfect place for you to learn. The sea is so shallow that you can walk and walk and still have your head above sea level. I would love to teach you how to swim one of these days. Would you like that?"

"Me swim? Huh. That will be the day, but I can try," he said, making her smile. Soon they were entering the small port of Mgarr. There was a long line of carts full of crops ready to be shipped to Malta. George could now understand why the Tal-Latini cargo boats had arrived at Cirkewwa point so fully loaded. The wooden farmers' carts were all pulled by a horse or donkey. Many of the farmers must have brought their dogs along too because there were a lot of them barking and running around. There were fishermen working on their nets getting ready to go out on their next trip and others preparing the smaller fishing boats, called Luzzu. These were painted horizontally in different bright colours with carved eyes on each port side. These, the locals believed, would protect any fisherman against all evil at sea. What a lovely, sheltered and majestic port it was. The moment George stepped onto Gozo, he felt a warm sensation he had never experienced before. It was as if the island or someone there was welcoming him. He was still lost in thought when he heard Lord Shembrie calling, "George, come on! We have to get going."

The magical feeling reminded him of the short story his mother, bless her soul, had recounted to him so many times as a child. He could still hear her clearly telling him that Gozo was the island of Ogygia, where the Goddess Calypso dwelled, around the year 800 B.C. The Goddess had held Ulysses captive on the island for seven whole years. The myth tells of Ulysses landing on the island's largest sandy beach, which the locals call Ramla Bay because of its red sand. Could it be that the same spell was still around? He was so caught up in his fantasy that he started to look around him to see if he could catch the source.

"Come along George! Let's get going," Lord Shembrie called out again, now standing beside a horse cab.

"What an enchanting place," George said, climbing into the cab. "I love it already."

They immediately climbed the hill facing the small Neo-Gothic church, dedicated to the Holy Lady of Lourdes. It added that final picturesque touch to this lovely small fishing port. As Gozo was only an island of sixty five square kilometres, it was not long before they passed the next village, that of Ghajnsielem, and then the next one too, that of Xewkija.

Before George knew it, they were entering the main street of Rabat; the city of the island. The city fort, called 'Ic- Citadella', the Citadel, was straight ahead. There it stood, high up on top of one of the many flat hills around Gozo, fortified and used by the Knights of St. John to protect the people during the Turkish siege. The karozzin made its way up through Corsa Street, the main street, and right past the open market where the locals shopped from carts at the square the Gozitans called 'It-Tokk' or 'the meeting place'. They pointed out to George the small square behind It-Tokk, where stood the Basilica dedicated to his own name patron, Saint George, built in the 17th century. George was interested in seeing it, but he was too shy to ask. The horse cab turned right towards the city gates of the Citadel in order to stop there to visit the Cathedral of Santa Maria and to say prayers. The church had been rebuilt during the years 1679 to 1713 by a Maltese architect by the name of Lorenzo Gafa. In 1716, Bishop Giacomo Cannaves dedicated the church to the Assumption of the Holy Lady, Santa Maria. In 1864 it became a cathedral. Its remarkable Trumplau dome was painted by Antonio Manuele of Messina in 1739. Locals still lived there inside the old city walls and an elderly man who they met outside was more than proud to recount to them some of the legends. From the Citadel they could see most of the island, including the village of Zebbug, high up on another flat hill. On his last visit to Gozo, Lord Shembrie and his family had passed through Zebbug, and had fallen completely in love with this small village overlooking valleys all round with breathtaking views.

Today, his instincts were telling him to go up there again. Since they had ample time before the birthday lunch at Xlendi, he told the driver to take them. Once there, Lord Shembrie told the driver to take the first left. In minutes, the cab stopped at a dead end and they found themselves looking at views of majestic valleys and the city of Rabat beyond. To their right there was a lane which was split into two, with two very large farmhouses. The one to the left was occupied, but the other was abandoned and for sale. Lord Shembrie loved the location and he wanted to read the 'for sale' sign. The sun had faded most of the writing but on closer inspection he could still see what it said: 'For Sale - Contact Toni Ta Lola, (Toni, Lola's son) at Xlendi Bay.' 'What luck', he thought to himself, 'that's where we're going next'. He had a good feeling about this. "Jane! Grace! Stay here and enjoy the view. I need to stretch a little. George, come with me."

"We won't be long," Lord Shembrie called back, and together they headed towards the house.

"My family loves Gozo and I always wanted to buy a property here. I have visited some very nice villages but this hill by far is my favourite place. Take this farmhouse for example. Come, let's go inside and inspect it."

"Do you think it's wise to walk onto somebody else's property without permission?" George asked.

"Please George. Nobody lives here. Look, it's practically a ruin. Come." The front door was only held closed with a rusty nail. It was no surprise that once Lord Shembrie touched it, the nail broke in half. "Oops, don't worry. Before we leave, we will use a big stone to hold the door in place again." Once inside, they were standing in a very large courtyard facing four inner doorways. Three took them into large rooms where the owners apparently used to keep the animals. The iron rings that tied the animals were still attached to the walls and they could see three mangers. The other large room was a

131

kitchen. A table and some broken chairs still stood in the centre and a few rusty oil lamps were also to be seen. Gingerly, they now walked up some of the loose steps to the second floor and the upstairs rooms. Both of these had metal beds, with badly torn hay mattresses and some old furniture. A few pictures of saints in large frames adorned the walls. The other room was for storing animal food and still had a few bundles of hay inside. They went up onto the roof and saw the most panoramic views Gozo had to offer. With the recent dry weather the fields had all tuned brown, but one did not have to close one's eyes to imagine the beauty of the lush grass and the wild flowers that came after a few spring showers and to realise that this place was absolute heaven. "I love it. I think I'm going to buy it," Lord Shembrie said. "It's a wonderful place indeed. The house itself needs a lot of work, but once renovated, it could look perfect. Gozitans live mostly off the fields and the sea but there are some talented masons here. I know I could hire as many of these as possible. I will have this farmhouse looking ship shape in no time. As for the woodwork, this I'll leave for you."

"Me? You're pulling my leg, right? I mean, I do live on Malta. I can't be in two places at the same time!"

"George, sometimes you are so naïve. You take the measurements and do the work in your workshop. All you then have to do is just fit them. It's not as unfeasible as it might sound." For a minute there, George thought that Lord Shembrie was going to make him stay on Gozo until he had finished all the work. "Now let's get back to the family and George, please don't mention a word of this. It's Grace's birthday, so let's just enjoy the day."

As George waited for Lord Shembrie to walk down the old stone steps, he took the liberty of having another gaze at the fantastic views the rooftop had to offer. A few pigeons flew out of their nesting holes, (called 'barumbara') at the sound of footsteps. A woman was walking out onto her roof, carrying the morning washing. Even though he was some distance away, with that first look, he felt the same tug and warmth he had felt earlier at the port of Mgarr. She smiled at him and her look instantly stole his heart. For a moment, George could not even think and he forgot who and where he was. He was about to raise his hand to greet the farm girl, but Lord Shembrie's voice interrupted him.

"George, come down, we don't have all day! Let's get going".

"I'm coming!" George replied, and taking one last look at her, he descended the steps to join the others. Back in the karozzin, George was still under the magic of the farm girl's smile. He sat in silence, recalling it again. Grace could perceptively sense something different about George's manner.

"George. Is something wrong?" she asked, thinking that her father may have said something to upset him.

"I'm fine," George replied, "it's all the fresh air, I guess. I feel so relaxed, I could fall asleep."

"Why don't you lean back and get comfortable then? Close your eyes for a while," Lord Shembrie suggested. Back on Corsa Street, the main street of the city, they now had to pass through St. Francis Square. Here they could see a lot of fine horses getting ready for the races. They would have loved to stop and watch a race, but they were short of time and so continued. At the next village, the small one named Fontana, just a short distance down the road, the cabman stopped his horse to give it a drink of water from the constantly running spring there at the local washhouse. On seeing such a handsome stranger inside the cab, the local ladies stared openly at George.

"George, please put the curtain down," Grace asked him, "you deserve better." The jealous Grace now called out to the cabman to move. "I think the horse has had enough to drink. Let's get going." The cabman did as Grace asked. Getting back into his seat, they continued on their way. The valleys on both sides of the street leading to Xlendi Bay were dotted with bamboo farms. Bamboo was used by both farmers and fishermen alike. The warm southerly breeze coming from the sea swayed the bamboo canes. In motion, it was as if the bamboo was waving to welcome its visitors. Only a short walk from the sea front stood an isolated little church. This tiny fishing village housed a couple of houses, a few fishermen's wharves, a seafront guesthouse and a nun's convent. Three fishermen's boats had just returned back to the bay to unload and to sell the catch of the day; mostly swordfish and silver bream. Lord Shembrie told Kelinu the cabman to drop them off and gave him the time of return. The four of them then walked along the sea front for a few minutes before deciding to sit at St. Patrick's Guesthouse. On seeing such elegantly dressed clients at the table, Joe, the owner, rushed out to wipe the table and to welcome them.

"Good afternoon," he greeted them.

"Good afternoon," Lord Shembrie replied.

"Are you having lunch or just something to drink?" Joe asked politely.

"Today we are here to celebrate a special occasion. It's my daughter's twenty sixth birthday today. We would like to eat the best fresh fish you can offer us, and of course a good bottle of your local wine."

"I have just bought a large swordfish from that fisherman right over there. You couldn't eat anything fresher. I can prepare some juicy steaks right off the middle, served with a fresh salad on the side and potatoes. Would that be to your liking?"

"That sounds perfect," Lord Louis answered.

"As for the wine, I do make my own, if you would like to taste it."

"Yes, that would be fine."

"Have you been to Gozo before?" Joe asked.

"Yes, but it has been some time now. We love the island and I have to admit that Xlendi is lovely. It is so relaxing here. Whatever happened to John, the previous owner?"

"He moved to Malta the day he retired and I haven't seen him since. Maria! Maria!" Joe called to his wife, "bring a jug of my white wine and four glasses."

Lord Shembrie tasted the wine approvingly and said, "Yes this will definitely do for now, but only fill three glasses; George here doesn't drink a drop. What do you care to drink George?"

"Cola will do for me," he replied.

The view, the sun, the sound of the sea, the fresh air and the food and wine were magical. To top it all, Grace had George. This birthday was definitely very different to her previous ones. Those were all shared with many affluent people, with expensive presents and heaps of exotic food. This was exceedingly more pleasant. She felt so happy and relaxed and would not have changed it for the world.

When Lord Shembrie went in to pay the bill, Joe told him that the wine was on the house, a small birthday gift for the occasion.

"Thank you Joe, that's very nice of you. Now, I wonder if you could help me. There is a farmhouse on top of the hill in Zebbug off Rabat Road, first left. It's up for sale. The sign says to ask for someone by the name of Toni, Toni Ta Lola here in Xlendi, to be exact. Would you know this man by any chance? I have an interest in buying the property."

"He is my cousin and he's over there near Karolina's cave," Joe replied. "There he is, the one with the big belly hanging out like a football! Come, I will introduce you."

"Not today. Today I don't want to talk business, with it being my daughter's birthday. Just ask him if he could meet with me this Wednesday up at the house, say at around one o'clock in the afternoon. Go see what you can do. I'll give you a good commission if I do decide to buy."

"I will go immediately," Joe said.

In only a few minutes, Joe hurried back to Lord Shembrie to tell him that Wednesday was indeed fine. Just then the cab returned to pick them up and the small group headed back to the port of L'Mgarr. Even before stepping onto the boat George felt sad to leave Gozo, and more so the Zebbug farm girl. Little did he know that Lord Shembrie was going to bring him back that very Wednesday, in just a few days' time. Grace had enjoyed a wonderful trip but she had missed her siesta and was tired.

Once back on Malta and in her father's car, she fell asleep. George too closed his eyes but not because he was tired, he just wanted to day dream about the woman he had seen on the roof. With her in mind, George asked to be dropped at Qormi, making the excuse of being a little tired himself. Grace would have liked to have had him near her for longer but he had given her so much already.

"Thank you George. I will cherish this birthday forever. Good night."

"Before I forget, I have a small birthday present for you Grace. Here." Grace opened a little blue box. In it she found an exquisite pendant made of fine crystal on a chain.

"Something small, I do hope you like it," George said, hoping that she would, with it being the first time he had ever bought a present for a woman.

"I love it. How thoughtful of you, thank you! I'll put it on right now," Grace replied, her eyes brimming with tears.

"Oh that looks beautiful on you darling," Lady Jane said.

"I'm so glad you like it. Happy Birthday Grace and have a good night. Today I had a great time. Thank you and see you tomorrow."

"Good night George. Sleep well and thank you for coming with us," Lord Shembrie said.

Once inside his house, George did not even stop to take his clothes off; he just threw himself straight onto the bed to dream about the girl and to think about what he could do. What if the Zebbug farm girl was already married or even courting? Maybe, he thought, it was foolish to dream about her. Anyway Lord Shembrie had not even bought the farmhouse yet and anything could still happen. Finally, exhausted, he fell asleep, still wearing his clothes.

Meanwhile, when the Shembrie family arrived at the villa, they found a surprise birthday gathering organised by the staff. They had prepared a birthday cake and some birthday gifts. Oh how Grace wished that George were there to share it too.

Early the next morning George woke up refreshed and ready to let go of all thoughts of the woman in Zebbug, but when Lord Shembrie told him that the two of them were to go again on Wednesday to see about buying the farmhouse, his heart jumped with joy.

"That's wonderful!" George answered, excitedly. "What I mean is, I loved Gozo and I don't mind coming along with you again to see it," George said quickly, trying not to sound too eager. That Wednesday, the meeting between the two men seemed to go on forever. All the time George sat outside on the wall looking out for the farm girl next door. It seemed an age, but suddenly he heard bells ringing and six goats appeared, each with a little bell tied around its neck, followed by the girl he had been dreaming of. There she was, walking behind her small flock, keeping them together in the herd using a long stick. She saw him and nodded a hello with the warmest of smiles. He started to walk in her direction, transfixed by her presence, but yet again the magic was broken by the sounds of loud talking and laughter.

"George, I've bought the farmhouse," Lord Shembrie said happily. To George's ears it was good news. It only meant that he would be returning.

"Congratulations; I'm sure you will enjoy it." On leaving the premises they had to walk past the farm girl, now sitting on the wall in the lane, watching her sheep.

"Il-gurnata it-tajba," they both said at the same time, wishing the woman a good day.

"Likom ukoll," she replied, wishing them the same. George could swear it was the sweetest voice ever. Not only did she look beautiful but she had the softest, most melodious voice he had ever heard. George stole another look at her as they passed and felt such a joy at simply seeing her there.

"I bought it for a very good price, an absolute bargain," Lord Shembrie said, breaking into his reverie.

"Of course Toni is by no means stupid. To complete the deal, I had to give him the contract to do all the construction work."

"What, even the woodwork?" George asked.

"No, that's all yours. I told Toni that you are my carpenter and why would I want to hire anyone else? I know you will do a fine job. He had no choice but to agree."

On the way back, Lord Shembrie was full of himself. All he talked about were the many shops and all the properties he owned, but George hardly took any notice. He was deaf, surrounded only by the image of the woman he had just seen. Lady Jane and Grace welcomed the news of the new property with open arms. They both loved Gozo, they said, and having a retreat there had always been one of their many wishes. During the next few months Lord Shembrie and George made several visits to Zebbug. The work was progressing far better than they had originally even hoped. Lord Shembrie had promised Toni an extra cash bonus if the construction work was completed before the winter rains. Due to this incentive,

Toni had hired a few extra men and they worked a six day week. With every visit George somehow managed to catch sight of the girl and these glimpses only served to captivate him more and more. Toni was amused at this and in response told George a little about her; that her name was Maria and that she was single. She was the youngest of eight siblings but the only one who still lived on the Zebbug farm with her mother. Now George could not wait for the day when he would be there without Lord Shembrie, so that he could get to know her a little.

By the middle of October, just a few months later, with Toni having finished the construction of the house itself, it was George's turn to install the windows and doors and to complete the kitchen. Lord Shembrie told George that he had organised with Toni to give him a place to stay in the same village. George needed a few weeks to finish the work but he could not have been happier. This would give him ample time to get to know Maria, the farm girl. George's apartment at Zebbug only consisted of two small rooms, yet George would have gladly slept in an open barn as long as he could see Maria.

The medicine Grace was taking worked miracles, and she looked as well as ever. Her friends were more than happy to see her out and about attending all kinds of parties. She had also regained all her old confidence and charm. She felt so alive and happy being around elite and glamorous people, but deep inside she still only loved George. Between thinking of him and enjoying the lavish parties she was attending, she was caught in turmoil. Yet her parents were thrilled to see her back to her old self again. They knew that sending George away to Gozo to work meant that their daughter now had a chance to see that there was life without him.

On his first day at the Zebbug farmhouse, George had hoped to see Maria the moment he stepped foot on the grounds, but she was nowhere in sight. After carrying in some windows, he went onto the roof and sat there for a while. On each previous visit, she had always been there. Then, sometime later, while he was still fitting the first window, he heard footsteps. Someone was on the property. Stopping, he looked around. It was Maria and she was coming straight towards the house. Taken by surprise, he did not know what to say or do. He had prepared for this moment for so long, yet now he was lost for words.

"Good morning George," Maria said.

"You know my name?" George asked, amused and delighted.

"Of course I do. Uncle Toni told me your name the day the rich man bought this house."

"You mean to tell me that Toni, the man who owned this house, is your uncle?"

"Yes. Didn't you ever wonder why I was always around on every one of your visits? Uncle Toni used to let me know when you were going to be here."

"Good old Uncle Toni!" said George, surprised. "Here I was thinking that I was just a very lucky man! Still, it's very nice to learn that you spoke of me," he said shyly.

"When Uncle Toni told me that you were asking about me, I liked it."

"Now I am embarrassed," George replied.

"Don't be. I didn't mind at all. As a matter of fact I had been looking forward to the day when we could meet one another properly, and here we are. Aren't you going to invite me in?"

"Yes of course! Do come in."

"I hope you're hungry. I have prepared something." This was more than George could ever have imagined. Putting her basket on the floor (a bixkilla,) George quickly grabbed a cloth to wipe the table.

"I'll do that. I have everything with me, including a tablecloth. You know I spent most of my childhood in this house, I know it blindfolded! I hope that you like cheese. I have brought some of my own."

"I love cheese," George answered, happy and excited.

"That's perfect. Prepare yourself for a cheese feast. I have fresh goat's cheese, dried as well as peppered. You can try them all," Maria said, as she took them out of her basket. George was very taken by her approach. She was so confident and sure of herself. He felt such pleasure being around her. When the table was cleaned and set, Maria poured fresh milk from a container. Holding the fresh bread to her, she started to cut the slices. To his surprise Maria was left- handed, just like his mother had been. This was something rare on the islands. Left- handed people were superstitiously believed to belong to the devil. Parents tried everything to persuade all left handed children in their families to become right handed, even sometimes tying the left hand behind the child's back until he or she became a right handed person. His mother and now Maria seemed to have got away lightly.

"I would have bought you some of our home made wine, but Uncle Toni told me that you don't drink alcohol."

"Is there anything Uncle Toni didn't tell you about me?" George asked jokingly.

"I don't know, you tell me!" she said, with shining eyes.

Over fresh bread, milk and Maria's cheese, they talked and got to know a little more about each other. Most women on the islands lived under the strong rule of men and some of them were in total fear of speaking to strangers. However, Maria was quite different on several accounts.

"Are you always this relaxed when you meet a person for the first time?" George asked.

"I am. With my family in farming long before I was born, running the farm meant that we always came into contact with a lot of different people, some more difficult than others. Anyway, you are not a stranger. I already know a lot about you."

"Oh, you do? So what more do you know, tell me?" Maria started to tell George what she had found out about him and George was impressed, but soon she started to put her things back in the bixkilla. "I really must be going now. My mother will wake up soon and start looking for me."

"When can I see you again?" George asked, feeling sad that she was leaving so soon.

"I'll be here tomorrow. My mother always has her daily siesta around this time. I could sneak out then, though my two sisters who are nuns, and my brother who is the priest, always come to visit at this time on Sundays."

"Tomorrow then it is; that's just wonderful. By the way, I've never tasted better cheese than yours. Thank you for the lovely lunch and for your company."

"Thank you, and George, you don't have to bring your sandwiches; I will enjoy preparing something myself. Is there anything you prefer?"

"No, not really, I eat everything," George said, all smiles.

"That's good. Tomorrow I will surprise you with another of my homemade specialties."

For the rest of the week Maria and George met every afternoon and with every meeting their friendship grew. Knowing that they could not meet up on Sunday, George returned to his house in Qormi after their Saturday rendezvous.

Once home, he made an effort to visit Lord Shembrie at the villa in Luqa. He wanted to tell him about the progress at the farmhouse after all. Grace was extremely pleased to see him around again. He was so good for her. She treated George well and with respect but George noticed that she was once again just like before, bossily ordering everyone to do her bidding. In just one week, she had become the scheming old Grace again.

During the following weeks Maria and George met daily in secret. No one seemed to suspect anything. It was as though they were living on another planet. During this time they shared some deep feelings and fell in love. Grace however had not been intimately involved with a man for some time. She knew that she should not try to seduce George as she might seem overbearing and possessive, so she started having an affair with a wealthy young man. But with this affair came something different. Unlike the other times, this time she felt somewhat guilty, as if she were cheating, even though there was no commitment or arrangement whatsoever between herself and George. Feeling this way, she ended the affair. "George, I miss you. Could you take some time off from Gozo? There are many things I would like to discuss with you," she asked him when he came to visit.

George never expected this. Caught off guard, he did not know what to say. He was so looking forward to his meetings with Maria and would not give these up for anything or anyone. Seeing her father in the room, George used his presence to his advantage.

"I wish I could but I did promise your father that I would finish off the work in Zebbug by the end of this year" George said loudly, making sure that Lord Shembrie had heard him.

"He is right," her father said. "I do want that house closed up before the New Year. I'm sure that George will finish it soon and then you will have plenty of time together."

His quick thinking had paid off and Grace left the room in a fury. By the beginning of December, the work on Gozo was coming to an end. Maria and George often thought about what was going to happen to the wonderful relationship they had built once George moved back to Malta, but neither of them had the courage to bring up the subject. On the first Monday of December when Maria and George met, they were in a very playful mood. When Maria ran out of the farmhouse she shouted after George to try and catch her.

"Catch me, if you can!" she cried out, entering into the open barn at the back of the farmhouse. Inside the barn, it did not take George too long to figure out where Maria was hiding, and jumping over the low bay which she had hid behind, he grabbed her from the waist. Maria screamed with delight. She tried to pretend to wriggle free but George had a good grip on her and started to playfully tickle her. They both laughed hysterically and rolled over, one on top of the other. "Stop it, George! Please stop it! I'm out of breath," Maria begged, and finally George did. While catching her breath, Maria looked at George's handsome face and eyes. For the first time in his life George knew that he had the woman of his life in his arms. The sun's rays shone through the open barn doors right onto her angelic face as her big dark brown eyes gazed into his. Maria had never looked as beautiful as she did at this moment. George could clearly hear his heart beating. He could not resist such beauty and slowly, very gently, he lowered his head and kissed her. It was the very first kiss for them. They were lost in the magic of the moment, which they had dreamt so many times of happening. They forgot the outside world and all they had been taught. George made love to Maria there in the hay; the ever so gentle and innocent Maria.

Coming back to reality and realising what she had just let happen, Maria pushed George away from her, then stood up and ran, feeling utterly ashamed of herself.

"Maria! Where are you going?" George yelled out, trying to stop her.

"Stay away from me!" she cried out breathlessly, running away. "You just stay away from me, do you hear?"

"Wait! Come back!" George yelled again, but Maria kept running.

Upset and confused, George did not know what to do. Back at home, Maria fetched some water. Closing herself in her bedroom, she started to wash herself. Still crying, she knelt in front of the statue of the Holy Lady on top of her dresser. Making one sign of the cross after another, she begged the Madonna for forgiveness. Feeling ashamed and dirty, she covered her head with a veil to go to confession. She did not want George to see her, so she went out the back way, jumped over a wall, and ran to the village church from a lane beside her house. Although hiding her face under her veil, Father Joe knew the voice of the young girl in the confessional box. Upon hearing Maria's confession, he was very shocked. How could the young and innocent Maria, who he knew so well, commit the worst sin of any unmarried woman? He could not quite digest it. He wanted to make sure that Maria was not a victim of rape, so he asked her if she knew the man and if he had forced himself on her.

"No. He didn't attack me if that's what you mean," she answered quickly, hoping that she hadn't got George into any trouble, "Father, I only have myself to blame. It was I who teased him. Father, I am so scared! Please forgive me. I cannot live without God and the Holy Host. I have shamed myself. I beg of you to help me."

Father Joe knew Maria's family as his own. Loretta, Maria's mother, was a saint of a woman, and three of Maria's siblings formed part of the Catholic Church Clergy. Yes, he was going to give her the pardon she was begging for, but he was going to make sure that Maria would never, ever repeat such a sin.

"Maria, you should know better. Intimate relations occur only after taking your marriage vows in front of God. Before I forgive you in the name of God, you have to promise to God now and in front of me that you will never see or talk to the man who did this to you ever again. Only then can I grant you the forgiveness you ask."

"Yes, I promise I won't see him again. Thank you Father," she answered right away.

"In the name of God the Father, the Son and the Holy Spirit, I forgive you all your sins. As for penance, I want you to say two Holy Rosaries every morning and every evening for a month." At this point he proceeded with the closing prayers and the blessing.

"Thank you Father," Maria said, as she made the sign of the cross. Out of the confession box, Maria recited two Rosaries.

Meanwhile back at the farmhouse, George was on the lookout for Maria. He did not want to leave before they had talked things over. His long wait paid off when his eyes caught her coming back from the village square. He ran to meet her halfway but once she saw him, she became afraid. She had just promised God that she was going to stay away from him and he was right there. Quickly, she turned around to walk away from him.

"Maria! Maria!" George called out; "Wait! I have to talk with you!" Hearing him calling out her name, Maria started to run and George ran after her, but seeing her run into a house, he stopped, realising that she clearly did not want to see him. Physically and emotionally tired, he dragged himself back to the farmhouse. Upset and disappointed, he packed his tools and returned to his place. During the days that followed, Maria was nowhere in sight and George missed her immensely. Feeling rejected, he worked hard all day, day after day, and before he knew it he had finished all the work. Sadly, he returned to Malta without even catching sight of the woman he loved and needed.

The next morning, George walked to his village church to confess. Father Vella was more than disappointed to hear of George's actions. Father Vella then explained the grievousness and the consequences of such a sinful act and George listened in silence.

Father Vella gave his penance and blessing. Having confessed, George felt a little better, but he could not stop thinking of Maria.

That Sunday, he was to turn twenty seven. Prior to the incident in the barn, George had hoped to ask Maria if she would consider becoming his wife. Had she accepted, he would have been ready to meet with her family, but now all this had changed. Feeling depressed, he was not looking forward to his birthday at all. What George did not know, was that someone was organising a surprise birthday party just for him. George had never celebrated in a big way. He had always just stepped next door to his godparents to have cake and a coffee, but this birthday was to be different. This year, Grace wanted to thank him for all the care and the kindness he had shown her during the past two years. Her plan was to host an elaborate Gala Dinner at her villa. She wanted to give him the best birthday she could, and so invited many of Malta's elite and wealthy.

On Saturday, while George was working away on a table at the villa, Grace came to his side to wish him a good day. "Good morning George."

"Good morning Grace."

"George, tomorrow I would like to take you out for your birthday, for dinner, just the two of us."

"I don't know. I mean, it's very kind of you, but to tell you the truth, I haven't been feeling so well lately." Grace didn't panic. She was sure that she could persuade him.

"I did happen to notice. Did you see a doctor?"

"No."

"Do you want me to call our family doctor over?" Grace asked.

"No, I will be fine. I'm sure."

"Maybe all you need is some fresh air and something different, something exciting. Please say that you will come tomorrow. It would do you good and it would make me very happy."

"To be honest, I was just going to visit my godparents and then stay at home and relax."

"You can't mean that? How could anyone stay at home, alone on his birthday? George, that is so boring."

"I guess you're right."

"I'm glad that you agree. Then you will take me up on my invitation?"

"Yes thank you, I'll come."

"You won't be sorry, I promise. Now, put your tools down. I am taking you into town, to my hairdressers. I will tell Father to drive us into Valletta."

"Why? I think that my hair is fine the way it is."

"George, please don't be offended. Yes, your hair is fine but you could do with a trim. Tomorrow you are going to be my guest and I want you to look your best." Too tired to argue and knowing how stubborn Grace was, George went along with her. When Paul, Grace's hairdresser, finished working on George's hair, George looked more handsome than ever and Grace loved it. "Do you like it George?" George did and he showed it with a smile. Once out of the hairdressers, she took him into the clothes shop across the road. With the help of a salesman, George was fitted out with an expensive three piece suit, a white shirt and a red tie. He looked so adorable. He always held that special place in her heart but seeing him in such stylish clothes for the first time, he again won her over. "You look so elegant," Grace said. "We'll take them all please."

"No! Please don't," George said. "These clothes cost so much money and when will I ever wear them again?"

"George, will you please relax? If you only wear these clothes tomorrow, it'll still be worth it. You look like a film star. Go ahead and pack them please," she told the salesman. Turning back to George, she continued, "and George, I have not finished with you yet. You need a pair of new shoes, so please be good and let me have my fun."

George could clearly see that he was dealing with the old Grace and he was not going to say another word. New shoes followed and now George owned a very expensive outfit indeed. Grace's shopping spree did not end here; she took George into another clothes shop and there he was fitted with the latest in casual dress. "My God, just look at you!" she said, admiring him in the big long mirror. "It's so easy to dress you, everything looks so good. I cannot tell you the fun I'm having. I want you to walk out of here wearing this outfit just as you are. Please, just pack the clothes he walked in with," Grace instructed the salesman, who was looking suitably envious. By now, George was going along with whatever Grace had in mind for him.

"All this shopping has given me an appetite," Grace commented as they came out of the shop. "Let's walk down to my favourite café; it's just at the end of this road." Arriving at Piazza Regina, they entered Cordina Coffee Shop, an elegant café renowned for its variety of daily fresh pastries, different coffees and elegant surroundings. "I have to go and powder my nose," Grace told George once she had chosen the table; "I won't be long."

Looking as handsome as he did, many women glanced over to look at George and it made him feel quite shy and nervous. Luckily for him, Grace returned before he left the table.

Her charming banter calmed George and she ordered two coffees and pastries. If he had predicted what she had in store for him that day, he would have refused to come to Valletta with her, but as the day wore on he actually started to enjoy it all. It was a nice distraction after the way Maria had deserted him. Amongst other topics, Grace told George about her Christmas holiday plans and commitments. George could not believe that one person could have so many events to attend. She was so full of energy and excitement. On leaving, they took a cab to head back home. Once past the village of Marsa, Grace told the driver to take the main road to Qormi. Once in front of George's house, she told the driver to stop. "Why are we stopping here?" George asked. "I still have some hours of work left to do at the villa."

"George, when are you going to learn to relax? Earlier, I asked my father to give you the rest of the day off and he agreed."

"Oh!" George answered in surprise.

"Did you really think that after such a morning I would let you return to work?"

"Thanks. Well. What else can I say? I enjoyed every minute of it. I had a wonderful time."

"You're most welcome. Before I go, George, could I ask you something?" George nodded his head.

"Could I escort you to Mass tomorrow morning? I would like to share most of your birthday with you, as you did for my last one on Gozo. I am sure that you still remember that day."

"I would like that. I was planning to attend the eleven o'clock Mass. Is that a good time?" George replied, without any hesitation.

"That's perfect. I will pick you up at ten thirty. Wear the clothes you're in, they look very good on you. Here, take your other clothes and your new suit. See you tomorrow morning."

When George closed the front door behind him, it hit him like a thunderbolt. He had just dated one of the richest and most beautiful women on the Maltese Islands. To top it all, she had bought him some wonderful presents. A luxury lifestyle would never be to his liking but having a taste of the rich life could make him change his mind. Feeling pleased and extremely lucky, he put on his three piece suit. Standing in front of the large Sotto Speccio in the mirror, he kept looking at himself. He did look like a film star. He also realised to his surprise that he could not wait to see Grace again.

When his godparents, Martin and Karmena came with their usual birthday cake to wish him a happy birthday early the next morning, they thought they had the wrong door. Sporting his new haircut and clothes, George looked so different. The expressions on their faces had George laughing. Inviting them in, he thanked them and then, over a few slices of birthday cake and a cup of coffee, George told them all about the events that had taken place in the last twenty four hours. Hearing him mention Grace's name made them none too thrilled. She had been nothing but bad news to him in the past and they didn't want to see George get hurt.

"We came to invite you over for dinner this evening like we always do, but I can see we're too late!" Martin said.

"I feel terrible but I did promise Grace that I would go to the villa. Thanks anyway," George said, without even thinking how his words had sounded. Martin and Karmena might have been offended but they knew that George did not mean to hurt them. They were now quite certain that George was entirely under Grace's spell. Wishing him a happy birthday again, they left before Grace was due to arrive. At exactly ten-thirty, George was at the front door ready and waiting.

"Good morning George and happy birthday!" Grace said, stepping down out of the cab.

"Good morning Grace."

"George, I want to walk up to church with you, if you don't mind."

"Mind? No, not at all," George said.

Grace had him eating out of her palm. Arm in arm, they walked up the main street. "Look, everyone is staring at us," she said, full of pride. It was true. Everyone was staring at them and this continued even during the Mass service. Some villagers were having

151

trouble placing the young, well dressed couple. There was a handful who thought they recognised George but even they were waiting for the service to end to make sure. However, Grace, always one step ahead of the rest, whisked George away into a waiting taxi outside before anyone even realised they were gone. Yes, they had disappeared, but the gossip had just begun. Everything was happening just as Grace had planned it, and after a relaxing journey along the seafront and a stop for a bite to eat, she returned with George back to his home.

"I will send a taxi to pick you up at around seven, so George, please be ready," she told him.

"I will, I promise," George replied. He had a short siesta and then, he started to prepare for the evening. Wearing his new black suit, he nervously bit his fingernails as he sat there waiting until the taxi arrived to take him to the Shembrie's villa.

"Lady Grace is almost ready. Please do come in," Joseph the butler told George on arrival at the Shembrie's estate. Once inside the large hall, George was greeted with a crowd of people. He was shocked. He did not recognise anyone. "Happy birthday George," Grace said, walking out of the crowd to hold him by the arm. They entered under the glittering lights of crystal chandeliers in the drawing room and glasses of champagne were passed to everyone present.

"Here's to you George, happy birthday!" Lord Shembrie announced.

"Happy birthday!" Lady Jane and the guests cheered. George was now introduced to the guests one by one. Some were political figures; the rest were several of Grace's closest friends. The second Grace left the room a few of the single ladies were at George's side within seconds. "Grace tells us that you are a new rising star! She told us that the film is already in production but she refused to tell us anything more, other than that. Please give us a small hint. Is it a love story?" one woman asked.

A film star! He wanted the floor to open up. He was fuming. 'How can she do this?' he asked himself. Luckily for George, Joseph the loyal butler came to his rescue. "George, Lord Shembrie would like to have a word with you, if you would kindly follow me."

"Thank you," George said, relieved. Excusing his quick departure from the cloying females surrounding him, he followed Joseph into the kitchen.

"I felt sorry for you back there George, I do hope you don't mind my intrusion."

"But Joseph, how could she do this to me?" George said, full of rage. "What gives her the right to fabricate such a scheme? I'm no rising star! Maybe I should just leave. I wonder what she'll come up with then!"

"I wouldn't advise it. I have never known Grace to give such a grand party for anyone before. She went through a lot to get the whole thing organised. This party means a lot to her. Please, for this one evening, do try and relax. It is your birthday after all."

"There you are!" they heard Grace say as she entered the kitchen; "the girls tell me that my father has asked to see you. My father is upstairs, so why are you in the kitchen?"

"It's entirely my fault," Joseph said, "I had to save the poor man from the ladies. They were devouring him. I hope I didn't overstep my position?"

"No, not at all. Thank you Joseph for protecting my knight from those hungry dragons! Now let's get back to the guests, shall we?" George didn't know what to think but he respected what Joseph the butler had said to him. Half an hour later, Joseph came to ask everyone to move into the dining room, as dinner was ready to be served. The table was lavishly laid. Only the very best china, silverware, crystal and fragrant flowers were waiting for them.

George had never seen such a beautifully laid table; it was fit for a king. The staff who George worked with stood in position and wore white gloves to serve him, like all the rest of the guests. He felt truly out of place. He was about to panic but just then Grace sat down by his side. He felt sure that she would lead him through it all and she did. After the delicious creamy pumpkin soup, a variety of food and sauces followed. Everyone was having a lovely time. When the desserts were served and the plates were cleared, Grace stood to ask for everybody's attention. "I want to thank you all for coming this evening. You have made George's birthday a very special one. In particular, I want to thank my parents for their support." Then, turning to George, she handed him a small parcel. "This is for you George, from my parents and I. Go ahead and open it." The room went silent and all eyes were on George. The guests could not wait to see what was in the box. When George eventually opened it, he pulled out an engraved twenty four carat gold pocket watch on a chain. Everyone applauded, except for George, who was speechless. He stood still looking at the magnificent present in his hand. It had even been engraved with the letters 'G.G.' on the front, and when George opened its face to see the time, it played a melody. "The new clothes wouldn't be complete without this gold pocket watch," Grace whispered to George. "Now, stand up and say something. Make it short and simple."

All eyes were upon George. He could feel his face becoming redder by the minute.

"Thank you Lord Shembrie, Lady Jane and Lady Grace," he started, "it is such a wonderful gift. I promise that I will cherish it for the rest of my life. Thank you, and thank you all for coming," he said, to a rapturous applause all around.

"Very good George, that was very good. I'm so proud of you," Grace said as he sat back down. George was sitting with some of Malta's elite and most prestigious of families but he could not wait until it was all over. George's handsome looks had created many admirers in the room. The Shembries would only honour someone special with such a lovely party. It was obvious to many however of Grace's feelings for George. Her eyes and her smile gave her away every time she looked at him. She was so proud and happy sitting there beside him. The guests were sure that they would be seeing more of them together in the near future.

"A very good looking man, keep him happy." "He is good for you." "Thanks for the invitation." "The food was excellent." "Thanks for a lovely evening." "What a lovely man." "He's terribly handsome. I would have been in a scrap or two over him in my younger years, I can tell you!" were some of the comments the guests made on leaving.

"Thank you so much," Grace repeated, as they all left, one by one.

At the end of the evening, the four of them now sat down. George had thought that the evening and the presents were over but Lord Shembrie apparently still had something else in store. Seeing that George was the source of his daughter's happiness, he wanted to give them more time together. "George, I want you to have some time off work over the Christmas holidays. I think that beginning tomorrow, work can wait. You are welcome to visit our home but just to relax. You could then return back to work on January the second. How does that appeal to you?"

"That would be very nice, but are you quite sure? You have given me so much already."

"Yes I am," he replied quickly.

Grace, as this point of the evening, was a little bit tipsy but she had overheard every word. She already knew what she wanted next. "George, I would like you to escort me to the New Year's Eve ball. Oh, please say yes. It would make me so very happy!" George was caught with his hands tied once again. After such a party and presents, he could hardly refuse her. "Oh, I knew I could count on you! Tomorrow, I'll teach you how to dance the waltz. It will be so much fun. You just wait and see."

"Dance? Me? Not a chance; I've never even tried before."

"You will. I bet you'll know a lot by Christmas day," Grace said.

George was enjoying the special attention Grace had been lavishing on him and so the next day, to please her, he tried dancing for the very first time. For Grace, having George hold her in his arms while she taught him the waltz was the happiest she had ever been.

By the time New Year's Eve came along, one could not exactly call George a professional dancer, but he could do a decent waltz. For that special night Grace had her hair done up and wore a special dress made for the occasion, which looked exquisite. She hired top hat and tails for George. They looked quite a couple together. The evening started better then she could ever have expected. George was totally relaxed and they danced and danced. She was having the night of her life and now she could not wait for midnight, the moment when she would kiss George for the first time. As the crowd chanted the countdown, chills went up Grace's spine with every count. At exactly midnight, Grace put her face up to George and touched his lips. It felt so good and she did not want to let go, but George pulled away. For some reason, the act of kissing reminded him of Maria on Gozo, the woman who he really wanted beside him tonight.

"What's wrong?" Grace asked, looking at him.

"Nothing, nothing," he murmured, embarrassed.

"I hope you didn't mind….."

"Mind what?" George asked, cutting her off.

"Me kissing you," she replied, reaching for two tall glasses of champagne from the tray a waiter was passing around. "Have some Champagne."

"You know I don't drink," George answered.

"There were a lot of things you didn't do or didn't know how to do up to a few weeks ago. Drinking goes with socialising. You'll get the hang of it, just like the clothes, the presents and the dancing. Now, let's drink to the New Year, to us, and your new life!" Grace had said all the wrong things. The last statements stung George, penetrating and bursting the bubble he had been living in since the day she had taken him to Valletta. He did not want to drink alcohol. He did not need the expensive clothes, parties and presents. Come to think of it, he did not need Grace or her high society life. Had he the courage, he would have run away from her right there and then, but he could not. It would not be fair on Grace, and it was New Year's Eve after all. He did not say much during the rest of the night and Grace drank one drink after the other. George could not even look at her anymore. She became drunk and George was smart enough to call a taxi to escort her home before things got any worse. By the time they got to the villa, Grace had fallen asleep. Her parents thanked George for bringing her home safely.

Unlike Grace, George could not sleep. He had somehow put Maria at the back of his mind but tonight she had returned. The more he tried to stop thinking of her and her well-being, the more restless he became. Eventually he fell asleep, but his night was filled with nightmares, strange reoccurring nightmares. When he woke up, he was sweating all over. After bathing, he made some coffee and then went next door to wish Martin and the family a happy New Year. George felt better to be with his own kind again. He did not want to leave the house and they did not want him to leave either, for they had missed his company, jokes and laughter. Martin invited George to stay over for the midday meal and George accepted readily. The setting at the table and the sauces on the meat were not anywhere near what the Shembrie's chef usually prepared, but it was Karmena's cooking and George ate it all. He even licked the plate clean to the laughter of his neighbours. After dinner, Karmena and her daughters cleaned up while Martin and George moved into the next room to relax over some card games. George had already forgotten all about the Shembries and felt just like his old self again.

At the villa, Grace woke up with a severe hangover. She could not remember anything that had taken place the night before. When her parents told her that George had brought her home totally drunk that morning, she felt awful. 'How could I do such a stupid thing?' she thought. She was sick for most of the day and so for once she was happy that George was not around. Luckily for George, the festivities had all passed. There were no parties to worry about. When George returned to work at the villa, Grace came to him to apologise for her behaviour. George was smart enough to let her take the blame and life returned to normal. Grace now returned to acting but she always found some time for George.

Late that January, Grace came home with some good news. She had landed a short role in a low budget movie. This was the break she had been dreaming of ever since her first day on set. The part was to be filmed in Italy as early as February and she had to be away for at least three months. Just the thought of travelling, living and meeting new people of another culture filled her with excitement. She was looking forward for the day of departure with great anticipation. Everyone was very proud of her. They all encouraged her, especially George. "Oh George, I wish you could come along too. I am going to miss you dreadfully."

"Three months will pass quickly. When you return you'll have so many tales to tell. It will be a wonderful experience. Seeing you all excited, reminds me of the day my sister got the offer from the Armstrongs to go to work for them in America. She took the opportunity when it came her way and look at her now; she is married, owns a house and a prosperous business. You will do well. I know it."

"Thank you George, you don't know how much your support means to me. I really mean it."

When Grace left for Italy, the villa seemed empty. Her parents missed her dearly and the staff too, even though life without her around was a lot easier. George now had ample spare time. Maria was always in his thoughts and the only way he could free himself from her spell, he realised, was to see her face to face one more time.

That March, George summoned up enough courage to cross over to Gozo and Zebbug to see her. He did not know what to expect, so when the horse cab arrived at the hilltop, he asked to be dropped off so he could walk the rest of the way. Little by little, he crept up the lane to Maria's house, and then he stopped and hid behind a big tree. Looking over the low stone wall, he spotted a woman wearing a head scarf and dressed all in black. She was sitting on a stool milking one of the sheep. George assumed it was Maria's mother. 'How unlucky,' he thought to himself. He had never even seen her mother around before and today of all days she was here. Even so, he had come a long way and he was not going to give up yet. He decided that no matter how long he waited, he had to talk to Maria and it had to be on this day. Carefully he straightened himself up and took a step backwards, only to step on some twigs, which broke under his weight. Startled, the woman stopped milking and turned to see who or what was there. To make amends, George came out of his hiding place to apologise. To his surprise, the woman dressed in black, was Maria.

Chapter 13

Maria and George

For a moment, George thought that Maria would run away, but she did not. "George. Is that really you?" she asked, looking straight at him.

"Yes. Please don't run away. We have to talk."

"Oh my God, it is you!" Maria said, pulling up her skirt to run towards him. Seeing her coming towards him, George ran to meet her half way.

Holding on to one another, Maria started to cry. "George, thank God you are here! My mother, my poor mother, she passed away." He had never even seen Maria's mother, yet he felt sad. Holding Maria tightly, he could feel her pain and he wanted to share her loss. Maria and George walked into Maria's house. "So when did it happen? When did your mother die?" George asked, as he sat down at the table while Maria put a pot of water on the burner.

"Just after New Year, on the second of January," Maria answered. "I went to wake her up only to find her dead. I yelled and screamed all the way to the police station in the square. The doctor said that she had died from a heart attack. Oh George, it was terrible. I kept on seeing her face and hearing her calling me for days. If it wasn't for my family's support, I don't know how I'd have coped."

"Maria, I'm so sorry," George said.

"And what about you, what brings you here? Did your boss send you to check on the house?"

"No, he didn't. As a matter of fact, he doesn't even know I am here. Maria, I came to see you. We need to talk."

"Yes, I think we do," Maria replied.

"The truth is I've never forgotten you. My head wanted to but not my heart. Today I came to find out where we stand. Only you can set my heart free."

"Is that what you want, I mean, to be free?" she asked, lowering her head and turning away from him.

"No. I want to hear you say that you love me as much as I love you. Only that would make me happy."

She turned to face him. Her face lit up with pleasure. "Really? Why yes! I love you George, I do! I really do!"

Over tea, Maria started to speak, back to that day, the day she ran away from the barn. Hesitantly she told him all about the confession and her promise to God.

"But today you broke the promise, why?" George interrupted.

"Only God could have sent you back to me. Only He knows how much I love you; how much I've suffered these last few months without you and how much I need you."

"Maria, will you marry me?" George asked her outright, excited with hope.

She wanted to leap with happiness but there was still something else she needed to make clear. "George. I have something to tell you. You'd better prepare yourself for what I'm about to say."

"What? What is it?"

"Taking a deep breath, she looked at him and said, "I am pregnant. I am carrying our baby."

"Did you say pregnant?" George asked, in shock and astonishment.

"Yes."

"Are you positive?" George asked.

"When I didn't see my monthly, I thought it was just late. This happens sometimes. With my mother's death, I totally forgot all about it, but when I started feeling unwell and vomiting, it all made

161

sense. I haven't had my period yet, so I must be. I didn't know what to do, I've been so scared, but God is great and He has sent you back to us."

"Yes He did, Maria. Does anybody know? I mean that you're pregnant; did you tell anyone?"

"No I didn't. I've been too afraid."

"That's good. That's really good. We have to get married as soon as possible. We have to save ourselves from scandal. Later, we can always say that the new born arrived early and unexpected. The clock is against us though. When can I meet your family?"

"How about this Sunday, we usually eat around noon? Yes, come around one o'clock. We will be expecting you."

"Good, that's one thing settled. Now listen to me, make sure that you don't tell them that you're pregnant. I don't want them to hate me before they've even met me. Tell them that a carpenter who has been working on the next door farmhouse has come to know you and that he has returned to ask for your hand in marriage. I don't expect you to move to Malta. It will be a lot easier if I move here. Yes, tell them that I have agreed to move here and to work the farm with you."

"George, that's wonderful, but are you sure? You would be leaving your house, your job, your friends and everything behind. You know that I would sell the animals and move to Malta, if you asked me to."

"I don't know if I told you but when I was a little boy, my mother used to visit and help out on a farm, bigger than yours. Being a widow with three small children, she used to take us along. Now, I can't say that I took to being a farmer, but I liked the animals. In a few months you won't be able to run the farm. Once we marry, there will be enough time before the baby comes for me to learn. I will be too busy to miss anyone on Malta. Anyway, if we are to be a family, my home is with you."

"Oh George, you are such a wonderful man. The farm does make a good income and we shouldn't lack the basics of a good and comfortable life." Maria had such a lovely face. Her smile came with that something special. George felt such warmth around her.

"My employer will fill my position in no time. There are plenty of unemployed carpenters out there. Anyway, I don't really care what Lord Shembrie thinks and does. I have a family to take care of now."

The time with Maria was intoxicating. The few hours flew by and soon George had to start heading back to Malta. The short visit had totally changed his life. That Sunday, as agreed, Maria introduced George to her family, Sister Maria Angelika, Sister Maria Concetta and Father Antonio. George had charisma and his looks were admired by all. Maria's family immediately liked him. Using the lines he had practised over and over again, George told them how he had fallen totally in love with Maria and that he had come to ask their permission to marry her. Having heard from Maria beforehand that she had fallen in love with George too, they were prepared. When he concluded by confirming that he was ready to move onto the farm, they truly believed that this match was made through their beloved departed mother, now in heaven. Maria desperately needed help on the farm but more so, also a man who could protect her. Nobody could fill both these positions more than a loving and caring husband. Yes, George had to be heaven sent they felt. With this in mind, the three family members asked him to return in a few days. Many years had passed since the days when men were checked before marrying a woman, but the same custom was still thriving and in use now. No one wanted to see a relative marry into a scandalous or troubled family. In George's case, this was going to be easy. Being a priest, all Father Antonio had to do was visit the village church in Qormi. When the Qormi parish priests spoke only praise for George there was nothing left to be done and Father Antonio was satisfied.

When the group met again later that week, George and Maria received the family's blessing; they could marry on any day. Knowing that the little one in Maria's womb was growing with each passing day, George asked to marry Maria the following Sunday. "Just the family if you don't mind," George stated firmly.

There were no objections. Preparations were discussed and agreed upon. Back on Malta, George went directly to tell his godparents about the upcoming nuptials. As expected, they were in shock. They had never known George to date any woman other than Grace and that was only during the last weeks of December. With the New Year, George had seemed to find himself again and this pleased them. But today, he had come and dropped a bombshell at their feet. Not only did he announce that he was going to marry in just days, but that of all the women on Malta, he had fallen in love with one on Gozo. To complete this astonishing news, he was going to live there too. Growing up around their six girls, they had always hoped that George would marry one of their younger daughters. They were very disappointed to say the least, yet they loved and respected him dearly.

"I love everything about Maria," George said with deep conviction in his voice; "she is warm and gentle, a wonderful person and pretty too. When I look at her, I forget the struggles of the world. I love her that much. I really do."

They did believe him. It was written all over his face. George had found real love. Congratulations were in order and they gave him their blessing. George then asked Martin, now in his late sixties, to honour him by standing in as his best man. "History repeats itself. I stood for your father a very long time ago and now I am honoured to stand by your side too. I proudly accept."

Happy and excited, George explained that the wedding was to take place in a very small chapel in the convent where the nuns, Maria's sisters, lived. He told them that her brother the priest was going to do the Mass Service. George had specifically asked for the wedding to take place at one o' clock in the afternoon, so that they, Martin and his wife Karmena, would have plenty of time to cross over and then to return home before sunset. Martin and Karmena had always supported George and they were not going to disappoint him now. Not only did they agree to go along with all the arrangements but they also promised that their children would take care of his house and all his belongings in Qormi.

The next morning, George went to the villa to give Lord Shembrie his notice. He thought that George was joking. "Come on George! It can't be true," he said, laughing it off.

"It is," George replied.

"How can this be? I mean, you have everything here. We are like family. It wasn't that long ago that our daughter went to all kinds of lengths to make you feel special."

"It wasn't like that and you know it," George retaliated defensively; "I didn't ask for that birthday party. As a matter of fact, before Grace came to me that Saturday, I had planned to spend my birthday alone at home. I only went along with it so that I wouldn't upset her. Yes, I admit that you have all been more than generous, but I have met the love of my life, and I'm going to marry her and move to Gozo."

"George, but you hardly know this woman! With your secure job here and your own house, you could have any woman you wanted. You are still so young, why rush into marriage? Shouldn't you make sure that she is the right one?"

George didn't want to hear anymore. He had come here to quit and that's what he was going to do. "I have met the woman I want for my wife. This I am sure of."

165

"Really, and what about our daughter?" Lady Jane asked, now entering the room, having been eavesdropping throughout the whole conversation. "Have you thought of her at all? She confided to me that your relationship has recently become closer. So what's happened to that, or, have you conveniently forgotten?"

"No I haven't. But let's be realistic. Grace and I are close but we could never be more than close friends. She deserves someone of her own station in life. I'm sure you agree. She has been in Italy over a month and a half already, and when she calls home, she repeatedly tells you that she is happy. She is among actors and film directors, people of high society, and I am happy for her. I am a carpenter, and that's what I'll always be. And anyway, marrying Maria and moving to Gozo won't mean goodbye. We can still see each other now and again. Don't forget that on Gozo, we are neighbours. You will always be welcome to visit our home."

They realised that there was some truth in what he said. Indeed, they would be thrilled if Grace were to marry a film star or a director. Little did they all know however, that in Italy, Grace was at that very moment crying alone in her room, her adventure having taken a turn for the worse. In Malta, Grace was a well known young woman of a rich family but on Italian soil she was no one. Grace had always chosen her men, manipulated them, dropped them cold and enjoyed it all in the process. In Italy, she was among men who had women ready to do anything for fame and fortune. Grace was very pretty with a stunning figure, but there this did not amount to much. There were many other women with the same qualities.

Almost from Grace's first day in Italy, men noticed that she thrived solely on male attention and she became an easy target to be taken advantage of. Most of the famous producers she met promised her roles in upcoming projects and she trusted them, but they were just using her. These sad experiences made her more than just angry. 'How can I trust another man again?' she wondered. There was only one man in her life and that was George the carpenter. That morning, while watching the sunrise out of the hotel balcony, Grace decided that once her contract finished and her feet were back on Malta, regardless of what anyone might say, she would publically declare her love for George.

Meanwhile, George was planning his wedding for that following Sunday and Lord Shembrie, although greatly disappointed, agreed to end George's work contract in order to give George time to prepare for his forthcoming nuptials.

"We wish you and your bride happiness George," he said, shaking his hand as they parted in good faith. After all, George was a fine young man, a hardworking and dependable employee and had showed the family nothing but respect.

On Sunday, everything went to plan. Martin and Karmena were picked up at the port of Gozo and taken straight to the church in Rabat where George was nervously waiting.

Maria was getting dressed at her sisters' convent while her brother, Father Antonio, was in the sacristy preparing for the wedding service. With a few minutes left, Father Antonio and several altar boys approached the altar to meet George and Martin. Soon, the organist started playing the famous wedding march. Maria appeared at the entrance of the church, dressed in a simple, pale, yellow dress. Maria felt that it was inappropriate to wear a white wedding dress, due to her mother's passing. Ironically, George was wearing the suit that Grace had bought him for his birthday. A few white bouquets were added to the church's interior. There were not many guests present; just Maria's relatives. The regular Sunday morning services had finished, with the last one at noon. These were always full with parishioners. That was why George had asked for the wedding to take place afterwards. When Martin and Karmena saw Maria, they were totally enchanted. She looked so pretty. During the sermon, Father Antonio said many beautiful words and wished his sister and her husband a lot of luck and happiness. After the service and the signing of the register, they headed down to Xlendi Bay to Uncle Toni's cousin's guesthouse for a four course meal. It was now time for Martin and Karmena to get to know Maria a little more.

"You were right George, Maria does remind me of your mother, God bless her soul," Martin said to him after a while. "She is a wonderful woman. Now I can understand why you feel as you do about her."

"Thank you. I do miss my family. I just wish they were all still alive. I do miss Mariella. Thankfully at least, I still have you to share my joy with today."

"We will always be your family George. You can count on us. We are so happy for you. Maria will look after you well. As you know, we've never been to Gozo before, but we can see why you love it here. It's such a beautiful island and I'm sure the Gozitan people will treat you well. You will do alright. But please, don't feel offended if we don't visit. We are getting on in years now and we hardly go out of our own house these days. But of course, you are welcome to come and visit us whenever you want."

"We will come, and soon. That I promise," George replied. Before they parted company, they hugged and wished each other well.

"Take care George, we will miss you," Karmena said "Thanks for everything and our regards to the family."

When George and Maria arrived back at the farmhouse, he lifted Maria into his arms and took her right up to the bedroom. Looking at his lovely wife, he realised what a very lucky man he was. Slowly and gently they removed each other's clothes and quietly they explored each other's bodies. Lovingly and tenderly their passion mounted and the two became one. Afterwards they lay beside each other, whispering and laughing as newlyweds do.

"Even though we've already got a head start, how many children would you like us to have?" George asked Maria.

"I don't know. A few, or whatever God sends. I promise to be the best wife and mother. George, you have made me so happy in such a short time. I do love you."

That evening Maria prepared a light meal. After seeing to the animals, they said the Rosary and prayed before retiring. In the early hours before dawn, Maria awoke to begin her daily duties, leaving George to sleep on. When George eventually woke too, he dressed and went to the kitchen. Maria was happily humming away to herself and on the table, George saw an enormous breakfast.

"Good morning my darling," George greeted her.

"Good morning, my dear husband!" Maria answered, giving him a kiss. "Did you sleep well?"

"Very well thank you, but tomorrow; make sure that you wake me up. I want to learn your routine and help you as much as I can."

"I will, I promise, if that's what you want. I was about to, but you were sleeping so deeply. By the way, did you know that you snore?" she said, smiling.

"I don't snore!"

"Yes you do," she grinned.

"Do I really?" George asked in a very serious voice, as he reached out for her hand to gently pull her next to him.

"Just a little but I love it," she replied, giving him a warm kiss. "It made me feel so safe knowing that you were there next to me. You are very warm; definitely better than my hot water bottle."

"Thank you, it's good to know that I have already beaten the competition!" George joked.

Maria enjoyed serving her husband his breakfast and George ate and ate. Afterwards she took him around the farm and showed him all the animals: five cows, six sheep, three goats, six chickens, two roosters and three cats. George could not believe that one tiny woman could handle all the farm work as well as attend to all these animals, and as if these were not already enough, she did other things as well. She grew her own herbs and vegetables, made her own wine and the delicious Gozo goat's cheese, not to mention the normal household chores. She was an extraordinary woman.

That afternoon, while Maria rested for a short while, George sat down to write a few lines to his sister. He wrote of the wedding and that he was extremely happy. He wrote all about Maria and explained about his new life on the farm on Gozo. He finished the letter by giving his sister the new address and said that he would wait with anticipation to hear from her. In a couple of weeks, George had settled down in his new lifestyle. In the process, he had met a few locals and already made some new friends, but being very busy, he did not go out much. This did not bother him at all though, for he had his darling Maria and he loved his new life.

When Mariella, George's sister in America, received her brother's letter, she was very surprised to say the least. Her brother had never mentioned girlfriends, but remembering that on Malta brief courtships were a very common practice, she understood and was very happy that George had found someone special. She did not have to carry the guilt of leaving her brother behind alone anymore. The next morning she sent George and his new wife a telegram of congratulations.

Seven weeks after their wedding, George announced Maria's pregnancy to the family. Sister Angelica, Sister Concetta and Father Antonio were thrilled with the news. They could not wait to meet the newest member of the family. George again wrote to his sister.

When Mariella got the letter, she started to cry. She herself wanted children badly but she was not so lucky. After trying for many months and with no result, her disappointments had turned into frustration and depression. Wanting to have a child at all costs, she'd had tests done at the best clinic available. However, the final results had proved to be unbearable; they were told that she would never be able to conceive. This news was shocking, painful and hard to digest. Austin was very understanding and he tried to make it as easy as he could for her, but nothing could fill the emptiness she felt within. Reading that her new sister-in-law was pregnant, she envied her but she was happy for them all the same. At least, through Maria and her brother, the family name could carry on. Thinking about her situation and her family back on Malta, Mariella decided to make a surprise visit there that summer.

In the meantime, Maria's belly started to show but she hid her advanced pregnancy well with careful dressing. Being so busy on the farm, George had not been to Malta at all, even though he had promised Martin that he would go. He wanted to take Maria there before she got any bigger and to show her the Qormi house. So leaving Maria's sisters to tend to the farm, they went that Sunday. Martin and his family welcomed Maria with open arms. Maria gave them some of her fresh goat's cheese and a few bottles of her wine. Over soup and baked macaroni, they talked and laughed. Karmena and Maria even exchanged cooking recipes. When Maria walked through George's next door house for the very first time, she liked it. Also, she could not help noticing how clean it was. Though closed for months, there was no smell of dampness; Karmena and her children were taking good care of it. After a short siesta, George took Maria to St. Sebastian Church and then back to Martin's house to give them back the house key and to thank them once again.

Chapter 14

Grace Returns Home

Grace's filming in Italy had come to an end. She was so looking forward to seeing George. Once the ship entered Malta's port she could not wait any longer. Taking out her new small binoculars, she walked onto the prow and started looking out for him. It did not take her long to catch sight of her parents however, standing by her father's car, all ready and waiting to greet her. George however was nowhere to be seen. All concerned, she barged through the crowd to be the first one down the gangway. Louis and Jane were so happy to see their daughter home safely, but after a quick embrace, her first question was about George.

"Where's George? I bought him something very special. Where is he? You did bring him with you, didn't you?" Her father could not bear to tell her the truth.

"George is down with a fever. Don't worry. He will be fine in a few days. So how did things go in Italy?"

Without George's welcome, the excitement seemed to have diminished and Grace sat quietly all through the drive to the villa. When they got to the front door the staff were all waiting for them, but their warm greetings did not excite Grace. The only person she wanted to see was George, and he was not there. She walked right past them as if they did not even exist, ignoring their welcome altogether. "Let's go into the drawing room," her mother said, "we've prepared some of your favourite food. I can't wait to hear all about your exciting adventure."

"That has to wait. I am not hungry, just tired. All I want at the moment is to have a hot bath please," Grace said, quietly.

"Of course my dear; I'll call the maid to prepare a hot tub for you."

After a relaxing soak, Grace came back downstairs. She knew her parents very well, so as they sat in the drawing room she only told them what they wanted to hear. Opening her large travelling trunk, she had many gifts for them, including expensive bottles of wines, liquors and cigars for her father and a set of pearl and gold earrings with a matching necklace for her mother, plus a few very expensive garments.

"Is this for me?" her father said, all excited, lifting up the big box near him.

"No, that one is for George. I can't wait until he opens it. Oh why did he have to be ill?" Her parents couldn't believe it. Even after such a long time away from Malta, Grace was still so attached to George. Feeling tired after such a long journey, Grace retired early.

The next day, during breakfast, Grace kept bringing George's name up repeatedly. In the end, she told her parents that she was going down to the village of Qormi to see him.

"No. You very well know that a woman alone is not allowed to visit a man, even when he is ill. It is just not proper," her father said.

"Then you come with me. I don't want him to think that I don't care after all he has done for me over the last few years."

"He is not alone, if that's what you are worried about. His godparents live right next door, as you already well know. They are taking good care of him. Besides, I don't want you to catch this Influenza. In a couple of days he will be fine."

"All I want is to say hello. Why you are making it so difficult?" Lord Shembrie could see that his daughter was as determined as ever. He was certain that she was going to visit George that day, with or without him. Asking her to walk with him, they went out and sat in the garden under the gazebo. "Grace, I have

173

a confession to make. Please don't get upset. I lied. I had to. George is not around because he is no longer my employee." Grace was about to stand up but her father held her. "I swear to God, I didn't fire him, believe me. George came to the villa and he resigned from his job here. I tried to keep him. I even told him that he should take some time to decide before he rushed into marriage."

"Marriage! What marriage? What are you talking about now?" Grace asked, extremely confused.

"I'm so sorry Grace, I really am, but George is married." Grace suddenly felt like she was in a long dark tunnel with no light at the end.

"I don't believe you! First you tell me that he is in bed with fever and then you tell me that you have lied to me and now you tell me that he is married! I don't believe you. I want to see George and I'm going to see him now! I want the truth and I want it from him." Standing up, she walked away.

"Grace for God's sake. Where do you think you are going?"

"I am going to Qormi to see George and don't try to stop me."

"You won't find him there. George does not live there anymore. He has married a Gozitan woman. They live on Gozo."

"Stop lying. My God, stop lying!" she said, putting her hands over her ears.

"I am not lying. Please stop and hear me out. I beg of you, it's true, really."

Grace stopped. "How could he? How could he?" she said, crying on her father's shoulder.

"Now, now, it's not the end. You have the whole world and your whole life in front of you. You will get over him in time."

"No I won't. George is the only person I need. The only man I want. Someone has stolen him from me, but it's not over yet. Whoever she is, she is in for a fight. I will win him back, you'll see!"

"Grace, George is married. Forget about him."

"That's easy for you to say! My heart is breaking. Just leave me alone do you hear, just leave me alone!" she said, running away. Closing herself in her room she cried and cried. This time around, Lord Shembrie went to tell his wife and Jane immediately went to her daughter's side.

"Oh mother!" Grace cried.

"I am so, so sorry. I'm here for you my dear child."

They cried together and when the crying stopped, her mother held her. Grace did not eat much that day and she did not say a word either. Lord Shembrie and his wife gave her all the room she needed but they hovered over her like a pair of hawks. Grace could not sleep; her heart was full of hate. She had horrible thoughts. Thoughts she could not control. She could clearly see herself fighting with this other woman. In her mind they fought, tearing hair out, yelling and screaming at each other. She could not take it anymore. Getting out of bed, she went into the garden for some fresh air but even this did not help. Returning to bed, she eventually fell asleep.

As the days passed, her early thoughts became nightmares, finally stopping only when she saw herself stabbing the other woman. She could see herself relishing the death of this woman lying on the floor and she could clearly see herself enacting this horrific killing. If she could not have George then no one could have him, she said to herself. At this point, she would wake in shock, breathless and sweating. Opening her bedroom window, she would stand there, trying to catch her breath. She did not want to return to bed for she was too scared to sleep.

In the meantime, Maria was having her own problems. She was experiencing terrible back pains and standing on her feet really hurt. Knowing that a doctor's visit could reveal the early pregnancy, Maria and George had never called him over, but today, they had to.

During his examination, the doctor found that the baby was resting on a nerve.

"How far did you say your wife is?" he asked George.

The baby was now in its seventh month but George had to lie. "She must have got pregnant on our wedding night on March the sixth."

"Are you sure? I would have thought that she was in her sixth month. Maria needs bed rest. Only that will help her. Call me if you need anything." Maria had hoped to keep on working on the farm until the delivery day.

"Don't you worry, I can handle the chores," George assured her, now that the doctor had left.

"You are such a wonderful husband. I can always count on you George."

As the days passed, Lady Grace became more and more depressed. She could not take the pressure any longer. She had to do something or she was going to find herself where she was two years ago, ill in bed, only this time round George would not be coming anywhere near her. She felt that without George she could not survive. She was desperate. 'The woman deserves to die,' she thought. Like all criminals, Grace was sure that she had the perfect plan and that she would get away with it. Grace knew that she could not use a horse cab on the day as it would take too long to get to Cirkewwa, the crossing point to Gozo, and she knew that she could not ask her father to drive her.

So, on Friday, she booked a taxi for Saturday morning. During dinner, at the table that same evening, Grace told her parents that she had a very important appointment in the morning with an Italian film director. "It might take most of the day," she told them, just to be on the safe side.

Obviously her parents were thrilled. Her father even offered to drive her, but being clever and prepared, she said, "Thank you father, that's very generous, but everything has already been organised by the film company, including the transport."

At the appointed time on Saturday morning, the taxi arrived at the villa. Grace was on her way to carry out her evil plan.

Chapter 15

A Death

It was June the fourteenth, 1939, and a lovely sunny day. Not being a fisherman's daughter, Grace knew nothing about the sea and she did not even think to enquire about the weather conditions. On this day however, the sea currents were very strong. Once the cab stopped at the port of Cirkewwa on Malta, Grace expected to see The Royal Lady, the same boat on which she had sailed on that memorable day, her last birthday. But on this day, The Royal Lady, now nicknamed by the Gozitans 'The Rolling Lady' due to its performance in stormy seas was nowhere in sight. At first, Grace thought that she had just missed it and she simply needed to wait for the next trip. Wanting to find out, she went and asked. To her disbelief a sailor working for the Gozo Mail Company told her that due to the strong currents, The Royal Lady was still sheltering back in the port of Valletta on Malta. Crossing over to Gozo was impossible.

"How long will it be?" Grace asked, totally shocked.

"There's no set time. As soon as the captain feels it's safe to set sail he will, but it could be hours and it might not even come at all." This was unacceptable to Grace. She had planned this for many nights now and she was determined to get it over with. It had to be done and on this day. Seeing a fisherman standing near a Luzzu, she walked over to him.

"Does this boat belong to you?" she asked.

"Yes madam it does."

"Good. Now, how much will it cost me to cross over to Gozo?"

"What, now?" the astonished fisherman asked, with a shocked expression.

"Yes! Now!" she replied crossly.

"Lady, you are joking right? I mean look at that sea; it's like a pot of boiling water. It would be suicidal!"

"You can go as slow as you want, I don't mind," Grace said, using all her charm to make him relent.

"Madame, this is not a car or a horse. It can't be done, sorry," he said, shaking his head and smiling. Grace always carried a large amount of cash on her. She liked doing things impulsively. Taking a few notes out of her purse, she showed these to the fisherman.

"These are all yours if you give it a try," she told him. Ricardo noticed that she had a lot of money in her hands. Having six children, a wife and being late on some payments, he fell for the temptation.

"You did say, even if I attempt to cross over, didn't you?" he asked, now biting on his lower lip.

"That's right. This could all be yours if you just try," Grace replied, in order to persuade him.

"Oh God! I must be insane. Madonna, Holy Mother of Jesus, please help me for I don't know what I am in for," he said as he pulled out the pendant of the Holy Lady hanging on a chain around his neck and kissed it. To the disbelief of all those around, including the cab driver who had driven Grace there and who had also hoped to make some extra cash by taking her back, Ricardo the fisherman helped Grace into his Luzzu.

"Ricardo! What are you doing? Where are you going?" the sailor shouted out.

"Ricardo! Are you mad? You will both drown!" another fisherman yelled.

Others agreed with them but to no avail. Ricardo started out, yet as soon as the little boat passed the sheltered walls of the port and into the open sea, the Luzzu went out of control, bobbing violently up and down and sideways. Being an experienced sailor, he knew very well that it was virtually impossible to make the trip to Gozo and predicting that the lady on board would now beg him to return back to the port, he decided to turn around. "Sorry but this is as far as we go. We have to turn back; we'll never make it!" he yelled at Grace, thinking that he had made a lot of money just for trying. But to his shock, Grace opened her handbag and pulled out a knife. "Keep going," she said; "you keep that rudder on course or I'll kill you. That I swear. I don't care much about my life but I am pretty sure that you do about yours!"

Ricardo could see the hate in her eyes. This lady was evil. The only way he was going to see his family again was to do as he was told. Up and down they went, over one wave and then onto another. Using all his skills and praying like he had never prayed before, Ricardo neared l'Mgarr, the port of Gozo. Stranded by the rough sea, a few Gozitan fishermen and the few farmers who had come to ship their crops over to the main island, were sitting having a cup of hot tea or a glass of wine at Gleneagle's Bar, just overlooking the port. When they caught sight of the small luzzu bobbing out at sea, they thought that it had come loose from its anchor. Yet, looking through his binoculars, Peppi informed them there were two people inside it. Before the barman knew it, everyone had rushed down to the port to help out in case the luzzu overturned.

"I told you we would make it," Grace triumphantly told Ricardo, as they made it to the breakwater of the small port. "Look at them. Look at those people. Everyone will be talking about you for a long time to come." Safely into the port, the Gozitan fishermen were furious with Ricardo.

"How dare you risk this lady's life?" one man asked as they helped the completely drenched Grace to safety.

"It was she who made me do it! I swear," Ricardo answered.

Seeing so many Gozitan men around her, like always, Grace the minx took advantage of the situation and she started to cry. "That's not true. When he heard the sailor telling me that the Royal Lady wasn't sailing, he approached me. He offered to bring me over for a substantial sum of money. I could see what the sea was like but he assured me that we would be just fine. I'm no fisherman. Stupid me, I believed him. I have never been so scared in my whole life. I even begged him to take me back but he refused. Look at me! I am wet and cold and still shaking. He could have killed me."

"No. No. That's not true at all. She is lying," Ricardo said in defence, "it was she who offered the money. When I wanted to turn back, she took out a knife and she threatened to kill me! Search her purse! You will find a knife. You have to believe me. Ask her to open up her purse."

"Here!" Grace said, opening her purse wide, "do you see a lot of money? Do you see a knife? Open his bag over there. You will find the money I paid him."

Poor Ricardo, for little did he know who he was dealing with. Grace had quickly placed some notes into Ricardo's bag while he was busy keeping the boat afloat. As for the knife, she had dropped this into the sea as soon as they had entered the port. Ricardo had quite literally been taken for a ride. He was angry but he stayed quiet, in fear of the fisherman and of what they might do to him.

"Lino, go for the police. I'm sure the lady wants to press charges," one said.

"No. I don't want any more trouble," Grace said, "what I need now more than anything is to get to my friend's house and to change from these wet clothes, before I get Pneumonia."

"Oh, you are a very lucky man indeed," one fisherman told Ricardo. "You give the lady back all her money, do you hear? Than you can shelter here until the currents calm down, and don't you dare

181

visit our shores ever again." Humble and frightened, Ricardo did not argue. After giving Grace the money, he took out his rosary beads and thanked the Holy Lady for sparing his life. Grace, noticing that a young muscular fisherman in the group kept staring at her, approached him.

"I really need to get to my friend's house as soon as possible. Could you please help me?"

"Where does your friend live?" Pinu the young fisherman asked.

"In Zebbug," Grace answered, as she pretended to sneeze to make him take pity on her.

"My uncle owns a car and he happens to be right over there. I'm sure that he would let me drive you," Pinu said.

"Oh. That would be perfect. Thank you."

It didn't take long. Uncle Manuel gave the keys to his nephew and they were on their way. Grace felt powerful and sure of herself. Not only had she made it to Gozo safely and at no cost, but she was in a car and in the company of a very handsome man. Yes, on any other day, she would have tried to seduce Pinu, but not anymore. Although married, George was still the only man she could ever want. At Zebbug, she made Pinu drop her off a fair way past the farmhouse. She did not want him to connect her with the death of George's wife in any way.

"I don't know how to thank you," Grace said to Pinu.

"I am happy that I could help. Can I collect you later?"

"No, I don't know how long I'll be here. You have a nice day and thanks. Thank your uncle too," Grace said, giving Pinu a large tip.

"Goodbye" Pinu said, waving out of the driver's window as he took another good look at her figure through the rear view mirror. Once the car was out of sight, Grace sneaked onto her father's farmhouse premises before anyone else could see her. As this was the first visit to the house since her birthday, all she could recall was the old place in ruins. Now she was standing in front of a completely different farmhouse. It was so lovely. The builders and George had done an excellent job and she loved it. "Amazing," she said to herself once inside. Everything was in place. The kitchen was compact. The dining room was very big and the living area had a big fireplace. There was still space for one bedroom on the ground floor and two bigger bedrooms upstairs. The views from all the sides of the house were out of this world. Then she stopped and the smile disappeared from her face; she remembered the real purpose of her visit. Opening a window slightly that looked out onto Maria and George's farmhouse, she looked through to see if she could catch sight of Maria, but she seemed to be nowhere around.

As the hours passed without any sighting of her, Grace got nervous. What if she had come all this way for nothing? Then, she heard some footsteps coming down the path. Taking a peek, she was stunned to see that it was George and he was alone. 'My God,' she thought to herself, 'he looks more handsome than ever.'

A heat raced through her whole body. She had repeatedly told herself that she could not let George see her anywhere near the farm. He would surely connect her with his wife's death. But, totally mesmerised, she ran down to meet him. Hearing the neighbour's front door opening, George looked in that direction. Seeing Grace at the front doorway, he walked over to greet her.

"Grace! It's you! What a wonderful surprise!" he said, as he walked over to her.

"Oh George, it is so nice to see you again. I've missed you so."

"It's good to see you too. Are your parents in the house?"

"No. I came alone. I'm all by myself. I just arrived a few hours ago."

"Oh! Why? I mean, how long will you be staying, if you don't mind me asking?"

"I don't know, a day, maybe two."

"So how was Italy? I hope that everything went well."

"It was fine. But George, first I want to thank you for the wonderful job you've done on the house. I love it. Why don't you come inside?" But George would not dare, especially knowing that she was on her own. He knew very well what she was capable of.

"Sorry, not today. I'll have to decline. I am sure your father has told you that I am now married. We are expecting our first child soon, isn't that wonderful?"

The last statement hit Grace like lightning. She thought she would choke and could not talk. Her body went cold. Instead of throwing things around and tearing her hair however, this time, she swung at George left and right, losing all control.

"How dare you! How dare you do this to me! I love you! You are mine! How dare you!" she kept repeating, while hitting George over and over again. George tried to stop her before she hurt him. He grabbed hold of her arms and pushed her away with all his force. Grace's foot stepped onto a rock but she then lost her balance, toppled backwards and fell, tearing George's shirt and some buttons off in the process. George expected her to stand up and come back at him, but she did not move.

"Grace!" George called, "Grace, please don't play any stupid games. Get up now, we have to talk." But Grace lay still. George got very worried and he gently knelt near her. He touched her but there was no response. Lifting her head off the ground, he felt blood on his hand. Her head had hit a rock. He tried to find a pulse but there was none; she was dead. George was horrified and cradling her to him, he started to sob. Seeing the rock on which she had landed, he got hold of it in his anger to throw it as far as he could, but using his left hand, it did not go a long way. What was he to do now? He wanted to go

184

for the police; it was an accident after all. But Grace was not just any ordinary woman. She was the only child of the very influential and powerful Shembries. They would prosecute him to his death. No, he could not take such a risk. He had a wife and the baby on the way to consider. He decided to tie Grace's body with a rope and then lower it into the well on the grounds, until he could work out a solution. After he did this, he covered the mouth of the well with a large piece of wood and returned to the house. Maria heard his steps and she called out to him. George ran to see what she needed, but on his way upstairs, he caught sight of his reflection in the hall mirror and instantly stopped. His shirt was covered with bloodstains. Quickly he ran out of the house and into his barn. Hiding the blood stained shirt, and changing into a fresh one, he rushed back to see Maria.

"George, I am so glad to see you," Maria said, "I've missed you so. My darling, the baby, he's been kicking all morning. Here, give me your hand," she said, placing it on her large belly. "There! You must have felt that one. Oh George, the baby is very strong. I'm sure it is a boy, a little Georgie. I just know it!" George started to cry. Maria thought that he was crying out of happiness and emotion but George was crying for very different reasons.

Meanwhile back at the Shembrie's Villa Ambrosia in Luqa, the Lord and his wife were becoming very concerned. Grace had not returned home. Worried, Lord Shembrie drove to the film agency that Grace was associated with to see how things were progressing. On learning that his daughter had not been anywhere near the agency that day, he wondered why she had lied. He had no clue where to look, so he returned home. By suppertime they were worried to distraction. Grace had never once missed her evening dinner, unless of course she had informed them beforehand. Hours passed and there was still no sign of her. Lord and Lady Shembrie could not take it any longer and called for the police.

Before they knew it, two policemen were at the house and they took down a full report. They could not list her as a missing person yet, not until twenty four hours had passed. Being from the same village, the two policemen were well aware of Grace's reputation. Once out of the villa, they even joked about it.

"Poor Shembries! When are they going to accept it? Their daughter has no morals. I bet you any money that she is having a great time in some man's bed as we speak."

"You've got that right! I'm sure we don't have to take this report seriously. She'll no doubt be back home by morning." Meanwhile the Shembries kept praying, hoping and waiting.

Back on Gozo, George tried to stay calm. That evening, he even managed to say the daily Rosary with Maria, as if nothing had happened. After the prayers, they wished each other a good night. But on this night, George was not planning to sleep; he had to stay awake to get Grace's body out of the well and to throw it down the edge of the cliffs behind her farmhouse. This would make it look as if Grace had accidentally fallen to her death. Maria was so used to his sleeping habits and him getting up to check on the animals, that on this night she was not disturbed. Sneaking back onto the next door property, George carried out his plan. Making sure that he had no bloodstains on him, he then returned to bed.

Meanwhile the Shembries could not sleep a wink. Grace had not shown up and at day break they called the police again. All the other police stations were notified and a search commenced. The police started visiting Grace's closest friends and acquaintances but no one seemed to have seen her. It was as if Grace had vanished into thin air. The Shembries usually kept a very low profile when it came to family affairs, but when they had received no feedback as to her whereabouts; they decided to involve the media.

"Read all about it, read all about it! Reward offered. Young socialite missing."

The first person to call the police was Joe the taxi driver, the man who had picked up Grace from Luqa that fateful morning. In the next few hours more witnesses came forward, including Ricardo and two Gozo fishermen, but the most important piece of information of all came from Pinu, who told the police the location where he had dropped Grace off in the village of Zebbug.

"Did you say Zebbug, Gozo? Well how about that?" Lord Shembrie said when the commissioner came to the villa. Looking at his wife, he went to check if the key to the farmhouse was hanging in its usual place. "Why didn't we think of it in the first place? The front door farmhouse key is missing. She must have taken it. Jane; get changed, we are going to Gozo. She has to be at the Zebbug farmhouse. That's where she is."

"But wouldn't she have told us?" Lady Jane answered.

"How could she, knowing how we would react?"

"Do you need any police assistance to take you there Sir? I could arrange a car," the commissioner enquired.

"No, thank you. We will take over from here. Before you go though, I really would appreciate it if you could gather a list of names and addresses of those who reported in. I want to thank them personally."

"Consider it done Sir."

During the long drive to Cirkewwa, Malta's port crossing to Gozo, Lord Shembrie and his wife had a lot of time to discuss in length the best way to approach the situation. They did not want to add to their daughter's depression. In the end, they agreed that if Grace did not even know about the involvement of the police and the media, then they would not even mention this. All they prayed and hoped was to find her safe and sound. Arriving at their farmhouse, they knocked on the front door. When no one answered, they tried the handle and found it was open. They went in and called out her name, but again, there was no answer. Everything was tidy and in order, including all the beds. In their rush, they did not even notice Grace's purse on a chair beside a wardrobe in the main bedroom. As the front door had been open, they knew that Grace could not be far away, so they went to search and call for her outside.

"Why don't I call next door? She might be there," Lord Shembrie suggested when again there was no answer.

"No, she wouldn't be at his house I'm sure. She hates his wife or have you forgotten? We know Grace isn't good at closing doors behind her; she must have forgotten to close it, that's all. It's obvious to see she didn't sleep here at all last night as none of the beds have been touched. She has to be at that hotel down on the main street in the city."

Together they drove down to Rabat. But to their disappointment, The Duke of Edinburgh Hotel had no one registered under a Miss Grace Shembrie. "Maybe she has registered under another name? She is young, brunette and was wearing a pink dress."

"Sorry, but at the moment we only have twenty guests and they are all men."

"Are there any other hotels on Gozo?"

"Only this one but of course there are some small guesthouses; one down in Xlendi Bay and another one in the village of Marsalforn."

"No, our daughter would only stay at a hotel. Jane, let's have a short rest, you must be exhausted after such a long trip." Holding her husband's arm, they walked into the hotel's back garden. Sitting on a cushioned bench, they shared a pot of tea.

"I'll drive back to the farmhouse. You stay here and rest for a while. Grace must have gone for a short walk. If I don't find her at the farmhouse then I will drop by to see George; he must have seen her at some point. Even if he hasn't, I'll keep asking around. Gozo is small and someone must have seen her somewhere. Before the day is over, we will find her."

"I will be here waiting. Please find her, find our daughter and bring her to me, I beg of you."

"I will my darling, I promise," he said, and then left the garden. On the way out he approached the hotel's receptionist and handed him some money.

"This is for you. Please take care of my wife. If she asks to rest for a while, put her up in the best room the hotel has to offer. I'll take care of it when I return."

"Thank you. I will take good care of her, Sir," James replied. Back at the farmhouse, Lord Shembrie called out for Grace many times but again there was no reply. George recognised the voice and went to meet Lord Shembrie before he could come knocking on his front door. Maria heard the calls too and she lifted her head to see out of her bedroom window. She caught sight of two men talking. One of them was her George, but she could not place the other one as she could not see his face. The shouting now stopped. The presence of her husband seemed to calm the other man.

"George! Thank God you are here. Grace has been missing for over two days. Please tell me that you've seen her! Please tell me that you know where she is!"

Full of guilt, George almost started to confess, but for the sake of his family honour he knew he had to carry out his plan.

"Sorry, I haven't seen her."

"George, according to several people, Grace crossed over to Gozo on Saturday. A man called Pinu drove her here. George, I'm sure she came to see you. My wife and I came earlier and she wasn't anywhere around so I came back to see if she'd returned. I've looked everywhere and I've called her name many times; if she was here she would have answered. George, please call her. If she's hiding she will come out; she'll do anything for you."

"Let's split up. You go that way and I'll search this way."

After a few minutes Lord Shembrie heard George calling.

"Lord Shembrie, Lord Shembrie, come over here! Hurry! I see something!"

Looking down the sheer cliff face, in the direction George was pointing at, Lord Shembrie could see a woman's body in a pink dress. She seemed to be motionless. "Oh my God, that dress, that's my daughter down there!" Frantically, Lord Shembrie started to scramble down to get to her side.

"Don't be crazy!" George said, holding him back. "Grace must have come too close to the edge where we are standing now. You'll surely suffer the same fate. Stay put, while I run for help."

"Oh my God, George hurry! Run, run!"

As soon as George informed the village policeman on duty at the village police station, the officer telephoned Head Office in Rabat. The two men ran to the scene of the accident.

"Here, tie this rope to that tree so I can lower myself down," Angelo, the policeman said, seeing a rope on the ground. But the rescue attempt was cut short. Angelo could see that the body was lifeless and he returned to the two men. "I'm so sorry, we cannot help her," the constable said.

"No, no, it can't be! How could this happen? Grace was so frightened of heights."

"A tragic accident indeed, I'm so sorry, I really am," George replied.

"Oh my God, my wife, my poor wife, she's at the Duke of Edinburgh Hotel as we speak. Oh my God, how am I going to tell her? God help me."

More police arrived and so did the ambulance. The body was brought up and the doctor pronounced Grace, dead at the scene. Her father wanted to hold her, to bring her back to life, but he was kept at a distance. "My daughter, my beautiful daughter, how could this have happened?" he repeated over and over. The doctor gave him something to calm him and then the police drove Lord Shembrie to his wife at the hotel, followed by the doctor and the ambulance. Beforehand, the doctor had told the ambulance driver to follow them. He was sure that Lady Jane would need medical assistance.

The police stayed behind until the car came to pick up Grace's body. Seeing that two policemen had stayed on the grounds and that they were checking around, George got worried. Everyone, including Lord Shembrie, seemed to have already accepted that Grace had died of an accidental death. What George did not know was that one of the officers was an experienced detective and an expert in such cases.

"What is going on out there George? Why were the ambulance and the police here?" Maria asked him as he went to her bedside.

"You'll find out sooner or later, so I'd better tell you. They have found a body next door. It's Grace, Lord Shembrie's daughter. She fell off the cliff."

"Oh my God, please don't tell me…."

"Yes she's dead. It's awful."

"That's so sad, her poor family. I could never go on living if something were to happen to our children. Let's pray for her soul and her family."

Down at the Duke of Edinburgh Hotel, the news was too hard to take and Lady Jane fainted. Grace's body was temporarily put into the Gozo morgue. The Maltese press did not take long to hear about the findings at the farm in Zebbug. Quickly they had their men travel over to Gozo to cover the story.

Meanwhile, back in Zebbug on Lord Shembrie's property, Detective John Mahon found some disturbing objects; two shirt buttons near a dried patch of blood and a blood stained rock, some distance away. Detective John Mahon had worked for Scotland Yard in England for many years before he retired and moved to live on Gozo. Trying to keep active on such a quiet island, he had voluntarily joined the Gozo police to help them whenever they needed his services. Putting the two findings into two separate plastic bags, he personally crossed over to Malta and to the laboratory for forensic tests. By now the news of Grace's death was already in all the local newspapers.

Those who knew Grace were devastated to say the least. A few political members and high society friends of Grace and the family even crossed over to Gozo to console her parents and to see how they could help them on such a tragic day.

The next morning Grace's body was transported to Malta. When the autopsy was completed, the results confirmed what Detective John Mahon had suspected; Grace had died from a fatal blow to the head. The bloodstains on the rock matched perfectly with Grace's blood type and the dried blood fingerprints on it belonged to a man with long and very rough fingers. Knowing that it was George the farmer, the next door neighbour, who had located the body, Detective John Mahon issued a warrant for George's arrest.

Crime on the small island of Gozo was so rare that it was almost unheard of. When the Gozo police got the call to pick up George Gawchi and to keep him in custody until two detectives arrived from Malta to interrogate him, they could not believe that they were talking about George the Maltese; a man who they had come to know and respect. Seeing Sergeant Leli Grima and three other policemen coming onto his land, George quickly came out of the house to meet them.

"George, you have to come with us to the police station."

"I can't. Maria is expecting and she is bedridden. I can't just leave her behind and on her own."

"Then I'll leave one of my officers here until one of her sisters arrives."

"That's fine, but I do need a few minutes with my wife in private. I have to tell her that I am leaving the farm."

"Fine, but I have to come with you," Sergeant Grima said.

"Why, don't you trust me? The bedroom is a private place. I said I want some time alone with my wife."

"Sorry George, but you don't have a choice. Either I come along or I'll have to take you down to the police station immediately."

"If that's how it is, then come, but you have to promise that I'll do the talking. I don't want you to upset her."

"Fine, but be quick," the sergeant said.

On seeing Sergeant Grima entering the room behind her husband and unannounced, Maria's instincts told her that something very bad must have taken place. "Oh God no!" she said, thinking that one of her siblings had had an accident or worse, died.

"Maria, don't get upset, nothing's happened," George said. "The sergeant came to ask me to go down to the police station, that's all. It seems that they need some information about Grace's accident. It's only a formality. I will be back in no time. The sergeant is leaving one of his men outside until one of the family get here."

"George, you don't look well. Your face looks pale. Are you ill?"

"No. I am fine, just fine. Now relax. I will be back soon. "

"George, please tell me once again that I have nothing to worry about."

"I promise."

"Please hurry back. I will be waiting for you."

"I will. I promise," George replied, kissing her.

George stayed calm and quiet all the way to the police station but when they told him that two detectives from Malta were coming to ask him questions, he became tense and started to breathe heavily.

"George, what's wrong?" a policeman asked.

"Nothing, I'm fine." Concerned, the same policeman asked George if he wanted a glass of water.

"No, I don't need any water. What I need is for you to take me back to my home. My wife is pregnant and she needs me. I don't want to stay here any longer!" George shouted out suddenly, standing up from the chair he was sitting on.

"George, please calm down," Sergeant Grima told him; "Maria's sister is already with her at the farmhouse."

"Sergeant, I didn't do anything wrong."

"Then you don't have to worry, do you?"

Some hours later, George was on the verge of a breakdown. He was about to complain again but just then, two men dressed in three piece suits and wearing hats, walked in. They were Inspector William Bonello and Detective John Borg. They introduced themselves, had a few words with the sergeant, and then two police officers escorted George into a room at the back. No matter what they asked George, he kept to his story. He said that he did not even know that Grace had been on Gozo and that he was very sad about her death.

"So George, you keep insisting that you didn't even know that Grace was on the island and that you had nothing to do with her death."

"That's right. How many times do I have to repeat myself?"

"I am going to show you something, something that might jog your memory," Detective Borg said, pulling out a paper bag and two clear plastic bags; one containing a blood stained shirt, the other a blood stained rock. George's eyes could not believe what he was seeing. He could not remember the blood stained stone but the shirt was exactly like the one he had been wearing when Grace died.

"We had a search warrant and we searched your farm. In the barn, we found this shirt."

George was exposed. Shaking, he covered his face in his hands. "George, this is your shirt, isn't it?" the inspector asked. "This is the shirt you were wearing when you hit Grace on her head with this rock, isn't it?"

"I didn't hit Grace with any rock, I swear I didn't," he said through his fingers, as his hands hid his face. "I didn't kill Grace, I swear. She fell onto a rock, yes, maybe that one, but it was an accident. I swear it was an accident. You have to believe me."

"George, you are under arrest for the murder of Miss Grace Shembrie," the inspector said. "You have the right to remain silent and you are entitled to a lawyer."

George was then fingerprinted, handcuffed and placed in a cell until he was transported to the prison on Malta. Sergeant Grima took it upon himself to go and face Maria with the sad news. In consideration of her condition, he called her family doctor to accompany him.

"So what happened at the police station?" Sister Maria Concetta asked the sergeant at the front door of the farmhouse. "And you, Doctor Pisani, why are you here and where is George?

"Could we please go inside?" Sergeant Grima asked.

"Yes please do, I'll put the kettle on."

"Sister Concetta, I have bad news. George has been taken to Malta. He has been arrested," the sergeant said.

"What for?"

"They think he had something to do with the young lady found dead on the cliffs."

"There has to be a mistake," she replied, making the sign of the cross. "George wouldn't harm an insect, let alone a person."

"Let's hope you're right but the truth remains that George is on his way to Malta's prison as we speak."

"My God, oh my dear God," she said as she sat down. "I don't believe it. My sister, how is she going to cope?"

"Maria is a strong woman. We have to pray to God that she can handle it, that's why I'm here," Doctor Pisani said.

"Maria doesn't have to know, not yet anyway. I have a better idea. I will tell her that George fell ill while he was at the police station. I will tell her that he was admitted into hospital. Tomorrow, I will tell her that he had to stay in the hospital for some tests. I am sure that George's name will be cleared by then. Why worry her for nothing? The news of George's arrest could make her lose the baby."

"That might just work," the sergeant said. "When I was upstairs with George a few hours ago, Maria did say that George didn't look too well. Coming from you, a nun, she will believe you."

"I wish I didn't have to do this but I am only doing it for my sister's own good; God, I beg you, please forgive me for what I am about to do," Sister Maria Concetta said, making the biggest sign of the cross that she had ever made. "You two stay here, and if you hear me scream, run upstairs as fast as you can. If you don't hear anything, then please see yourselves out."

Keeping as calm as she could, Sister Maria Concetta told Maria the bad news.

"I knew it. George didn't look well. What did they say he has?" Maria asked.

"They are doing tests. Sister Maria Angelica and Father Antonio are at the hospital. Unfortunately these things do happen. As for you, you need to stay put and rest." Maria took her rosary beads out of the drawer of the night table and they started to pray together.

When the inspector conveyed to the Shembries the news about George, they wanted revenge.

"My God, are you telling me that George killed our Grace? Louis, I want George dead," were Lady Jane's first words. Lord Shembrie could not agree more. He wanted George's blood more than anything in the world. Getting on the phone, he called his lawyer, Dr Luigi Bayada to come to the estate.

"My angel, my Grace, my only child; she was going to be twenty seven in nine days' time. Her mother and I had already planned big things for the day and now this man, this murderer has taken her away from us forever. I want you to hire the best prosecutor on the island. I want George Gawchi to hang. Only the rope will win Grace justice."

"I felt sick the moment I heard. I promise that I'll get you the best prosecutor and that George will hang for this," replied Dr Bayada.

"Just do it. Pay whoever and whatever he asks for. I'm ready to buy George's death at any price, even if I have to sell my soul to the devil."

From the villa, Dr Bayada went to see the most successful prosecutor on the island who was Dr Karlo Cardona, a lawyer who had never lost a court case. Many insinuated that Dr Cardona bought some   style, but nobody had ever proved it. To make   na took the case, Dr Bayada gave him Lord Shen   cheque.

                    about the death of Grace; horrible, just
hor   st have some hard evidence to arrest George.
I'll   Lord Shembrie that George is as good as dead
an   my condolences."

)r Bayada went to a few village squares to
s   e told everyone that the murderer had raped the

197

poor woman before he had thrown her off the cliff edge. This false rumour spread like wildfire. Now everyone wanted George's head.

Meanwhile, locked in a cell under heavy security, George was permitted to choose his defence lawyer but none came to mind. George had never needed a lawyer before in his life. Yet only an hour later, a policeman escorted a lawyer to George's cell; his good friend, now Dr David Pach. Having read the newspapers, Dr David Pach had not been able to believe what he was reading and so came to see for himself.

"David, I'm so glad to see you!" George said, startled at seeing him and also unaware that his friend was now a registered lawyer.

"George, what's going on?"

"David, I didn't kill her. I swear to God, I didn't kill Grace. It was an accident," said George.

"George, take a couple of deep breaths." George did.

"George, I have graduated and I'm a registered lawyer now. I came to see if I could help."

"You're a registered lawyer?" George said, still shaking.

"I am. George, have you appointed your defence lawyer?"

"Not yet. But now I do know who I want to defend me. Please David, say that you will."

"George, before you jump to any decisions, please hear me out. I've only just graduated. If the information I've heard is correct, the Shembrie family has already appointed a certain Dr Karlo Cardona, the best prosecutor money can buy and the best in the business. He has never lost a case. George, during the last few years, I've come to know a few excellent lawyers, so let me check and see what I can do. You'll need a very experienced lawyer even to have the smallest of chances."

"But I want you," George replied.

"George, Dr Cardona will be asking for your head. Do you understand that?"

"A minute ago you said that this Dr Karlo Cardona, this prosecutor, has never lost a court case yet, am I right?"

"Yes."

"So this means that whoever I get to defend me in my case only has as much chance as you! David, I need someone who I can totally trust, and you are that person. Oh God. Why did this have to happen when my poor wife is in the last stages of her pregnancy?"

"Your wife is expecting?"

"Yes she is."

"George, you must realise that if I take your case and lose, I will regret it for the rest of my life. It's a big responsibility."

"Yes, but if you don't and I hang, wouldn't you feel the same way, knowing that the other lawyers might have had me in the bag from the start? David you are my only hope. Please, I beg of you, please help me."

"I do see your point and I can see where you're coming from. Before I commit myself though, I need you to tell me everything that took place on that day. I mean everything." George started recalling the events but he had hardly finished three sentences when a policeman escorted a priest into his cell.

"George, how are they treating you?" It was George's brother in law, Father Antonio.

"How's Maria? How is she?" George stood up and asked, all concerned. The presence of another person in the cell made Father Antonio hesitate. "Father Antonio, this is my good friend Dr David Pach," George said, introducing them. "He is a lawyer. I trust him completely. How is Maria? How did she take the news?"

"Maria doesn't know the true facts just yet. We've told her that you felt unwell while you were at the police station and that you've been admitted into hospital."

"And she believed you?"

"Coming from Sister Maria Concetta, yes, she did. This evening she'll tell her that you have to stay at the hospital overnight to have some more tests done. By tomorrow afternoon this ridiculous accusation of you killing a woman should be all cleared up. We'll have you back home before she even suspects anything took place, isn't that right Dr Pach?"

"I don't know. George was just telling me about it all as you came in. George, do you want to tell us what happened?"

"I'll start from the moment I saw Grace. She came out of her house and she called out to me. I have to admit, I was very happy to see her again after so many months. I was excited to hear all about her overseas trip. We talked for a few minutes and everything was fine, until I told her that my new wife and I were expecting a child. All of a sudden, she lunged at me like a wild animal, hitting me hard all over. I pushed her off me. I had to. She lost her balance and fell backwards onto the ground. I called out her name but she didn't move. Shaking all over, I knelt down beside her. I said her name again but she just remained there, motionless. When I lifted her head off the ground I felt blood running down my fingers. Then, I saw the rock her head had landed on. She was dead. I wanted to run for help but I got scared. I was scared that no one would believe it was an accident. I couldn't think straight. I panicked and decided to hide her body inside the well until I could work out what to do."

"Oh my Dear Lord," Father Antonio exclaimed.

"George, you shouldn't have touched the body," David said, "this is bad. Dr Cardona already has the upper hand. You played an alibi. George, I do honestly think that you need the second best lawyer on the islands to have any chance at this."

"No David, I want you to represent me. I'm one hundred percent sure of this; I beg you."

"All right then. All I can promise is that I will do my very best."

"Thank you, that's all I ask of you. Thank you David," George said, feeling a lot better.

"George, as of this moment, you mustn't speak to anyone about the case except me. Sorry Father. Now let me go and get the paperwork done. I'll be back soon."

When Dr Pach retuned, George signed the papers, officially appointing him as his defence lawyer. Saying their goodbyes to Father Antonio, the two policemen escorted Dr Pach and George into a room so that the two could talk in private. Dr Pach listened carefully to every single word George had to say, as if his own life depended on it. When George finished he could clearly understand what had taken place and why. If he had the power to decide the verdict, he would certainly let George go free under the act of self-defence. But George's life didn't depend on him. This was to be judged by ten independent jurors in court. The biggest disadvantage was the fact that George had tampered with the evidence in order to deceive the law.

Dr Pach now asked to have the bail hearing set for the next day, in order to get George out on bail and back to his wife. This was granted and arranged for the afternoon. By early morning, small groups of people took to the main street of Valletta, holding all kinds of signs condemning George to death. Stopping periodically in front of the court building, they shouted and demanded justice. They wanted George to be hanged.

For security reasons, the police van transporting George to court had been instructed to drive through the back streets. At exactly three o'clock the hearing began. After some harsh and strong statements incriminating George, Dr Cardona returned to his seat.

George had stayed strong through it all, pleading not guilty to all the accusations brought against him. Taking the floor, Dr Pach asked the Honourable Judge to release George on bail so that George could return to his pregnant wife and to attend to the farm. But these pleas fell on deaf ears. Not only were all pleas rejected, but the Honourable Judge set the trial to be heard in just two weeks' time. Dr Pach strongly objected, saying that he needed more time to prepare his case thoroughly. Again his plea was rejected. Little did Dr Pach know that the prosecutor had met earlier with the judge to agree on the trial date and had asked to have the case heard as soon as possible, knowing that the percentage of the Maltese public were behind him.

George was then taken out through the back doors and driven back to prison before the crowd, who were still protesting on the main street, even noticed. The front pages of the local newspapers were all about the murder. 'The Case of the Century,' one newspaper called it. The editors also printed the dates of the hearing and when Grace's funeral was to take place that Saturday. By eleven thirty on Saturday morning, Luqa's village square was packed with people. The Kappilan kept the church doors closed in order to control the crowd. Inside his church, he had reserved the front rows for the family, the elite and for the high personnel. When the hearse arrived, the crowd went silent. By the time the coffin was placed in front of the altar steps, hundreds of people had filled the church, packing the doorways and spilling outside. Lady Jane, Grace's mother, was too frail to attend. She had been given sedatives to make her rest.

During the moving service, Lord Shembrie sobbed out his pain from behind dark sunglasses. Having his closest friends around him, he held on. When the funeral service was over, the huge crowd moved outside and waited. Then a woman in the crowd approached Dr Cardona, the prosecutor.

"How much are you ready to pay me for some solid information in the case against George?" she asked, keeping her identity well hidden under a black scarf.

"Who are you?" Dr Cardona asked her.

"How much do I get?" she asked again.

"I have to hear what you have to say. Then we'll talk money."

"We can't talk here. I'll meet you down the road. At the corner of St. Anthony's Street, do you know the spot?"

"Yes. I'll be there soon."

The lady hidden behind the scarf was none other than Guzeppa. She was one of the people who had seen George push Grace to the floor in front of his Qormi house on the day she had suffered the stroke, a few years earlier. She had come in order to cash in. When the two met again, Dr Cardona liked what he heard. This case was one of the most important cases of his whole career and the information was as good as gold. However, he wasn't ready to pay Guzeppa yet, not even a penny. "Come down to my office to sign a statement."

"I want my money!" Guzeppa said crossly.

"Woman, I can take you right now down to the police station and have you charged for withholding evidence. On the other hand, if you co-operate, I promise that when I win the case, I will reward you generously."

Guzeppa got scared and went along with Dr Cardona's demand. When she left his office, he went to the police to get the list of names and addresses of the last people who had spoken to Grace. During the next eight days, he visited and saw them all, both on Malta and on Gozo, except for Ricardo the fisherman who was out at sea. Everybody agreed that George should get the rope for such a crime. He felt satisfied; he seemed to have everyone behind him and in his investigation he did not intend to leave any stone unturned.

When he returned from his visit to Gozo, he stopped at Ricardo's home again. This time he was in luck and Ricardo was there. "As soon as I stepped ashore, I heard about the events of her death. I don't want to talk about that woman," Ricardo said at the doorway; "her name alone gives me the creeps. I am sorry that she has died but…"

"Murdered. She was murdered," Dr Cardona jumped in to reply.

"Murdered? Whatever, that is sad. But I tell you, that woman was no angel. Do you know that she tried to kill me that day I took her over? No, of course you didn't."

"Are you sure we're talking about the same Miss Grace Shembrie?" Dr Cardona asked.

"I am. That woman promised to pay me a good sum of money just to try to take her across to Gozo but the second I turned the boat around due to the rough seas, she took out a knife and threatened to kill me. Her eyes were as cold as ice. I still get chills thinking about it. I tell you, that lady was possessed by the devil she was. I've never felt so scared in my whole life."

Dr Cardona didn't like what he was hearing. He had to find a way to silence Ricardo.

"Have you mentioned this incident to anyone?"

"Yes. I told those Gozo fishermen when we arrived safely into port but they didn't believe me. I can see that you don't believe me either. Please go away and let me be."

"But Ricardo, I do believe you."

"You do?" Ricardo answered, arching his eyebrows, showing his big brown eyes.

"You see, Grace loved Gozo," continued Dr Cardona, "and she'd been planning to spend that weekend on Gozo for weeks. She was desperate to get away. Now there's no sin in that, is there? God bless her soul, she didn't even tell her parents. She wanted to be alone. Then, this George, this murderer appears at her doorstep and he takes her life. Ricardo, tell me, do you have any children?"

"I have six and I love them all."

"Then you must understand what Grace's family are going through, having their only daughter murdered. If this George Gawchi, her murderer, walks on our streets again, all of our daughters including yours are in danger of being killed. He has to die."

"I never thought of it that way. You're right. This man has to die."

"Now, going back to the day, do you remember the amount Miss Grace offered you?"

"She showed me some notes, but to tell you the truth, I never got to count them."

"Would you say it was around this amount?" he asked, taking out a bundle of notes.

"I'm not sure," the fisherman replied.

"I'm ready to give you them all if you promise to forgive her."

"I will, I promise," Ricardo answered, seeing that he had a better deal. "This evening, I'll be offering some prayers for her soul, I promise."

"Before I hand these over, I ask you for two more things. First, to encourage all your friends and relatives to join the protest march in Valletta tomorrow, and secondly, that you don't tell anyone about our little meeting. If you do, you will definitely regret it."

"My mouth is sealed. I have never seen you. Good day Sir."

"Goodbye Ricardo."

Once the prosecutor had driven away, Ricardo, relieved that he had finally gone, quickly closed himself into his garage and counted the notes, which were a good sum of money indeed. Taking out some nails which he kept in a rusty tin, he exchanged them with his small treasure.

Maria's siblings had kept their bedridden sister believing that George was still recovering from a small operation. In the meantime, the farm chores had been given to Jamri, their cousin. With each passing day, Maria became more anxious. What if her George, her loving husband had died and they were all hiding it from her until after the baby was born? Just the thought alone scared her to death. After yet another sleepless night, she was ready to face the truth. Confronting her sister, Sister Maria Concetta, she demanded to know the complete truth. Sister Maria Concetta could not lie anymore and with a lot of difficulty and shame for all the deceit, finally told Maria the truth.

"How could you, how could you all lie to me, my own family?" Maria shouted. "I know what that Grace Shembrie woman was capable of! George told me many a story about her. My husband is in prison and here I am, lying in this bed as if nothing has taken place. George needs me more than you know, and I'm going to him, with or without your help."

"But Maria, the doctor said you should stay in bed!"

"I know what the doctor said. Now, are you going to help me pack or should I do it myself? I'm going to see George and then I'm moving into my Qormi house until George is released."

Sending Jamri to fetch the other two siblings, Sister Maria Concetta started to pack. As much as they tried to change Maria's mind, Maria stuck to her decision and in a few hours they were on their way to Malta. At the prison, Maria sat in the waiting room behind a big glass partition and George was sent for. When George heard about her visit, he did not know what to do. He had been worried sick about his wife and her health. He had longed to see her and now that she was only steps away, he wondered if his presence was good for her. Calming down, he dried his tears and followed the officer to the waiting room.

"Maria. I am so sorry, I am so sorry," he said, as he broke down sobbing at the sight of her.

"My darling George, I didn't know, they never told me! But I'm here now. Together we will fight it and win it. I know that you didn't kill that woman. I believe you."

"Maria. I love you so much."

"I love you too George."

They talked and prayed until Maria could not keep her eyes open any longer. Before they parted, Maria promised George that she would visit every day. In Qormi, Martin and Karmena welcomed the four of them into the kitchen and served them some hot food while her daughters went next door to prepare the beds. As soon as Maria had finished her soup, she asked to be excused. She was totally exhausted.

Chapter 16

The Trial

On Saturday the twenty-third, the trial day, the man who earned a living renting out jackets and ties off his cart, situated by the fountain across from the court building, had predicted a huge profit for himself. Knowing that many of the poorest of folk were hoping to be present for what the newspapers were calling 'the trial of the century,' he had loaded onto his cart everything he had in stock. He was right, for in only a short time, he had rented out every single item of clothing. When courtroom number four opened its door to the public waiting in the hallways, the immense crowd rushed in to get a seat. They pushed and shoved each other like a herd of wild cattle. The police tried to regain control but they were outnumbered. Courtroom number four was packed in no time, leaving many in the corridors. They were not going to give up however, and tried to squeeze inside before the doors were closed shut. The police asked the crowd many times to stop the pushing and to move away from the doors so that they could be closed, but to no avail; they just would not listen. Concerned for their safety, an officer went to the chamber to tell the Honourable Judge about the situation. To make it easier for all, the judge gave permission for this one time only, for the hearing to go ahead with the doors open. For this verdict the court had appointed ten jurors, all men. If all ten were to find George guilty, then George would hang. However, if one voted against the rest, then George could only be given a jail sentence. When George entered the courtroom, the crowd jeered him. Keeping his head down, George walked up the wooden steps and onto the stand. Standing at the right of the Honourable Judge, George looked tired and resigned, but once he lifted his head and caught sight of his wife sitting behind Dr Pach, he regained some courage. When the Honourable Judge, Michael Formosa, entered the courtroom, all went silent. The trial of the century was about to begin.

After George had been sworn in, Dr Pach, his defence lawyer, took to the floor. Approaching George in the stand, he bluntly asked him:

"George Gawchi, did you, or did you not, kill Miss Grace Shembrie?"

"No, I didn't," George replied, looking straight at his wife who was holding her rosary beads tight in prayer. Many in the crowd shouted "Liar! Liar!"

Using his wooden mallet, the Honourable Judge quickly restrained order.

"George, you said in your statement that the deceased, Miss Grace Shembrie, came at you with her fists, right at the point when you told her that your wife was pregnant, am I right?"

"Yes. She started hitting me left and right. She went crazy."

"Objection!" Dr Cardona interrupted, "he cannot talk about the deceased in such a way."

"Objection granted. Erase the last three words off the record," the judge stated.

"George, did you know the deceased Miss Grace Shembrie, before that fatal Saturday?" Dr Pach asked.

"Yes."

"How long, would you say you had known Miss Grace Shembrie?"

"For over two years," George answered.

"So I ask; why would the late Miss Grace Shembrie attack you? One would think, that having known each other for that long, she would have been more than happy to learn that you were becoming a father."

"Maybe she was jealous," George replied.

"Jealous of what; were you two lovers?"

"No, never, we were just good friends. But she did say that she loved me on more than one occasion. She must have been a bit jealous of my wife Maria."

"And what was your reply to her whenever she told you she loved you?" Dr Pach asked.

"I never encouraged her."

"George, after your arrest you told the police that the deceased, Miss Grace Shembrie, fell backwards, hit her head on a rock and that's when she died. Am I right?"

"Yes. That's exactly what happened," George answered.

"Could you please tell us what happened next?"

"When I realised that she was dead, I got really scared."

"Scared of what?" Dr Pach asked.

"Scared, that if I went for the police, the police would not believe it was an accident. I have a wife and a baby on the way. I panicked."

"You panicked?"

"Yes. I didn't know what to do next. I had to do find a way to protect my family name."

"Thank you. No more questions your honour."

Dr Cardona took the floor. "George, you say the deceased, Miss Grace Shembrie, attacked you. That she did this after you told her that your wife Maria was carrying your child and that she did it out of jealousy. You tell the court that you had to search for a cover up in order to protect your family name. You used the word 'panicked;' a strong word. Yet, you calmly told Lord Shembrie, the victim's father, that you didn't even know his daughter, the victim Miss Grace Shembrie, was on Gozo. You lied, and then, you pretended you'd located her lifeless body, when you knew exactly where you'd thrown it. To top it all, you even helped out. You rushed to the village police station; very clever indeed! You had them all fooled, didn't you George? Now, let me ask you a simple question; how would you describe your personality? Would you say that you are vicious, bad tempered or calm person?"

"I don't understand the question," George said, looking directly at his defence lawyer.

"Objection your honour;" Dr Pach said, standing. "I cannot see where Dr Cardona is going with this question."

"Objection overruled. George, answer the question," the Honourable Judge Formosa asked.

"I'm a calm person," George replied.

"George, have you ever hit anyone?"

"No."

"Could you repeat that please?"

"I said no. I have never hit or raised my hand to anyone."

"Would the court please address Miss Guzeppa Zammit to the witness stand," Dr Cardona asked.

This unexpected announcement caught everyone in the courtroom by surprise. Who was this witness? Sworn in, Dr Cardona started with his questioning. "Miss Guzeppa Zammit, could you please tell the court your full name and where you live?"

"My name is Guzeppa Zammit, nicknamed Tal- Fekrun. I live in Qormi."

"Could you please tell the court whether you have ever met or seen George Gawchi, the accused here today?" Dr Cardona asked, pointing his index finger at George.

"Yes I have. I live just around the corner from his house. He used to work next door in his workshop."

"When you say his workshop, do you mean the garage he owns that's attached to his house on St. Sebastian Street?"

"Yes, of course I do."

"Please answer the questions with a yes or no."

211

"Yes."

"Can you tell the court what you saw on January the tenth, 1937, over two years ago, in front of the aforementioned garage?"

"I saw this man, George Gawchi, pushing a woman to the ground with all his force."

"Keeping in mind that you are under oath, I ask you, do you, Miss Guzeppa Zammit, remember the woman who the accused, George Gawchi, pushed to the ground? Answer me only if you are sure of her name please."

The courtroom went totally silent. One would think that everyone in there had instantly disappeared into thin air. Miss Guzeppa Zammit was sure that her answer was going to condemn George Gawchi to the grave. She had never thought it through. But here she was today, in court, and under oath, and she had to tell the truth. The only two people in that whole courtroom who knew about the episode were George and Dr Pach. Miss Guzeppa Zammit felt so guilty that she could not bring herself to say it aloud. Dr Cardona became impatient. "Miss Guzepppa Zammit," he said, calling out her name in a loud voice and startling her; "I shall repeat the question. Could you please give us the name of the woman George Gawchi pushed to the floor that day?"

"It was.... It was...... it was Miss Grace Shembrie, the deceased," she mumbled under her breath, as she lowered her head in the process.

"I didn't quite hear you, could you please repeat it and louder?" Dr Cardona asked, to make sure that everyone in the courtroom heard her.

"It was Miss Grace Shembrie, the deceased!" she repeated.

There were no doubts now. The crowd went wild. Men from all corners of the room were seen putting their fists up in the air. Some individuals standing in the back rows started pushing to get at

George. The scene was too much for Maria and she fainted. Her family called and shouted for help. Seeing his wife in distress, George jumped out of the witness stand to get to her side. Noticing George coming his way, Lord Shembrie got out of his seat to confront him. Only the quick interference of the police stopped a possible riot.

"Leave me alone! Leave me alone!" George shouted. Two policemen handcuffed him and dragged him away into a back room to safety as Maria was quickly escorted onto the terrace for fresh air.

"We have him," Dr Cardona told Lord Shembrie. "The people are all behind us. George will surely hang."

"Order in court, order in court!" The Honourable Judge repeatedly shouted, fiercely using his hammer to get the crowd's attention. But the crowd kept screaming for George's blood. When eventually the crowd did calm down, the Honourable Judge announced that the trial was adjourned, to be continued in a week and this time behind closed doors. By the time this was announced, George was already on his way back to his prison cell.

When Maria had recovered, she asked to be taken back to the courtroom, only to be told that the trial had been adjourned. "Is that good?" she asked Dr Pach.

"It gives me more time to do some research. Yes, it is good."

"So where's George now?" she asked.

"He was taken back to prison where he is safe."

"I want to see him," she insisted.

"Not today. Today you need to rest." Transport was arranged and Maria, together with her siblings were taken to Qormi, while Dr Pach headed straight to see George. As always, George's first thoughts were of his wife. "How is Maria? Please don't tell me that she's lost the baby?"

"No George, she's fine. She's at the Qormi house. Her family are there with her."

213

"Thank God for that. I was sure she had lost the baby," George said.

"She could do, if she has any more stress."

"I agree."

"Going back to Guzeppa, I remember you telling me about the incident back then, but never in a million years would I have thought that one day it would come back to haunt us. Thank God the crowd went wild when they did. I didn't have anything to counter Guzeppa's statement with. You were a condemned man but for some unknown reason, God has given us another chance and we have a week. I have to use it wisely; I have to come up with something."

"Maybe you should tell the jurors that the very next day after the incident Grace's father came over to my place and hit me with his cane."

"George, the trial is about Grace's death. It has nothing to do with Lord Shembrie. Guzeppa's statement has us with our backs to the wall. George, you need to pray like you've never prayed before. We have to find something, anything to counter Guzeppa's statement."

That afternoon Dr Pach dropped by to visit a few lawyers' offices to ask for advice, but none seemed interested. They were all afraid of Dr Cardona and his influence. That evening Dr Pach went through everything he had gathered on the case, including the reports of the doctors and the forensic experts, yet, he could not put a finger on anything that might help. Overtired, he tried to sleep but it was impossible. Then something came to mind. He remembered his visit to the bar in Luqa's square. George had asked him to find out why Lord Shembrie had gone to Qormi and hit him, accusing him of causing Grace's illness. A man there had mentioned a certain maid by the name of Lina, an employee of the Shembries who had been unjustly fired. He realised that he had to find this Lina and speak with her. Later that day he went to Mario's bar. The barman recognised him. "Nice to see you again sir, I remember you," Mario said, greeting Dr Pach.

"You have an excellent memory."

"I never forget a face," Mario replied proudly, with a smile from ear to ear.

Over a couple of beers, Dr Pach found that the lady he was seeking lived just around the corner, in house Number Fifteen. He left the bar to find her.

"How can I help you?" Eva, Lina's mother, asked the young, good looking and elegantly dressed man at her front door.

"My name is Dr David Pach and I'm a lawyer. I was told that a Miss Lina Micallef lives here. Is she in by any chance?"

"That's my daughter. She's not in trouble is she?" the worried mother asked.

"No, not at all"

"Please, do come in," Eva asked.

"Thank you."

"Sorry about the mess, we are in the middle of cleaning," Eva said, as they walked into the sitting room.

"If you're busy I could come back later."

"No, please take a seat. Lina is in the back room washing some clothes. I'll go and get her." Eva was a widow and Lina was her only daughter. "Lina, stop what you're doing, we have a visitor, a lawyer. He is asking for you. Have you any idea what he wants?"

"No mother."

"Go and change into another dress and comb your hair."

"Lina will be along soon," Eva told Dr Pach, once she had returned to the sitting room.

"Would you like some coffee?" she offered.

"You're very kind but no thanks. I'll only be a few minutes."

The moment Lina entered the sitting room with her warm smile and long ebony hair, Dr Pach was quite taken aback at her beauty.

"Lina, this is Dr David Pach."

"Good morning Miss Micallef; it's a pleasure to meet you. I mean, nice to meet you. I mean ......good morning."

"You're sure you don't want some coffee?" Eva asked again, "we were just about to have some."

"Then I will, yes thank you," he said, changing his mind.

"Miss Micallef, you used to work for Lord and Lady Shembrie at Villa Ambrosia. Am I right?" Dr Pach asked, as soon as her mother had left the room.

"Yes, but please, don't call me Miss Micallef. I'd feel more comfortable if you called me Lina."

"Lina. Going back to what I came for. I heard that you were unjustly fired from your job on the Shembrie's estate, is that right?"

"Who told you?"

"It doesn't matter, it's not important. I came to talk to you about George Gawchi, the carpenter from Qormi who used to work there. I'm sure you know who I mean. You and the late Miss Grace Shembrie used to visit his workplace in Qormi together, am I right?

"Miss Grace Shembrie is dead. Please let her rest in peace."

"I didn't mean to disrespect the late Miss Grace Shembrie, bless her soul, in any way. I am George Gawchi's defence lawyer; we go back to our childhood days. He didn't kill Miss Grace Shembrie, it was an accident. He told me how it happened and I believe him. George could never be a murderer."

"Everyone else seems to think he is. Anyway, whatever happened between the two of them, no one deserves to die."

"I couldn't have said it better myself. No one deserves to die. But if the jury finds George Gawchi guilty and he gets the rope, then that would result in two dead people, due to what I strongly believe was simply an act of self-defence."

Just then, Eva came into the room carrying a tray with coffees and biscuits. "Do you take sugar, Dr Pach?"

"Thank you, but I am leaving. Lina, I've changed my mind," he replied, standing up from the chair; "thank you for your hospitality. I should have known better than to involve you."

"Involve her in what, may I ask?" Eva responded.

"Mrs Micallef, as I told you, I am a lawyer. I'm the defence lawyer of George Gawchi, the man accused of killing the late Miss Grace Shembrie."

"Good heavens!" Eva said, spilling some coffee.

"I came to see if your daughter could help me out in the case but now I realise that I've made a mistake."

"Wait," Lina said. "I do believe George is innocent, I really do. How can I help?"

"Lina, are you out of your mind?" her mother shouted.

"Mother, I met George many times. He is a very honest man. Grace used to drive him crazy; I know that more than anyone. If George says that he is innocent, then he is. I have to help him."

"If you get involved in this murder case, the whole village will turn against us! Heaven knows what will happen to us. We could be forced out of house and the village. Stay out of it I tell you."

"Your mother is right," Dr Pach said.

"For a minute there, I thought you were different from the rest but now I can see that you are also scared of Lord Shembrie. On the day I got fired, I kept silent, but when I got over it I swore that I would never give in to injustice again. Please sit, have a coffee and tell me how I can help. I want to listen at least."

An exchange of questions, answers and warm smiles followed between the two while Eva listened. In the end, Lina agreed to testify. Not only did Dr Pach have something to use to keep the trial going, but he was going to see this beautiful woman sitting in front of him again, a woman who had very quickly stolen his heart.

"I'll send a car to pick you up; Saturday at eight sharp. Please don't get cold feet, don't change your mind as your statement means everything to me at this point. If you don't show up, George will definitely hang."

That Saturday, a large crowd gathered in front of the court building, shouting and condemning George to his death yet again. At exactly nine o'clock, George was sworn in. The second part of the trial was about to begin. The last statements on record were read and Miss Guzeppa Zammit was sworn in, but the two lawyers did not have any questions to ask her and she was told to step down. George was then sworn in again. "George, do you recall the incident?" Dr Pach asked, approaching George.

"Yes. I do."

"Could you please explain what took place that day?"

"While working at the villa owned by the parents of the late Miss Grace Shembrie, the deceased, she started to befriend me, sometimes stopping me from my work just to be at my side. Before things could get complicated, I decided to stop working at the villa. Unexpectedly, she started dropping by at my shop, asking me to return to her family's villa. I told her nicely that I had other contracts to finish but this didn't stop them visiting me."

"Excuse me for interrupting," Dr Pach cut in. "George, when you say 'them', who are you referring to?"

"Miss Grace Shembrie always came in the presence of one of her maids, a certain Miss Lina Micallef."

"Objection Your Honour; who and where is this Miss Lina Micallef?" Dr Cardona asked.

"Your Honour," Dr Pach proceeded, "could the court please call Miss Lina Micallef to the stand? She is just outside the door, waiting in the hallway."

Lord and Lady Shembrie were surprised to see Lina, the ever shy and quite lady they had once employed, as she walked past them with her head held high to stand in the witness box. Dr Cardona was dumbfounded. He had no idea what Miss Lina Micallef had up her sleeve. Sworn in however, the questioning started.

"Miss Lina Micallef, did you work as a maid for the Shembrie family at Villa Ambrosia during the time when Mr George Gawchi, the accused, worked there?"

"Yes, I did."

"Under oath I ask you now; how would you describe the accused, George Gawchi?"

"He is a kind, honest and nice man. I'd say he's a real gentleman."

"Could you please tell us why you and the late Miss Grace Shembrie paid visits to his workplace in the village of Qormi?"

"The late Miss Grace Shembrie, God bless her soul, wanted him back at the villa."

"Did George Gawchi try to stop these visits?"

"Yes, every time."

"So why didn't the late Miss Grace Shembrie stop?"

"The late Miss Grace Shembrie liked George Gawchi, a lot. I can honestly say that she loved him."

"A certain Miss Guzeppa Zammit, here in this court room, sitting right there in the second row, has claimed that on January the tenth, 1937, over two years ago, on one of the late Miss Shembrie's visits, she saw George Gawchi, the accused, push the late Miss Shembrie to the ground. Were you present with her on that day?"

"No, I wasn't."

"Why not?"

"I had already been unjustly fired by Lady Jane Shembrie, the mother of the deceased, here present today in the court room; my ex-employer."

"Thank you. No more questions Your Honour."

"Your Honour, members of the jury; I don't understand the point of this witness. Her statement has nothing to do with the case. Miss Lina Micallef is purely seeking revenge. Her statements have to be erased off the records," responded Dr Cardona.

"Dr Pach," the Honourable Judge said to the defending lawyer, "I will have Miss Lina Micallef's statements removed, unless of course, you can give me reason not to do so."

"Your Honour, the reason for her presence and questioning are to prove to all present here today, that the late Miss Grace Shembrie was most probably in love with the accused. That's why she attacked my client George Gawchi when he told her about the expected birth of his child" explained Dr Pach.

"I see. Dr Cardona, do you want to cross examine the witness, Miss Lina Micallef?"

"No, your Honour."

"Miss Lina Micallaf, you may step down," the judge told Lina.

Lina's unexpected appearance in court and her statements had thrown Dr Cardona. There were no more witnesses left and the time had come for one of the two lawyers to convince the ten jurors in their favour.

Taking the floor, Dr Cardona began; "Everyone can see that George Gawchi, the accused on the stand, is a very strong man. Look at him! I'm sure he could fight a bull to the ground. A man with his physique doesn't have to use much force to get a woman off him, but he did, on two occasions with the late Miss Grace Shembrie. However, I don't want to go further with this issue, so let's move on. I ask the court to please exhibit the items related to the case." A policeman uncovered three items on a table, standing close to the seated jurors. Each item was enclosed and numbered in a separate clear plastic bag.

"In bag marked 'Number One'," Dr Cardona continued, "we have two shirt buttons, found on the ground where the victim died. In plastic bag marked 'Number Two', we can see a blood stained rock, again found in the same area. The blood group is a perfect match to that of the late Miss Grace Shembrie. Also, the fingerprint experts found that the fingerprints on the rock are identical to the left hand fingerprints of the accused, George Gawchi. In bag marked 'Number Three', we see a blood stained shirt, which was found hidden in one of the barns which George Gawchi owns, right next door to the Shembrie's property in Zebbug. Please keep in mind that the two buttons came off the shirt in bag Number Three. Please also note that the blood stains on this same shirt match perfectly to that of the victim, the late Miss Grace Shembrie. Gentlemen of the jury, let me tell you what took place that day, the day Miss Grace Shembrie was taken away from this earth and from her loved ones. George Gawchi might not have loved the late Miss Grace Shembrie the way she loved him, but he liked her, he liked her a lot and who wouldn't? The late Miss Grace Shembrie was one of the prettiest ladies on the Maltese Islands. She had showered him with attention and presents as recently as this past December. On learning that she was alone at the farmhouse, far away from her parents who were in Malta, he took the opportunity to try and lure Miss Grace Shembrie into her house in order to force himself on her….."

"That's a lie! That's a big lie!" George yelled from the stand.

"Order in court!" The Honourable Judge shouted out. "Dr Cardona has the floor. Dr Cardona, you may carry on."

"Thank you Your Honour. Knowing that George Gawchi was now a married man, the late Miss Grace Shembrie obviously rejected him but George wasn't going to give up. Grabbing her by the arm, he pulled her towards the house. Miss Grace Shembrie fought to get away from him. She tried to stay on her feet by holding onto his shirt, but he was too strong. He unbalanced her and she fell to the ground, pulling off the two buttons in the process. On the ground and under his weight, she started to scream. George Gawchi had to stop her before his wife could hear. Seeing a rock nearby, the one we have here on the table in front of us, he picked it up and struck Miss Grace Shembrie on the head, killing her instantly."

Here, Dr Cardona picked up plastic bag Number Two and with the rock held in his hand, showed the jurors how the fatal hit had been delivered. "Hiding the body inside the well," he continued, "George Gawchi then went into one of his barns to hide the blood stained shirt he was wearing, the same shirt we have here inside bag Number Three. Later that night, George returned to the well, took the body out and threw it off the cliff edge nearby. He wanted everyone to believe that the late Miss Grace Shembrie had accidentally fallen off the cliff to her death. His alibi almost worked and today, here he is, begging for mercy. Members of the jury, before you decide your verdict, think hard and think clearly. Think of the late Miss Grace Shembrie, a talented and beautiful young lady; the apple of her parents' eye and a young woman who had everything to live for, only for this man to steal it all away. George Gawchi killed Miss Grace Shembrie for his sexual lust. Her parents and all the people of Malta want justice; they want you to send Mr George Gawchi to hang. They want him dead and away from their children. Only the rope can justify his horrible actions. Thank you."

Dr Cardona's words were to the point. His interpretations of what had taken place were very clear and believable. Walking back to his chair he looked at Lord Shembrie for approval and the Lord nodded his head, seemingly satisfied. It was now Dr Pach's turn to take the floor.

"The way Dr Cardona has explained the events of the day make us believe that he was there, watching it all from a tree! He is very clever and well known for his dramatic final speeches. I have to say, that for a while there, he almost had me believing that it did happen that way! But then, ladies and gentlemen of the jury, Dr Cardona did something which blew his made-up theory out of the window." Then, turning towards the Honourable Judge, Dr Pach asked permission to ask George Gawchi another question.

"Mr George Gawchi, I am going to ask you a very simple question. Are you a left or a right handed person?"

"I am right handed," George replied.

"Thank you." Dr Pach now walked over to the table where Dr Cardona had placed the bag containing the rock. Holding the rock in his right hand, just like Dr Cardona had done before him, he continued. "You see, the late Miss Grace Shembrie died from a crack found on the left rear side of the skull. The records show clearly that the fingerprints on the rock were that of George Gawchi's left hand. If George Gawchi had wanted to kill her, of course he would have naturally picked up the rock with his right hand to strike her, but this wasn't the case. The records show that in his statement given to the police, we understand that George Gawchi's right hand was holding and cradling Miss Grace Shembrie's head off the ground, and that when he saw the fatal rock and became upset, he threw it with his left hand as far away as he could. Being naturally right handed and throwing it with his left hand, it didn't travel far; that's why it was found only three meters away from the patch of blood on the ground. Also, a rock held in the left hand could never hit the skull on the left rear side, as in this case; it would be impossible. Go ahead and try it! So, I can't but thank the prosecutor Dr Cardona for highlighting the true facts based on the evidence he gave. Gentlemen of the jury, before you decide on your verdict, think of what I have just explained to you. The late Miss Grace Shembrie did sadly fall and take a fatal blow to the back of the head, just as George Gawchi claims. But, ladies and gentlemen, it was an accident. George Gawchi is innocent. Thank you."

However, Dr Cardona's reputation of being the best in the trade was to shine through again. By the time Dr Pach had finished, Dr Cardona had already thought of a way to turn Dr Pach's impressive speech back in his favour.

"Honourable Judge, could I take the floor again?"

This trial was getting exciting and the Honourable Judge allowed him to go ahead. "Please," the judge said.

"Dear jurors, do not let Dr Pach throw sand into your eyes! What if the late Miss Grace Shembrie had got away from the accused, George Gawchi, for even a few seconds? What if the accused George Gawchi had hit her while she was crawling away from him on her hands and knees after having simply fallen? In this situation, anyone holding a stone in his left hand could easily hit the fatal spot, couldn't he? Of course he could. Don't let Dr Pach trick you. George Gawchi did indeed kill Miss Shembrie." Dr Cardona seemed to have saved himself the embarrassment of losing a court case and to an unknown lawyer, but Dr Pach still had something left to say.

"Your Honour, can I have the floor again please?"

"Yes," the judge granted.

"Thank you." Dr Pach now walked over to the juror's bench and this time stood as near as he could. "I'm sure that you, just like me, have clearly heard the prosecutor Dr Cardona say the word 'if' and twice. 'What if' she had got free from the accused for a few seconds, 'what if' he had hit her while she was crawling away; he said one right after the other! Gentlemen of the jury, court cases are not judged on 'ifs;' court cases are judged on facts and real events. One cannot convict, or worse, one cannot hang a person unless one is absolutely a hundred percent sure of the true facts. Thank you."

This time Dr Cardona had nothing with which to counter Dr Pach's last statement. He felt choked and the questioning ended. The Honourable Judge and the jurors left the courtroom to decide on the verdict. When inside the voting room, the judge, fearing for their safety, told them that for this trial only, the individual votes would be anonymous. When all the votes were in and counted for, they returned to their respective seats.

As the Honourable Judge stood up to announce the verdict, George stood with his eyes tightly closed, praying and hoping that God would set him free.

"Mr George Gawchi," the Honourable Judge said, "you have been found guilty of second degree murder in the death of Miss Grace Shembrie by seven counts to three. You will not hang, but you will spend the rest of your life in jail, behind bars and without parole."

Exhausted and very emotional, George slumped to his seat. His life was spared but he had no idea what life imprisonment would mean. Lord Shembrie stormed out of the court room. The photographers in the hallway outside waited in anticipation to photograph Dr Pach. He had instantly become a name. Congratulations and interviews were in order.

Dr Cardona felt angry and disappointed. He had lost one of the most important cases he had ever taken on. He had failed and so hid from the media. When Maria heard the result of the verdict, she praised the Lord for sparing her George from death.

Chapter 17

The Aftermath

After things had calmed down, Dr Pach went to see Mrs Eva Micallef to ask her if he could court her daughter Lina. Eva could not have been happier; her daughter had found an honest and wonderful man and she blessed the union. At the Shembrie's mansion, Lady Jane could not cope with the outcome of the verdict. The news left her devastated and she had to be placed on medication.

With each passing day, Lord Shembrie grew to hate the world and everything in it, most of all George Gawchi and Dr Pach. Revenge was imminent. Finding out that Dr Pach was courting Lina, he paid two men to torch Lina's house down during the night. The men threw burning glass bottles of kerosene at the upstairs windows. Lina and her mother were terrified but managed to escape unharmed. For their safety, Dr Pach moved them into one of his family's properties.

Through the love and care of Martin's family, Maria found the support she needed to cope with all she was going through. In August, she gave birth to a healthy baby boy. Holding the little new born gave her so much pleasure and hope. When George was told that he had become a father, he thanked God with tears running down his cheeks.

Dr Pach asked permission to allow George to see his wife and baby in private and it was granted. The reunion was very special and emotional as Maria and George hugged, cried and held each other. The baby made them forget all the sadness they were facing. Maria asked George to name the little one but George gave her the choice. She told him that she wanted to name him Georgie, little

George, after him. George could not have loved her more. The baby was baptized on that same day.

Having so much time alone in his prison cell, George had a lot of time to think. The one thing that haunted him most was the fact that the day would come when other children would ask Georgie about his father's whereabouts. How would they react towards him when they found out that his father was in prison? He needed to talk about it with Maria.

"When he comes of age, I will find a way and I'll explain that you were unjustly imprisoned. I will tell him the truth. He will be fine," she said.

"Maria, family scandals never die on Malta. These are passed on from one generation to the next, as you know. Georgie and the next generation have to be spared."

"George, you are scaring me. What are you saying? " Maria asked.

"I want you and Georgie to get away from Malta. I want you to have a fresh start away from all of this. I think that the two of you should go and live with my sister in America. She will love you both and she will take care of you, I know she will. Take Georgie to America and start a new life."

"George, I will never leave you. How could you even think of such a thing?"

"Maria, this is a very hard decision, please don't make it any harder. I'm in prison for life. What kind of a husband and father can I be in here?" he said sobbing, with tears running down his cheeks.

"You are a wonderful loving man, George. We are a family. Now stop all this nonsense and let's pray. God will guide us through."

As they were praying, little did they know that Mariella, George's sister, was already half way on a journey; her destination

Malta. This was to be a surprise visit, to see the family and the island that she had missed so much.

Meanwhile, Lord Shembrie had pieced together a terrible revenge plan on George's family; an eye for an eye. Through a third party, a man was offered an enormous sum of money to carry it out. The hired assassin had been following Maria's movements for some time now, and saw that she always used the same narrow lane in between some fields whenever she made her prison visits. It made it the perfect place to carry out his evil plan.

When the day arrived, the assassin on his horse waited until Maria, holding the baby in her arms, was half way down the lane, and then trotted slowly in her direction. Maria loved horses and she could not wait to see it more closely, but to her shock and disbelief, once the horse got nearer, it charged right at her. Holding her baby tightly to her, she turned around and ran as fast as she could in the opposite direction, but the horse was a lot faster and it hit Maria hard in the back, throwing her to the ground and trampling over her. The assassin was sure he had killed Maria, and even as he kept galloping away from sight, he was already savouring his huge reward for a job well done. It was an amount that would see him rich for life.

Twenty minutes later, a farmer noticed Maria on the floor. Going closer to check on her, he could hear a baby crying. Jumping off his cart, he knelt down and carefully turned the woman onto her side to get to the baby. Picking the little one up, he could see no cuts; the blood stains seemed to belong only to the woman. Checking the woman's pulse, he felt faint heartbeats. She was barely alive. Quickly, he placed the little baby into an empty box that he had on his cart and then carefully lifted the unconscious woman onto it too. Joseph knew this area for he had fields here and he headed straight to Mr and Mrs Ellul's villa, the nearest residence.

"Don't move her," Mr Ellul said as he looked at the woman, "she's in bad shape. Monica! Monica!" he called out to his wife.

"Get some blankets, quickly! You," he pointed to the farmer, "you stay with them while I call the hospital."

In a very short time Maria and her baby were rushed by ambulance to the hospital. A doctor checked over the child. Little Georgie was a very lucky baby and his mother had protected him well. He had not sustained any serious injuries, only shock and bruises. On the other hand, Maria had suffered multiple injuries to the head, ribs and back. She also had internal bleeding, which put her life in grave danger.

An inspector, five policemen and Joseph the farmer were now at the scene of the incident. They could see that one of the woman's shoes was at least two meters away from where Joseph had found her. They even noticed the fresh footprints in the soft mud, indicating that she had tried to run away from her attacker. An investigation was opened.

Maria had always informed Karmena beforehand of her prison visits just in case someone came asking for her. Maria would then be sure to return home by five o 'clock, but on this afternoon it was almost six o' clock and she had not yet returned. Worried, she told her husband and together they went to inform the village police station. The policeman on duty called St. Luke's Hospital, only to learn that a woman and a baby boy had been admitted to the emergency ward that afternoon. The person on the other end also informed him that the mother was in a coma and that no one knew who she was.

When told, Martin asked if the person on the line could describe what clothes the mother had been wearing. The answer confirmed that it was Maria. Her clothes matched the description.

"Oh my God it's Maria! What about the baby?" Martin asked.

"I'll ask....... the baby is fine," the officer said, before hanging up.

Being from the same village, the constable knew that Maria was George's husband, who was in jail and that Maria's next of kin lived on Gozo. "Her sisters, the nuns, both live in the convent in Rabat if I remember rightly. I will telephone the police there, to inform them of the incident. Poor Maria, as if she didn't have enough things on her plate; I sure hope she makes it. It will be a while before her family can be at her side."

"You're right. I think that we should let Dr Pach know. Someone has to go to Maria and he is George's best friend. I am sure he would want to know."

"Yes, I think that's a very good idea. I'll come with you," the policeman said. Seeing the police as well as Martin and Karmena at his front door, Dr Pach knew it had to be bad news.

"What's happened?" he immediately asked.

"Maria and the baby; they've had an accident. They are in Saint Luke's Hospital," Martin said.

"Do you know what happened?"

"All we know is that Maria is in a coma, but the baby seems to be fine."

"My God, did you inform her family?"

"The police on Gozo have been informed," the policeman said.

"I have to go to them. Martin, Karmena, I can drop you home on the way," Dr Pach suggested, putting on his jacket.

"Could we come with you?" Martin asked.

"That would be better."

At the hospital, they were told that someone had attacked Maria and that she was fighting for her life. Dr Pach asked if he could see her. Looking at her swollen, bruised face, he felt so angry. Who could have done this?

Meanwhile, Karmena had gone to check on little Georgie. There he was, safe and sound, sleeping in the arms of a nurse. By the time Maria's three siblings arrived, Maria's situation had worsened. They prayed and prayed for her recovery but Maria slipped away. None of them had ever predicted anything like this. God had spared little Georgie's life but had taken Maria's instead.

Leaving the two nuns, Dr Pach drove first to Martin and Karmena's home and then with Father Antonio in the car, he drove to the prison. 'How was George going to take this loss after all he had already been through?' Dr Pach and Father Anthony wondered. When they met George face to face, the heart breaking news was devastating.

"No! No! This can't be!" George cried out, hitting the wall with his fist.

On this day even Father Antonio could not find any words to comfort his brother-in-law. The news of Maria's death spread quickly through the islands. In just a few weeks Malta had experienced two terrible fatalities, both connected to one man; George Gawchi. Could it be that there was a link between the two? everyone was now asking. The police asked the public to come forward if they had any information which could help them in the case, but this time no one did so.

Two days later, Maria's coffin was placed onto a small boat and taken over to Gozo. At the port of Mgarr, the coffin was met by a large number of Gozitans and clergy, as well as her immediate family members. They solemnly followed the cortege to her home village of Zebbug, where a Mass Service was led by her own brother. Maria was then buried in the village cemetery right behind the church. Baby Georgie was for the moment under the care of Maria's siblings, the nuns at the convent, in Rabat, Gozo.

Back in prison George tried to focus on the future of his now orphaned child. The best solution he could think of was to ask Martin and Karmena to foster him into their family. They were the only people he felt he could trust to take care of his precious boy, and after all, they did have five grown up daughters still at home to help.

Chapter 18

Mariella's Visit to Malta

During her long trip, all Mariella thought about was her family. The brother she had missed, meeting her new sister-in-law Maria, and holding the baby. As she believed her brother was living on the farm on Gozo, Mariella planned to spend her first night at the house in Qormi. As the large ship entered Valletta's Grand Harbour, her body was covered with goose bumps. She could hear the Maltese language being spoken all around her as she walked off the ship, and it was music to her ears. She felt so good to be home again. Once she had passed through customs, she called a taxi to collect her large trunk, a trunk full of lovely presents for family and old friends. On the journey to Qormi, she kept looking at the wooden balconies and at the familiar views, bringing back so many wonderful warm memories. Malta and America had been good to her, yet these were two different worlds. Savouring it all, it was not long before she arrived at her old home.

After unloading the trunk at her front door, the driver wished her well and drove away. The front door and those of the neighbours' still had the same dark green paint she always remembered. Taking a deep breath, she knocked on Martin's door to surprise them, as well as to ask for her house key. Seeing Mariella at the door, face to face, Karmena went numb. Never in a million years did she expect to see Mariella like this, so unexpectedly.

"It's me, Mariella!" Mariella said, stretching out her arms for a welcome hug which never came.

"Is something wrong?" Mariella asked, still waiting to be embraced.

"What a lovely surprise. I can't believe you're here! Is your husband with you?" Karmena asked.

"No he isn't. He stayed back home to take care of business."

"Welcome home my dear, welcome," Karmena said, "please come in. I'll call someone to help you with the trunk. It's so nice to see you back."

"Martin, it's Mariella, she's back from America!" Karmena shouted to announce their visitor.

"Who?" Martin answered from the kitchen.

"Mariella! Angela's daughter! Come! We need your help." Martin and all his children now came rushing into the front room to hug and to welcome Mariella back.

"I haven't heard from George for a while," Mariella said, as soon as she stepped inside.

"Did Maria have the baby? Is it a boy or a girl?" she wanted to know happily.

"Oh, they have a lovely boy. They named him Georgie," Karmena answered.

"Oh, I can't wait to hold him in my arms."

"Mariella look at you, you look so much like your mother, God bless her soul. You must be hungry after such a long journey. Let me make you some coffee and sandwiches while Sonia and Bernadette go to prepare your house," Karmena said, dreading the thought of being the one to have to tell her the bad news.

"How can I refuse your home brewed coffee? I could smell the aroma of the beans the moment you opened the door! Maybe I should take you back with me to America. They would love your coffee. You would become rich in a very short time and I'm not joking!"

Over a bite to eat, Mariella could not stop talking about her life in America. Everything seemed so different and new to Martin's family. They were mesmerised. It was as if Mariella had landed from

234

another planet. Karmena invited Mariella to join them for dinner later in the evening but Mariella was feeling tired and she politely refused, intending to return and talk more the next morning. This worked out for the better. As much as Karmena had meant the invitation, she had also hoped that Mariella would decline the offer as she needed time to prepare herself for the questions regarding George. When Mariella left and was settled in her home, Martin walked up to Dr Pach's house.

"Mariella, George's sister is back from America, she's here at the house! She's come back to visit the family."

"Good heavens!" replied Dr Pach. "Does she know about George and Maria?"

"I don't think so. She's as happy as can be. When she asked about the baby, Karmena told her that Maria had a baby boy, and then we changed the subject. We only spoke about her life in America."

"You did well."

"Martin, tomorrow I'll come to your place, at eight. We'll then go together to see her; if someone has to tell her about it all, it had better be me."

"Yes, it would be a lot easier for us if you could do it. Dr Pach, thank you, and see you tomorrow. Good night."

In the morning Dr Pach kept his word and at eight o' clock knocked on Martin's door. Then they went to see Mariella who was happy, though a bit surprised to see them both standing there on her doorstep so early. "Good morning Mariella and welcome back. I heard of your return from Martin when I called to visit. It's so nice to see you again," Dr Pach said.

"David! It's so nice to see you. You look well. Good morning Martin. Please, do come in."

"David is a lawyer now. Everyone knows him as Dr Pach," Martin told her, as they sat at the kitchen table while Mariella put the kettle on.

"A lawyer, oh, very impressive for a young man who I only remember as a bird watcher!" she said, with a twinkle in her eye. "Congratulations are in order David, or should I say Dr Pach?"

"Please call me David. I always felt like family to you and your brother. Your mother, God bless her soul, loved me as if I were one of her own."

"She did, yes, she really loved you."

"Mariella, it's not easy to tell you what I'm about to say," he began, when she had served them the coffee, "but it is better you hear it from me."

"What is it? Please don't tell me that something bad has happened?"

"It's about George's wife, Maria. She died."

"Oh my God," Mariella said, putting her hands over her mouth in disbelief. "My poor sister-in-law; I didn't even get to meet her. Did she die giving birth?"

"No, nothing to do with the baby's birth, it's more complicated than that. It's a long story."

"When did it happen?" Mariella asked.

"Recently; only last week."

"Oh my God, I have to go to my brother right away. The poor man, he must be devastated. He needs my support. I am ready to pay anyone who could take me to Gozo and to his farm. I do not want to waste any more time."

"Mariella, your brother is not on Gozo; he is not at the farm."

"Then, where is he?"

"Brace yourself. Your brother is in Cordine, in the prison. Mariella, I am very sorry."

"Are you telling me that my brother killed his wife?"

"No, nothing like that."

"Then why is he in prison?"

"He is charged with the murder of another woman, an acquaintance."

"That's impossible. My brother could never hurt a fly. I want to see him!" she demanded.

"Mariella," Martin said, as he put his hand around her shoulders to console her, "please let Dr Pach finish. What he has to say will hurt, but you have to hear him out." During the whole story, Mariella couldn't stop crying. It was as if someone was stabbing her in the heart, one hit right after another.

"How could this be?" she asked, lost for reason. "I feel as though I've lost ten years of my life just hearing about it. David, you have to find a way to free my brother, I beg of you."

"Like I told you, the lady was a Lord's daughter, one of the most powerful and influential men on the island. If it wasn't God's will, your brother would have hung."

"But you said that my brother is innocent; I just don't understand."

"He is. All those who know George believe that, but he was judged and given a sentence. There was nothing more I could do. In time, I promise that I'll do all I can to find a way to reopen the case."

"Please, can someone take me to my brother? I want to see him."

"I knew you would say that. I can take you there now. We can leave whenever you're ready, but I have to prepare you. I don't know how he will react to your unexpected visit, so please, if you don't mind, let me talk to him first," Dr Pach explained.

"I'll be ready in two minutes," replied Mariella.

At the prison, George was told of his visitor. "Please bring him in."

"Today Dr Pach has asked to see you at the window." George followed the officer.

"George, how are you?" Dr Pach asked.

"I'm depressed. At night I can't sleep a wink anymore. The thoughts of Maria's death and the uncertainty of my baby's future are slowly killing me."

"George, there is someone here to see you, someone you know very well."

"I'm not in the mood to talk to anyone, except you of course."

"George, this woman has come a very long way. I think you should see her."

"Come a long way? Who is she?"

"It's your sister, Mariella. She is waiting to see you as we speak."

"That's impossible! It can't be."

"She arrived yesterday, unexpectedly. This morning I spoke with her and told her everything. I had to. Then she asked to see you."

"I can't, I'm too ashamed. I can't. Tell her that I'm not ready to see her yet," George said, standing up quickly to return to his cell.

"George! George, please don't turn your back on me!" Mariella shouted out, running into the visitor's room. George had longed so much to hear her voice that he could not just walk away. "George, I'm here for you. Please talk to me." When George turned around, Mariella looked exactly as he had always remembered her; young and beautiful. Looking at George's sad face, a face that she now hardly recognised, Mariella wanted to cry. Dr Pach left the room to give them some space. "George, I'm so sorry. I should have never left you behind. I'm so sorry. George, I promise that I'll do all I can to get you out of here."

"Mariella, I am innocent."

"I know. David, or should I say Dr Pach, and Martin told me so and I believe them and you."

"Mariella. My wife, my poor Maria was killed. We were so happy. We were so looking forward to starting our family. Everything was perfect."

"George, now you stay strong, do you hear? I will get you out of here, I promise."

"Mariella, please don't get involved. I am sure that my wife's murder had something to do with Grace's death. I'm sure that Lord Shembrie wanted his revenge and got it. I already carry Maria's death on my shoulders. If something were to happen to you too, I don't know what I would do. A few weeks ago, I told my beloved Maria, God bless her soul, to take the baby and to go to America and live with you. I wanted her and our son to start a new life, far away and safe from Lord Shembrie and his power, but she didn't listen because she loved me, and now she's dead. You are my son's only hope. Mariella, God has answered my prayers. That's why you are here. Please tell me that you will take my son back with you to America."

"But Georgie is your son and you are his father. Let me call Dr Pach over. Let's see how we can get you free first."

"Mariella, Dr Pach has been my saviour. I owe him my life. If it wasn't for him I would be dead. Let him guide us. Yes, do call him in; the three of us have to talk."

Dr Pach asked for them to be given a room so that they could talk in private and this was granted. Together they discussed what needed to take place. Throughout it all, Dr Pach promised George that he would do all he could to help them both. They agreed that the next step was to take Mariella over to Gozo, so that she could meet

Maria's family and see the baby. At the convent, Maria's sisters; Sister Maria Angelika and Sister Maria Concetta, were very surprised to see the visitors but they welcomed Mariella with open arms. Mariella told them how sad she felt that she had never got the chance to meet Maria. They talked for a short time and then they took her to see baby Georgie. There he was, sound asleep in his crib. One look at him and Mariella's heart weakened. He was adorable.

"Pick him up, please go ahead," Sister Maria Concetta told Mariella in a low voice.

"But I might wake him."

"You've come a long way not to cuddle your own nephew."

Mariella had for many years longed to hold a baby and today she had the chance to do so and one of her own flesh and blood too. Very gently, she lifted baby Georgie out of the crib. To her surprise, the baby did not wake up. Sister Maria Concetta fetched a comfortable chair so that she could sit. Gazing at her small nephew sleeping on her lap gave her an incredible feeling of joy. Very gently she touched his face. Oh, his skin was so soft and he smelled so lovely that she just had to lift him to her face and kiss him. After a while Mariella slowly put the little one back into the crib and then Maria's sisters invited her and Dr Pach to stay for lunch. Even with all they had gone through over these last few months, Maria's sisters had a lot of respect for George. They told Mariella that they had never blamed George for anything that had taken place and that they truly believed he was innocent. Through their Catholic teaching and meditations, they believed that what humans cannot understand in this world, God will explain in the afterlife in His heaven.

After a few hours, Dr Pach told Mariella that they had to start heading back to Malta. The sisters felt sorry to see them leave. They liked Mariella's company so much and they asked if she would like to stay the night. The convent had many bedrooms unoccupied and Mariella gracefully accepted. Now she could not wait to hold baby Georgie again.

"Mariella, I will see you on Tuesday at your house at around nine o' clock," Dr Pach said before he left the convent.

"Yes, and David, I want you to know how much I appreciate all you've done for George and I. Thank you, really." Dr Pach was more than pleased with the way things had worked out and he left the convent feeling satisfied. When little Georgie woke up, Sister Maria Concetta showed Mariella how to prepare a baby's bottle and then gave her the baby to nurse.

"Go ahead and feed him."

"Are you sure?" she said, "I've never fed a baby before."

"We saw you with the baby earlier and you hold the baby's head well," Sister Maria Angelica said, smiling. Mariella was enjoying it all and she even successfully got him to burp. "Did you hear that?" she asked excitedly.

Putting little Georgie back into his bed, they sang him some lullabies until he eventually fell asleep.

On Tuesday, Mariella felt sad to leave her nephew's side to cross over to Malta but in the days that followed, she visited Gozo and the convent regularly. With each visit, they got to know each other well and became close, like a real family. Mariella became totally bonded with her nephew and she just could not have enough of him. She even found the courage to tell Maria's sisters of her brother's wish for her to take the baby to America.

"Our sister, God bless her soul, never kept any secrets from us. We know that your brother had asked her to go and live in America with you, only for her to refuse because she loved him so much. But now that she's gone and we've got to know you, we too have come to believe that it is the best thing for the child. If it is still your brother's wish and you want to adopt baby Georgie, then you have our blessings."

"I feel like crying," said Mariella, "for you are offering me the world."

"We're sure that our dear departed Maria would have wanted it this way."

"But what about your brother, Father Antonio; what does he think?"

"We have all discussed Georgie's future many times since your arrival on Malta, and he too wants only the best for the baby. You have his blessing also."

"Thank you. I will talk to my brother again about the subject. If he is sure of this then yes, I will take Georgie and I promise that I'll raise him in the Catholic faith. I am sure that David, or I should say Dr Pach, will help me with the adoption papers. We will be meeting again shortly, I'm sure. Thank you, thank you," Mariella said, feeling so moved. Before she left, she kissed and cuddled the baby over and over again.

"See you soon Mariella," the sisters said as they took the baby from her arms. She already felt sad to leave him behind.

Every time baby Georgie's name was mentioned, George could clearly see how Mariella's face lit up with excitement. "You can't wait until you hold Georgie again, can you?"

"George, your baby is so adorable. He looks like an angel."

"Mariella, I'm sure that you will be a great mother, and I know that you would be the best person to raise him."

"George, I do want to and I know that I'll be a very good mother, but I want you to make sure that you are totally certain about all this. It would be very hard on all of us, if you changed your mind later on in life."

"I'm sure that my heart will break in two when you both leave Malta, I have to admit that, and I will hurt for the rest of my life; but yes, I do want you to have my child. After all, he is your very own flesh and blood. God must love you and Austin very much."

"We will love him with all our hearts," Mariella answered, trying hard not to cry.

The next day Dr Pach and Mariella went to see George together. George stood by what he had said, and so Dr Pach started filling out the legal adoption papers. During the next few weeks, Mariella continued crossing over to Gozo to be with her nephew, sometimes staying over for a few nights in a row. When the adoption papers were all in order and signed, Mariella finally became baby Georgie's legal mother. On the day Mariella took the baby out of the convent, all the sisters and Father Antonio were present to hug and say their last goodbyes to her and to the baby they had come to feel so close to. During the drive back to Malta, Mariella could not stop thinking that through her mother's love in heaven an incredible miracle had taken place. Mariella felt so fulfilled. Back in Qormi, Karmena was ready to teach Mariella everything a mother needed to know about caring for and raising a child. After all, she had raised six of her own. George did not want to make it any harder than it already was, so he asked Mariella not to bring the baby along with her when she came to visit. On their last meeting, George and Mariella cried and cried. It was going to be the last time they would ever see or meet each other. Before she left, George had two more things to tell his dear sister.

"The gold cross that our dear mother gave me, it is still in the same box, in the same place where father always kept it. Take it and pass it on to Georgie. I will never be able to cherish it, but at least he will, and Mariella, please don't forget our promise. Never tell Georgie of his real parentage. From this day on, you are his mother and Austin is his father. Now, please go before my heart breaks in two and may God bless you all."

In just a few short months George had lost everything but he accepted his destiny. At least his son had a future to look forward too. Dr Pach, Maria's siblings and Martin's family were all present when Mariella and the baby boarded the ship. On this day, they stayed on the dockside waving until the ship was out of sight. Mariella had already sent a telegram to let her husband know that she was on her way back, but she did not mention the baby. She wanted to surprise him. Arriving in America and looking at the statue of Liberty, standing for justice for all, Mariella could only thank God for the best gift He could have ever given her.

For the past few hours Austin had been waiting near his car in anticipation of catching sight of his lovely wife. When he saw her on the prow of the ship, he ran to the jetty to greet her with a bouquet of red roses. When Mariella appeared at the exit door, he noticed that his wife was holding something in her arms.

"Look! Look what God gave us!" she cried out, with a happy shining face as she walked off the gangway.

"Is that a baby?" Austin said, with wide open eyes.

"Yes! Yes! And he's ours! Look at him. Isn't he perfect? Isn't he the prettiest baby boy you've ever seen?"

"Where did you get him?" Austin asked.

"This is my brother's baby, George's baby, now ours."

"I don't understand. Don't they like children?"

"It's a very long story. I will explain it all later. Oh my darling, I can't believe it! We have a child! Here, hold him," Mariella said, as she very carefully handed him the precious bundle. "Oh Austin, I'm so happy, I could cry." Austin kept looking at the baby in his arms and then he kissed the little one on the forehead. "What's his name?"

"He was baptized George but on the way here, I was thinking of changing it to Giorgino. You always said that if we'd had a boy, you would have called him Giorgino, and here he is; our Giorgino."

"Mariella I love you so much. We three are going to have such great times together. We have so much to look forward to."

The household help welcomed Mariella and the new addition, presented as Giorgino. Seeing them so happy and cheerful brought her tears of joy and baby talk was heard all over the house. Taking the baby with them, Austin and Mariella drove to buy the crib that Mariella had stopped by so many times to look at in the past. Back at home, after the baby fell asleep, Mariella started to tell her husband about all the things that had happened and everything she had gone through during her stay on Malta. Austin could not believe that one man could pass through so much and still manage to stay sane. Putting his arms around his wonderful wife, they prayed together. They did not get much sleep that night as they both kept waking up to look at the baby. Their lives had literally changed overnight.

Chapter 19

George and World War 2

Back on Malta, George felt his misfortune with every day that passed. Only the frequent visits from his brother-in-law Father Antonio, his friend Dr Pach and prayers stopped him from taking his own life.

Lady Jane, the late Grace Shembrie's mother, never recovered from her daughter's loss and she gradually became very ill. She passed away peacefully in her bed. Lord Shembrie may have thought that having Maria killed would have helped him to feel better, but it only added to his guilt. After Maria's death, he became too scared to leave his estate grounds. In time he became a lonely and depressed man.

In 1938, Dr Pach married Miss Lina Micallef.

In the New Year of 1939, the German dictator, Adolph Hitler was fast becoming a power house. As he moved to take over France, Europe seemed doomed for war.

When IL Duce, Mussolini, the Italian dictator, became Hitler's allied partner, he turned his eyes to Malta's strategic position, right in the middle of the Mediterranean Sea, between Sicily and Africa, and he prepared to take over the small islands. However, being under British rule and British intelligence, the people of Malta were aware of this, and as a result had started reopening the old shelters and finding caves suitable for the locals to run into and shelter once the air raids began. They had even placed some anti-aircraft artillery posts around the sea fronts as defences. Needing all the help that they could muster, they took all the prisoners out of the cells, including George.

On June the eleventh, 1940, Il Duce sent his first aircrafts over to induce the first air raid on the Maltese Islands. This was the beginning of what was to become the most bombed area for its size during the whole of the Second World War. On that very hot summer day, the Islanders saw nine Italian Macci fighters followed by a few bombers approaching at an altitude of about twenty thousand feet. The Air Force quickly sent out their three Sea-Gladiator biplane fighters, known as Faith, Hope, and Charity to defend the island's air space. Finding air resistance and losing some planes and lives, the Italians returned seven more times and carried out air raids on Marsa's dockyards. On this day alone, Malta lost civilian lives, with others wounded. George wanted to do his part and in time was stationed to help at Fort St. Angelo. With many losses, he was promoted to a gunner, dropping planes day in and day out. There he stood, proud to be Maltese, ready to face all the flying German Stuka 87 and all that the Junkers 88 threw at him. No matter how many blistering bullets showered his post, killing the others around him, George was never hit. His officers nicknamed him 'George the untouchable'. In that year, 1940, Malta encountered over two hundred air raids. During the months of January, February and March of 1941, the Maltese pilots and gunners hardly slept at all. Malta was raided almost continuously, day and night. One day in March 1941, while George was returning to his barracks, a Stuka 87 came in low out of nowhere and shot a magazine of bullets, creating havoc, before its suicidal pilot crashed the plane into a service hanger. The bullets and the blast injured and killed many soldiers, leaving destruction everywhere. Looking around, George noticed a jeep on fire some distance away. Through the black smoke engulfing it, he clearly saw a soldier waving for help. The jeep looked as if it was going to explode at any second, but this did not stop him and George ran to the soldier's aid. The soldier was unconscious when

George reached the vehicle. Dragging him out, George lifted him onto his back and started to run for safety, but before he could get far enough the jeep blew up, throwing them both to the ground.

George felt a little dizzy but he was sure he had not been hit. Crawling back to the soldier who he had just pulled out of the jeep, George was in for an amazing surprise. The officer, alive but only just, was none other than his old time friend David, Dr Pach. "Over here! Over here!" George yelled and waved at the closest jeep in sight, "over here, hurry!" he yelled again. George knelt beside his friend and holding him, he started to call his name. "David, David, hold on! It's me George, George Gawchi, please don't die. I beg of you, please don't die. Oh God, don't let him die." Seeing that David's leg was bleeding heavily, George took off his shirt and tied it as tightly as possible around it. When the soldier in the jeep came to their aid they placed David in the back and then sped off to the medical unit. The damage to David's left leg was severe and the doctors were not able to save it. They had to amputate. George stayed close to his friend until Lina, David's wife arrived.

"George, they tell me that if it wasn't for you, David would have died. Thank you!"

"You don't owe me anything; I would die for David any day. Today, I know why God saved me from being hanged. Had David not saved my life then, I wouldn't have been able to save his life now; it's incredible, isn't it? God does work in all kinds of mysterious ways." Now George and David were bonded more than ever.

On the fifteenth of April, 1942, Sir William Dobbie, Governor and Commander in Chief on Malta, conveyed a message sent from King George VI of England to the island of Malta. It read:

'TO HONOUR HER BRAVE PEOPLE I AWARD THE GEORGE CROSS TO THE ISLAND FORTRESS OF MALTA TO

BEAR WITNESS TO A HEROISM AND DEVOTION THAT WILL LONG BE FAMOUS IN HISTORY'.

On the eighth of December, 1943, Malta was in for another historic visit. This time it was none other than Franklin D. Roosevelt, the President of America, bringing with him an illuminated scroll from the people of America containing the following citation:

'IN THE NAME OF THE PEOPLE OF THE UNITED STATES OF AMERICA, I SALUTE THE ISLAND OF MALTA, ITS PEOPLE AND DEFENDERS, WHO, IN THE CAUSE OF FREEDOM AND JUSTICE AND DECENCY THROUGHOUT THE WORLD HAVE RENDERED VALOUROUS SERVICE FAR ABOVE AND BEYOND THE CALL OF DUTY. UNDER REPEATED FIRE FROM THE SKIES, MALTA STOOD ALONE BUT UNAFRAID IN THE CENTRE OF THE SEA, ONE TINY BRIGHT FLAME IN THE DARKNESS, A BEACON OF HOPE FOR THE CLEARER DAYS WHICH HAVE COME.

MALTA'S BRIGHT STORY OF HUMAN FORTITUDE AND COURAGE WILL BE READ BY POSTERITY WITH WONDER AND WITH GRATITUDE THROUGH ALL THE AGES. WHAT WAS DONE IN THE ISLAND MAINTAINS THE HIGHEST TRADITION OF GALLANT MEN AND WOMEN WHO FROM THE BEGINNING OF TIME HAVE LIVED AND DIED TO PRESERVE CIVILISATION FOR ALL MANKIND'.

FRANKLIN D. ROOSEVELT.
December 7th 1943

On the twenty-eighth of August 1944, the Maltese heard the last sound of sirens, which had wailed over three thousand, three hundred times. Malta was now out of the war and George was a war hero. Dr Pach and his wife Lina had survived the war too. Not only did Dr Pach, now back to court duties, get his friend George pardoned, but he also managed to get George a government contract. George was to make the wooden beds for the hospitals. What a memorable day that was. George was not only a free man again but he now had a future too.

With Qormi being the neighbouring village to Luqa, where Malta's main airport was situated, George and his neighbours were very lucky that their houses were not damaged. The first thing on his mind was to visit his godparents and their family, to find out if they had survived too. When he knocked on Martin's door it was Filippa who opened up. "I came to see how you all are. I have been vindicated. I am now a free man. How's everyone, how are your parents?"

"George, I am so happy for you. Please, come in."

Inside the kitchen George met the other four sisters; Lola, Giovanna, Maria and Cetta. They were all still single and living together. George asked about their parents, Martin and Karmena.

"Father, God bless his soul, died during the first month of the war of old age."

"I'm so sorry. He was such a wonderful person. What about your mother?"

"Mother is still alive; she is in her bedroom."

"Could you please tell her that I'm here? I'd like to see her, if she wouldn't mind."

"George, she is totally bedridden and her health is very poor. She is also blind. Come, I'm sure that she would want to have a word with you." Slowly they walked into the bedroom. "Mother, Mother can you hear me?" Filippa gently asked.

"Yes," Karmena replied.

"Mother, guess who's here? Guess who's come to see us? It's George, George Gawchi your godchild."

Very slowly, Karmena stretched her arm out and George held her hand. "George, how wonderful to know you survived the war too. God is good; there was never a day when I didn't pray for you my dear boy. George, I hope that you are a free man now after such a long war. I hope that God has rewarded you with your freedom."

"Yes, I am a free man."

"Praise to the Lord Jesus Christ, now I will die a happy woman. Please George, come closer, I want a hug." George slowly and gently leaned and hugged Karmena. "You skin smells just like the day you were born. Oh what a day that was, the day you came into this world. You were always so special. God bless you my dear godchild. God bless you George."

"God bless you too. I love you Karmena," George replied.

Leaving her to rest, the group now moved back into the kitchen. "I'm so moved," George said, drying his tears.

"George, you were always very special to mum and dad."

"How is your sister Katarina? How are Toni and the family? Please tell me that they are alive too?"

"Yes they are alive. They have three children and they are back at the farm now. I will let them know that you are moving back to the house. I'm sure that they will want to see you. After all, it was your dear mother who got them back together again all that time ago."

"Yes, please do. Tomorrow I will be visiting Gozo. I want to see Maria's family. Then I'll come back and settle here for good." Here they sat down to talk some more over coffee.

At the convent on Gozo, Sister Maria Concetta and Sister Maria Angelica welcomed George with great respect, as they always did. When George told them that he had been pardoned, they blessed the Lord Jesus Christ for His kindness. When he showed them his war medals, they were very proud to have such a man in their family. Together they went to see their brother, Father Antonio, who embraced George. They sat and talked for a long time, mostly about George's war experiences. In the end they asked him what he wanted to do with the farm in Zebbug. "The place brings too much pain. You can have it," he said.

"Cousin Jamri's children have been running it for the last few years. I'm sure they will be very happy when I give them the news. George, I just want to tell you that we always knew you were innocent. God has given you the justice you deserve. George, you are always welcome to visit, for you will always be family to us," Father Antonio said.

"Thank you and the same goes for all of you. Whenever you are on Malta, you know where I live. I'll be waiting. God bless and goodbye," George replied, full of emotion.

Chapter 20

Giorgino's upbringing in America

Right after the air raid on Pearl Harbour, Austin was called up for war duty. To safeguard his family, Austin called on the Franciscan monks to care for them in their monastery until his return. They loved the small child. He was such a breath of fresh air to have around. They read him many verses and passages from the Bible. Even at such a young age, Giorgino was very obedient. He listened to every word without interruption and then asked questions. His innocence, vision and understanding were a pleasure to watch. He definitely was a very special boy.

After the war ended, it was time for the family Di Philippe to say their goodbyes to the Franciscan monks who had looked after them. On this day, all of them gathered at the door of the monastery to say farewell to the young boy they had become so fond of. Before they departed, Austin and Mariella thanked them for their generosity, kindness and hospitality. Some years later, at the age of fourteen, Giorgino told his parents that he wished to re-join the same seminary, at the monastery where he had stayed during the war years. He told them of his wish to become a Franciscan priest one day.

Austin and Mariella had hoped that Giorgino would stay under their roof longer and maybe run his own small business one day. They even planned to send him to university. But today they were caught off guard and decided they needed to talk.

"He is still young," Austin told Mariella, "but if this is what he wants, then I think that we should let him try this."

"God has shown us many signs over the years that he might be heading to serve Him. The Catholic drive to teach God's will is in his mother's blood after all and Maria, God bless her soul, does have three siblings in the Clergy."

"He's such a wonderful, lóving and caring young man. If the day comes when he is ordained, I'm sure we'll be very proud," Austin agreed.

"You have such a lovely way of seeing things in life. I'm sure his mother is looking over us even now and my dear brother would be so proud. We are so lucky to have been blessed with such a child."

In joining the friar novices at the monastery, Giorgino's studies and meditations progressed rapidly. Sometimes he prayed and meditated for hours at a time and everyone loved to hear him preach. He had such a lovely way of explaining things. At the age of eighteen, his knowledge was at such an advanced stage that a year later he was ready to dedicate his life as a priest in the Franciscan Order. On the day he was due to be ordained, his parents asked him to choose a challis to his liking. For the occasion, Giorgino, now called Father Giorgino, also chose and recited his favourite passage of the Bible: Matthew: chapter 25, verses 34 to 40:

"Come, you who are blessed by my Father, inherit the kingdom prepared for you from the foundation of the world; for I was hungry and you gave me food, I was thirsty and you gave me something to drink, I was a stranger and you welcomed me, I was naked and you gave me clothing, I was sick and you took care of me, I was in prison and you visited me.'

Then the righteous will answer him, 'Lord, when was it that we saw you hungry and gave you food, or thirsty and gave you something to drink? And when was it that we saw you a stranger and welcomed you, or naked and gave you clothing? And when was it that we saw you sick or in prison and visited you?' And the King will answer them, 'Truly I tell you, just as you did it to one of the least of these who are members of my family, you did it to me."

Of course, he did not forget his parents either. Standing there on the altar and in front of all present, he thanked them for their care, for his upbringing and for their religious teaching and understanding of him, for being there to listen and for their never ending support.

"Through you I've been so blessed. I love you both," were his closing words.

After the service, congratulations were in order and then there was the dinner. Afterwards, Father Giorgino told his parents about his dream. He wanted to build a church, his own church, a monastery with many rooms, where he could shelter and feed the poor and the homeless who came to knock on the door. Austin and Mariella were so moved by his words that not only did they encourage this wonderful idea but were also ready to fund him the money he needed.

This was not the only present Father Giorgino was given on this memorable day. His mother had something else very special to give to him. "This is for you. I didn't have to buy it; it belongs to you," she said, handing her son a small box containing the gold cross that Salvu, his ancestor, had received from the Grand Master of the Knights, Jean de La Valette so many years ago. "It belongs to our family," Mariella continued, as she pulled it out on its chain. "My mother passed it on, on her death bed. It's been in our family for many, many years. It is now yours to keep."

"What a beautiful cross and such a treasure. I promise to wear it until my dying day. Thank you Mom." Mariella helped him put it on. After all these centuries, the cross and what it symbolised was at last around the neck of a man, who, just like the Knights of the Order of St. John, was ready to help the sick, the poor and the homeless.

A few weeks later, Father Giorgino flew to Rome to sit with His Holiness Pope Pius X11 himself. His Holiness was so fascinated by the young priest and his dream, that he invited him to stay a few extra days and he accepted. Even though The Vatican and Rome were very exciting, Father Giorgino could not wait to set foot back on American soil and to search out the right location for his monastery. Getting professional advice, he was told that the care of the poor was something much needed in Detroit, Michigan. Father Giorgino agreed to look into it.

When his parents heard about it they encouraged him, even though this meant he would be moving. In a few months the land was bought and the land permits for the monastery were in order. The construction finished on schedule and from the opening day, the Monastery of St. Francis of Assisi in Detroit, Michigan, saw many people come through its doors in need of food and shelter. In time, other clergy members and volunteers joined Father Giorgino in fulfilling his dream. Of course Austin and Mariella missed him terribly and so finally decided to sell their house and move to live there also, to Detroit, Michigan.

Chapter 21

George and Life after the War

Working on the government contract and with the love of his neighbours and the visits from Dr Pach and his wife Lina who already had four children, plus visits from Toni and Katarina and their children too, George's life was full and happy. All the children who came to visit with their parents called him 'Uncle George' and they meant the world to him. Seeing so many children growing up around him gave George much pleasure, but deep down, whenever George found himself alone, the pain of not knowing anything about his own son hurt him deeply. Oh how he wished that he could see his son and his sister once more, even if it was for just a minute, even from a distance. When George retired, he seemed to dwell on this wish even more. He felt helpless. One day he confided in his dear friend, Dr Pach.

"I understand completely. I feel for you, I always did. Back then, you did the right thing. George, why don't you go to America and do something about it? I can help you with the passport documents and I can contribute a sum of money to help you. When you come back we will all be waiting for you, whatever the outcome."

"Thank you. It's just that, as you know, I did promise my sister that I would never, ever look for them."

"I know, but I still believe that one has to listen to one's heart. Whatever you decide, I will back you up and help you."

Two weeks later George summoned up enough courage to go, and he went to Dr Pach's home to start filling out the documents for his passport. The English language lessons he had taken during his younger years had come in handy during the war time and now

257

would prove even more useful with him going to America.

Just weeks later, arriving on Long Island, George could not believe the sight in front of him. Humble as he was and having lived on such a small island as Malta, George was now stunned to be looking at something totally amazing and different. There were high buildings which seemed to reach to the sky, all kinds of makes of cars and many, many people of all different cultures. The fast movements were a new energy. He felt like a child in a fantasy land. Taking his sister's address out of his coat pocket, he asked about its location and whereabouts.

Changing two trains, he eventually arrived at the street. Just as Mariella had described in her letters, there in front of him was a very big house indeed. He had found it, but what was he to do next? Surely, he could not just walk and knock on the front door. Hiding behind a big tree trunk, he sat to think. Luckily, after just a few minutes, he heard a car starting up on the driveway. George peeked from behind the tree trunk and saw two men. 'Surely the driver has to be Austin, my brother-in-law', George thought. He waited until the car got closer and then walked onto the path and waved. The driver now stopped the car. "You must be Austin Di Phillippe," George asked.

"Sorry, I'm not, but I did buy this house from him some years ago."

George's heart almost missed a beat. Had he already come to a dead end? "Would you know where they moved to Sir, if you don't mind me asking?

"I don't know the address if that's what you mean, but they did say that they were moving to Detroit, Michigan."

"Detroit, Michigan. Is that far Sir?" George asked.

"It's a train journey from here. Do you know where the train station is?"

"Yes, I just came from there," George replied.

"Then go back and take the direct train. It's that simple."

"Thank you Sir," George said kindly. George was very tired but still decided to take the train. When he finally arrived it was already late at night and he felt shattered. He needed to rest. Finding a guest house right in the city centre, he booked a room for two nights. After a long night's sleep, George woke up refreshed. Going onto the main street he stopped at a cafe to have something to eat and drink. Sitting at the table George saw a gentleman reading the newspaper. Looking at the front page, George could see that it was the Sunday paper. Walking over to the gentleman, George politely asked if there was a Catholic church in the area. "Why, yes of course, it's just a two kilometre walk down the street from here." In church, George made the sign of the cross. The twelve o'clock service was about to begin. The priest gave a very good sermon. When George came face to face with him to receive Holy Communion, George felt something very warm and special and could not take his eyes off him.

"The Body of Christ," the priest repeated again when George did not respond.

"Amen," George said, now taking the Host. Back in his chair, George stared at the priest throughout the rest of the service. What was it he was sensing? Was it that his face reminded him of his brother-in-law, Father Antonio on Gozo, or was it maybe God telling him that this man could help him find the whereabouts of his family? After all, on Malta, clergy members knew almost everyone in the village where they practiced. When the Mass Service finished, he decided to see if he could have a word with the priest. Seeing a cleaner wiping some chairs, George walked over to ask where he could find him.

"Do you mean Father Giorgino?" the cleaning lady replied.

"I don't know his name to tell you the truth, but he preached at the twelve o' clock service."

"That is Father Giorgino. He is always ready to receive everyone. I just saw him going into the back garden about five minutes ago. He loves his flowers. Just walk through that hall there to the left and keep walking to the end. You will see a green door. Open it; that's the door to the garden. Go, I'm sure he'll see you."

When George got into the garden, he could see that Father Giorgino was in his undershirt. George thought that he might embarrass him, catching him without his robe, and he was about to leave, only to hear the priest calling out to him. "Hello there! Can I help you?"

"I can return another time," George answered politely, without even turning around.

"I can see you now, really. Come and sit with me." George walked to where he was standing. Father Giorgino picked up a shirt to put over his undershirt, but just before he managed to button it, George saw something hanging around his neck that made his knees buckle. Father Giorgino was wearing the gold cross that he himself had given to his own sister many years ago; the same gold cross that his mother had given him on her deathbed. The possibility of finding his son was too much. His feet started to give way and George began to lose his balance. Only Father Giorgino's quick reaction stopped him from falling to the ground. "Mother! Mother! Quickly! Get some water!" Father Giorgino called out, "hurry!"

Mariella heard her son calling and she quickly ran to the back garden. She took one look at the older man's face that her son was cradling in his arms and the water basin slipped right out of her hand. Even though so many years had passed, Mariella knew that face very well. She was sure that she was looking at her brother, George.

"Mother! The water, you dropped it," Father Giorgino said to his mother.

George could not believe that he had found his family. He was speechless.

"Mother, please help me take this man inside and onto a bed. He needs a doctor." Together they slowly walked indoors. George felt so blissfully happy to be holding onto them; the two people he loved most in the world.

"Mother, please, call the doctor."

"What is your name?" Father Giorgino asked, as he sat next to George and helped him sip some water.

"George. My name is George. I am a visitor here, just passing through."

"I am Father Giorgino and this is my monastery. The doctor will be here shortly. You can shelter here for as long as you wish. We will take good care of you."

George did not want this moment to ever end. He was the happiest man on earth. "I am feeling better already," he said.

In a while Mariella came in with the doctor who examined George. After the examination, he told them that all George needed was some rest, and that he might be suffering from low blood pressure. Mariella knew better. "We will take good care of him."

"Thank you; I won't be any trouble. I will be leaving soon, I promise," George said.

"Would you like some fresh vegetable soup?" Father Giorgino asked, "My mother makes the best vegetable soup around; I'm sure you'll like it."

"That would be very nice."

When Mariella came back with the hot bowl of soup, Father Giorgino excused himself and left the room. Alone with her brother after all these years, Mariella could not keep her emotions in any longer and placing the soup on the dresser, hugged her brother as tightly as she could. Holding each other after so many years, they cried and cried. During this emotional moment Mariella kissed her brother's forehead as she ran her fingers through his white hair.

"I'm so sorry," were George's first words, in choked Maltese to his sister, "I am so sorry that I broke my promise. I don't want to mess things up for you……please forgive me, but I couldn't just die without at least looking for you. I wanted to see my son and I longed to see you both before I died. You and Austin have done a marvellous job with him, I can see that. I am so proud of you. Now I will return to Malta and die a happy man."

"George, stop, please listen, "Mariella said, talking in Maltese. "I don't want you to go anywhere. My beloved husband Austin died some years ago. You and Giorgino are my only family now and God has brought us together again. I still can't believe you're here! After Austin died, there was many a time when I wanted to come back to Malta, to see you, to tell you all about your son, but I never got the courage. George, Giorgino is your son. We have to tell him. You've suffered enough."

What both of them were unaware of, was that Father Giorgino had momentarily returned to ask his mother for something, but hearing his mother and the stranger talking in a language he had never heard before made him realise that they must surely know each other. They seemed to have a lot to say, so he gave them space. He had never known his mother to keep any secrets from him and he was sure that she would tell him about this man later. George and Mariella had a lot to catch up on. He told her about the war and how he had become a free man. He told her all about Dr Pach's family; that Martin and Karmena had passed away and a lot more. Mariella could have listened to her brother forever. She adored him and having him in front of her felt wonderful.

"George, you have to come and stay with me, at my house. This is where you belong. You said that you are staying at the guest house up the street. Later on we will help you collect your belongings and bring them here. Please stay with us. You have to accept."

"But how are we going to explain all this to Father Giorgino? What if he won't forgive me?"

"Your son is the most wonderful person on this earth. All his life, all he does is forgive and give hope to others. Finding you after all these years will be God's best present; a gift for all that he's done for others. He will love you like no other son could love a father; I can assure you of that."

"I have invited George for dinner at our house this evening, I hope you don't mind," Mariella told her son when he joined them in the room.

"Mother if that's what you wish, then he is more than welcome." Father Giorgino could sense the happiness his mother had been feeling since this man arrived. His first thoughts were that they may have courted many years ago, before his father had met her. Since his father's death, his mother always looked sad and lonely. It was lovely to see her face shining again. After dinner that evening, they moved to sit and relax in the large living room. Mariella now told her son the truth about George and who he really was.

Father Giorgino was moved to hear that his father had suffered so much for him to have a secure future. "Oh my God," were his first words as he walked over to hug his father. Right there, they asked George to move in with them. That evening, when the three of them sat around the table to say prayers and to thank the Lord Jesus Christ for reuniting them again, George got very emotional seeing his sister holding his mother's rosary beads. He was now sure that their reunion was the work of his mother's soul, smiling upon them from heaven.

In the days, weeks and months that followed, the three shared many more emotional moments as they recalled stories from their past. George wanted to help by attending to any of the woodwork that Father Giorgino needed doing and Father Giorgino generously accepted his father's offer as he badly needed a carpenter. Mariella in turn was thrilled to hear about this and financed any of the tools and machinery that George needed. Their love flourished and in time this healed George's past pains and he could not have been happier. He daily thanked the Lord Jesus Christ for all He gave them, but by far the best moment of the day was when he knelt down in front of Father Giorgino to receive Holy Communion out of his son's own hand. He was so proud of his son and the Holy Host filled him with such peace within. Father Giorgino continued to call Mariella 'Mother', after all that was what she was to him. Of course, now he even had his father. He felt totally blessed.

George sent a telegram to inform his friend Dr Pach and Martin's children that he had found his family and that he would be staying in America for an indefinite time. The days and weeks that followed were filled with stories of their lives. Finding out that he had two aunts and an uncle in the Clergy, Father Giorgino could not wait to visit Malta. Together they planned a holiday for the coming year.

When the three of them arrived on Malta, they found Maria's family and George's friends waiting. Together they shared many unforgettable memories. Father Giorgino could easily have stayed on Malta for the rest of his remaining life, but his life was the Church and his people in Detroit, Michigan.

George or Mariella could have stayed behind in Malta too, but there was no way that after finding one another again that anyone could keep the three of them apart. Before they returned to America they met with a notary and legally signed over their home on St. Sebastian Street to Martin's five daughters.

Back in America, God blessed them with many wonderful years. When George and later Mariella passed away, Father Giorgino buried them both in the back garden of the monastery under the big oak tree, surrounded by an area awash with colourful flowers.

When Father Giorgino died, he too was laid next to them. At last the three of them rested together and forever more, never to be separated again.

THE END